W9-BOK-095

ROUGH JUSTICE

ROUGH JUSTICE

Brad Smith

This first world edition published 2015
in Great Britain and 2016 in the USA by
SEVERN HOUSE PUBLISHERS LTD of
19 Cedar Road, Sutton, Surrey, England, SM2 5DA.
Trade paperback edition first published
in Great Britain and the USA 2016 by
SEVERN HOUSE PUBLISHERS LTD.

British Library Cataloguing in Publication Data

Smith, B. J. (Brad J.) author.
  Rough justice.
  1. Trials (Rape)-Fiction. 2. Suspense fiction.
  I. Title
  813.6-dc23

ISBN-13: 978-07278-8560-9 (cased)
ISBN-13: 978-1-84751-669-5 (trade paper)
ISBN-13: 978-1-78010-723-3 (e-book)

All Severn House titles are printed on acid-free paper.

Severn House Publishers support The Forest Stewardship Council™ [FSC™],
the leading international forest certification organisation. All our titles that
are printed on FSC certified paper carry the FSC logo.

Typeset by Palimpsest Book Production Ltd.,
Falkirk, Stirlingshire, Scotland.
Printed and bound in Great Britain by
TJ International, Padstow, Cornwall.

ONE

The trial began Thursday morning. It was late spring and the day dawned cool and clear, the rising sun showing yellow-red to the east. Rose City looked nice at that time of year, bright and clean with the promise of summer on the air. The lake was blue-green under the morning light, the April floods having long since abated. The city parks along the shore sprouted tulips and lilies and mums. Sailboats were docked at the Lancaster Club and the bars along Fremont Street were opening their outdoor patios, the umbrellas and awnings popping up like the flowers in the park.

Kate woke up just past seven, and lay there in bed for a time thinking. Looking out her bedroom window after rising, to the faultless sky, she told herself it was a good day for beginnings. A good day to take him down.

She had decided a couple of days earlier what she would wear, settling on a black knee-length skirt and a maroon silk blouse. She had a jacket to go with the skirt in the front hall closet. Thomas Grant, the prosecutor, had suggested only that she dress conservatively. She assumed the other three women had been given the same instruction. Grant wasn't specific on the question of wardrobe and Kate hadn't expected him to be. He came across as being more substance than style. A tall slump-shouldered man in his fifties, with thinning black hair and a bit of a gut, he himself favored standard two-piece suits of dark blue or brown. Kate doubted he thought much to what was in fashion. His conversations with her had been straight and to the point. He talked as if a conviction was inevitable.

David was making pancakes when she went down to the kitchen. The table was set and beside her plate was a white rose that looked as if it had spent the night in the fridge. Kate picked up the flower and held it to her nose a moment. It smelled faintly of leftover pizza. She moved over to kiss David as he whipped the batter with a wooden spoon.

'You're a sweetheart,' she said.

'Oh, I know.'

'And so humble.' She poured a cup of coffee and sat down. The morning paper was on the table.

'You made the front page,' David said. 'Bunch of nothing . . . the first day of the trial, stuff like that. Browning spouting off. Time to correct this terrible wrong. Blah, blah . . .'

Kate looked at the story. There was a file picture of the old man from several years back, from a past campaign no doubt, and one of lawyer Browning exiting a courthouse somewhere, his heavy-lidded eyes and jowly face turned to the camera, his expression confident while at the same time contemptuous of the media he was facing. Kate was named in the article, as well as the other three 'accusers', as the paper awkwardly referred to them. Reading between the lines, one might conclude that the reporter was of the opinion that Joseph Sanderson III – or The Mayor, as he was widely known – was the victim of frivolous charges, and that those charges would be dismissed forthwith. Kate realized, though, that she was hardly unbiased enough to be interpreting anyone else's leanings. The phone rang and she reached for it.

'Hey, there.' It was Frances, her voice raised against some clattering racket in the background. 'Just calling to tell you I'm thinking about you. I'll see you down there later.'

'What's all the noise?' Kate asked.

'I'm out in the barn. Just changed the plugs in the cultivator and now Perry thinks he's adjusting the carb.'

'I was going to do that,' Kate said.

'That's pretty good,' Frances said. 'Except you wouldn't know a cultivator from a laying hen.' She paused a moment. 'You OK?'

'I'm good.'

'Walk in that courtroom with your head up.'

'You really don't have to tell me that.'

'I know. I couldn't think of anything profound though so I kind of went Jimmy Stewart on you. I'll see you there.'

'You're my favorite aunt, Frances.'

'I'm your only aunt. And I love you.'

'Bye.'

She hung up the phone as David brought her the pancakes. She had no appetite but began to eat anyway, partly because he had gone to the trouble and partly because she knew it was going to be a long day and she needed to eat. After a moment, he sat down across from her with his own plate.

'Can I cook or what?' he said as he made a show of digging in.

'You added water to a box of mix,' she told him.

'And I did it beautifully.' He chewed a mouthful and then swallowed, watching her. 'Nervous?' he asked.

'Yeah.'

She took a drink of coffee and looked back at him. He hadn't shaved yet and she could see the spot on his right jaw line – a perfect circle the size of a dime – where his whiskers refused to grow.

'Relieved,' she said then.

'Yeah?' he said. 'Why's that?'

'Because it's here,' she said. 'All these years, it's like I've been out there in the . . . I don't know . . . in the wilderness. Who's the guy in the Bible who was in the wilderness?'

'Moses,' David said. 'Moses was the guy in the wilderness.'

'So I was raised a heathen.' Kate shrugged. 'Point is – one way or the other, I'll be finished with it. I don't have to think about it every morning, I don't have to have this fucked-up reaction every time I see his picture in the paper.' She paused. 'Wondering if it was my fault.'

'You were fifteen years old.'

'I know. But the question's always there.' She stood up and walked to the counter for more coffee. 'You don't know what to think because you've got nothing to compare it to.'

'I'll tell you what I think,' David said, and he stood up. 'I think you're my hero.'

'Dale Earnhardt's your hero,' she said. She took his face in her hands and kissed him. 'You're going to have to shave and put on a clean shirt if you're walking into that courtroom with me.'

'OK.' He turned to go.

'How long was this Moses dude out there in the wilderness?' she asked.

'Forty years.'

'Shit,' she said. 'I guess I got off easy.'

*   *   *

Miles Browning was fastening the Shelby knot in his tie when the phone rang and the caller announced that his car was waiting. Browning gave the tie a final inspection and took his pants from the back of a chair and pulled them on. He slipped into the suit jacket and stepped into the bathroom for a quick look at his hair and then gathered his briefcase and left the room. He shared the elevator with three software salesmen who were in town for some sort of convention. They were comparing hangovers when Browning got on. One of the salesmen, red-eyed, his chin bleeding from a razor cut, asked if he was there for the convention.

'I'm afraid not,' he said, without looking at the trio. When the elevator stopped he was the first off.

The waiting car was a three-year-old Buick. Browning had instructed his assistant to procure a used vehicle to transport The Mayor and himself to and from the courtroom. With the media this trial would attract – had already attracted, in fact – it wouldn't do for the accused and his counsel to arrive every day in a new Mercedes or BMW, especially when the accusers were working-class women. The Buick was a rental and it fit the bill.

The Mayor was in the back seat of the car as Browning slid in, placing his briefcase on the seat. The driver was a pretty young woman, no more than twenty-five. She had blond hair tucked beneath a poor boy's cap. Browning looked at her face in the rear-view mirror for a moment before turning to The Mayor.

'Morning.'

'Good morning,' The Mayor said. 'Sleep well?'

'I did,' Browning replied. 'And you, Joseph?'

'Like a baby. I feel like I could go ten rounds with the heavy-weight champion of the world.'

'Not that anybody knows who that is these days,' Browning said.

The Mayor laughed and looked out the car window. He was wearing a navy blue suit, with a white shirt and scarlet tie. His tie clip had a Masonic symbol on it. His hand on the seat between the two men was thin and blue-veined, dotted here and there with liver spots. He was robust, though, for a man in his eighth decade; his gray eyes were sharp and he still possessed the voice of a country auctioneer.

'Say, have a look over here, Miles,' he said. 'That fieldstone building is where William Lyon Mackenzie holed up for a couple of days back in 1837. After your guys chased him out of Toronto. There's a plaque on the opposite wall that tells all about it, or at least somebody's version of it. The place was an inn back then. Now it's an expensive restaurant with lousy food.'

'But one with provenance,' Browning said. 'Does the plaque say whether William and the boys paid their bill?'

'I'm afraid it does not,' The Mayor said. 'History is little concerned with such . . . minor indiscretions. Don't you agree?' The old man turned to Browning as he asked this.

'I suppose.'

'History judges on a larger scale. History forgives.'

The courthouse was of recent construction, a forgettable design of glass and concrete located on the east edge of the downtown core, where most of the old buildings had been torn down and replaced in the past twenty or thirty years. There was a sizable assembly of media out in front – TV, radio, print – and there were vans bearing station logos parked haphazardly on the street, cables running here and there, monitors mounted on tripods. Browning glanced at the throng as the Buick pulled to the curb and the driver got out. He watched her as she walked around to open the door.

'I don't know who chose our driver, but this is her last day,' he said to The Mayor.

The Mayor regarded the pretty blond woman a moment and he nodded. Eight or ten reporters closed in on the two men as they stepped out of the Buick.

'You can engage,' Browning said quietly, 'but keep moving.'

'Mr Mayor,' a man holding a microphone called out. 'How are you feeling about today?'

'Happy,' Sanderson told him.

'Happy?' This from two or three people.

The Mayor and Browning moved through the crowd. 'Happy to finally put these charges to rest,' The Mayor said. 'To speak my piece at long last. I've been living in silence for nearly two years.' He smiled. 'You guys know better than anybody how alien a concept that is for me.'

'Did you rape these women?' a woman reporter asked.

Browning looked for the call letters on her microphone but the mike was turned away from him.

'Of course not,' The Mayor said.

'Mr Browning!' the first reporter called. Browning saw now that the man was from RCTV. He recognized him from the previous night's newscast. Browning slowed slightly, turned toward him.

'How do you like your client's chances?' the man shouted.

'His chances?' Browning replied. 'This is not a lottery. I'm not interested in chance. I'm interested in truth. And the truth is that these charges against my client should never have seen the light of day. This is character assassination, pure and simple. But you needn't take *my* word for it. Stick around and you'll see it is so.'

He and The Mayor reached the steps and it occurred to Browning that the old man was purposefully lagging, enjoying the ride. He was back on the stage he'd strutted for so long, back in the game he'd played so well. For the press, opportunity was fast slipping away and questions were flying now.

'Are these women lying, then?'

'What are their motivations?'

'Is there a civil suit in the works?'

'Mr Browning, what are your expectations?'

Browning, cherry picking, got the question he wanted. He stopped just outside the main doors to the courthouse. The Mayor stopped too, his expression one of calm benevolence.

'My expectations?' Browning repeated. 'Why, thank you for asking me that question. Perhaps I should apologize for being such a simple man, but I expect the same thing every time I walk into a courtroom.' He paused, waiting for the question. He seemed impatient, waiting for the reporter's intellect to catch up with his.

'And what is that?'

'Justice,' Browning said.

And he and The Mayor went inside.

Kate was meeting the other three women for the first time. This was by design, as the prosecution was determined that the defense would have no grounds to suggest any collaboration among the four. In pre-trial discussions, Browning had gone a step further and requested that any three of the accusers not be allowed in the courtroom while the fourth was testifying. Judge Oliver Pemberton – who'd been brought in from Ottawa to preside – had considered and then dismissed the motion, reasoning that the four would be giving testimony on four separate incidents, with no common evidence tying one to another. When Browning had argued that each might still appropriate from the others, whether in detail or inference, the judge had reminded him that the women's statements were already in the disclosure, and that any straying from those statements would, in fact, be detrimental to the prosecution's case. And that had been that, although Browning, in defeat, did not seem particularly dismayed by the fact.

Prosecutor Thomas Grant had an office down a wide hallway from the main courtroom and it was there that Kate met the others. She guessed the other three women to be anywhere from thirty to forty years old. Maria Secord was dark-haired, slightly heavy, attractive and outgoing. She had a harsh smoker's voice, and a tattoo on her neck that she'd managed to hide partially with a turtleneck sweater. There were rougher edges that the sweater did not hide. Debra Williams was tall and rail thin. She had washed-out blue eyes, and lank blond hair. She wore an inexpensive suit of ivory cotton. She worked as an assistant golf pro somewhere in the city, Kate had been told, and she had the cool detached manner of someone who'd grown up around country clubs, even though that apparently wasn't true. She spoke in clipped sentences and had a look of resolve about her that seemed practiced yet not quite perfected. Amanda Long was the quiet one; she was quite overweight and had beautiful brown eyes that never rested, darting from place to place like those of a feral cat looking for escape. She wore a long sweater dress over pants. Her fingernails were bitten to the quick, her fingertips red and raw from the effort.

The four of them sat uncomfortably in Grant's office, on hard wooden chairs which lined the wall, while the prosecutor sat on the edge of his desk and talked to them. He told them the case would be a marathon, not a sprint, and that it would ebb and flow along the way. Piling on the metaphors, he described a criminal trial as a series of skirmishes, and he went on to say that whoever won the key skirmishes would win the war. He advised them, most emphatically, not to lose their tempers under cross-examination, that doing so would be playing into Browning's hands. Saying this, he looked pointedly at first Maria and then Kate. He concluded by emphasizing that they held a distinct advantage in what was to come because they – and not Joseph Sanderson III – were telling the truth.

The speech came off as a pep talk and was uncharacteristic of Grant, at least of what Kate had seen of the man, and she wondered if he was trying to convince himself of their chances, as much as them. As he was speaking, she glanced from time to time at the other three women, trying to decide who might be the weak link in the bunch, wondering if it might be her. But she didn't feel that way, not at this moment. Then again, it had yet to begin.

And then it did. It was like a blur, moving single file down the hallway and into the noisy courtroom, where a dozen conversations merged into a jangle of words each indistinguishable from the other, the talkers gathered in groups – clerks and lawyers and spectators and cops. The chatter subsided briefly as they entered, as nearly everyone turned for a first look at the four, then the talking resumed, although at a significantly lower volume.

They were led by Grant to a long wooden table marked PROSECUTOR. There were five chairs waiting, and plastic bottles of water on the table, and legal pads, with sharpened pencils at the ready. Miles Browning was already present, installed at an identical table on the far side of the courtroom. He was leaning forward, talking to a young guy in a black suit. Between the two was Joseph Sanderson III.

The Mayor.

He gazed unflinchingly at the four women as they entered, his expression that of a kindly grandfather attending a graduation or wedding. Kate looked back at him, but found she couldn't hold it for long. The realization unnerved her and after a moment she forced herself to turn to him again. But he was no longer watching them, having diverted his attention to the spectators behind them. Kate turned, saw David among them. He smiled and then winked. She glanced about the crowded gallery for Frances but couldn't find her.

The jury was already in the box. Seven women, five men. Kate regarded the twelve, watched them fidgeting, saw them casting quick looks at her and the others before looking away. She wondered if they were nervous too, and she wondered if anybody in the building was not. But then she glanced again at The Mayor. He was not nervous. Whatever he was – and she knew too well some of what he was – he was not nervous, not about this, and quite possibly not about anything. Which was why he could sit there and present himself as the congenial relative, why he could smile and nod to various people in the room like it was a ribbon cutting and not a criminal trial.

Judge Oliver Pemberton walked in and the place fell silent. Moments later Grant was on his feet, addressing the jury. Kate was surprised just how quickly it had begun. After all these years of waiting, how could anything seem sudden?

'There are four things you need to know,' Grant said, starting out. He was standing directly in front of the jury box, his hands in his pants pockets, his belly overhanging his belt. 'And really, they are the only things you need to know. That's the simplicity of this case. There are no gray areas to consider, no mitigating circumstances, no intricate points of law to argue. There are just four things you need to know. One – Joseph Sanderson the third raped Debra Williams. Two – Joseph Sanderson the third raped Maria Secord. Three – Joseph Sanderson the third raped Kate Burns. And four – Joseph Sanderson the third raped Amanda Long.'

As he went down the list, Grant moved away from the jury, crossing the courtroom to the table where the four women sat. As he named each in turn, he stopped in front of her and paused before proceeding. Upon finishing, he turned back toward the jury.

'Those are the four things you need to know.'

Kate looked at the defense table. Browning was doodling on a legal pad, his glasses on the tip of his nose. The Mayor had removed his own glasses and was meticulously cleaning them with a cloth. There were two others at the table now, a man and a woman, presumably assistants or co-counsels to Browning. Of course one of the two was a woman, and of course she was sitting beside The Mayor.

Grant then gave a brief history on the specifics of each attack, offering the dates, locations and some, but not all, of the details. His pitch was even and controlled, and he gave no indication that the actions that he described disgusted him, or enraged him, or had any effect on him at all. He might have been describing a play he'd seen recently. When he had finished the narrative, he walked back to the table where the women sat.

'These sexual assaults – these rapes – all took place between sixteen and twenty years ago. Does that fact make these crimes any less egregious? Of course not. Justice delayed is justice denied. As a jury, you can do nothing about that delay. However, you *can* do something about the denial.' Grant pointed a long forefinger at The Mayor. 'The defendant here is a man recognizable to most of you, probably to all of you. He was the mayor of Rose City for almost thirty-two years. He has received the Order of Canada. He has dined with prime ministers, diplomats, royalty. He has been a public servant with scores of achievements to his credit. And . . . he has raped these four women.' Grant turned back to the jury. 'That is all you need to know.'

Grant sat down and Browning stood up. He smiled and nodded in the direction of Grant and then he removed his glasses and placed them on the table. He had a number of papers in his hand. After a moment he put these on the table as well, taking a moment to arrange them in an orderly fashion. Finally, he turned to the jury.

'I was never very proficient in math,' he said. 'But I do know the difference between one and four. And I can tell you that there is only *one* thing you need to know. Joseph Sanderson the third is innocent of these charges. And I will demonstrate to you that fact. Now we may be here for a week or we may be here for a hundred weeks. It matters little to me. All that matters is that when you leave here, you will be utterly convinced of the innocence of this man. You may very well leave here confused as to why these accusations were ever made in the first place – but you will be utterly convinced of my client's innocence.'

Browning then provided a rambling biographical sketch of The Mayor's life, rife with personal details and mentions of his more notable professional accomplishments. Grant had, of course, already alluded to some of these and it occurred to Kate that he had done so to pre-empt Browning in his own opening. Still, Browning managed to touch upon most of the key events of The Mayor's seventy-two years on the planet. His scholastic achievements in university, fifty years gone, were noted, as was the fact that he had skipped the third grade. Kate wondered what the jury was expected to do with that little nugget of information. Do over-achieving eight-year-olds rarely grow up to be rapists?

When Browning had finished the details on his Norman Rockwell print he turned again to the matter at hand, shifting from folksy biographer to indignant defender of truth.

'Who are these women who have brought forward these charges?' he asked, standing by the jury box but looking defiantly at Kate and the others. 'I don't know the answer to that question. I have tried mightily to understand, to see what is in their hearts. I don't know what unfortunate circumstances have combined to bring them here, what harsh conditions would prompt them to invent these malicious accusations. But I do know there is hope for them, as there is for all of us, no matter our trespasses. I believe that as much as I believe in the judicial system we are about to implement here today. But first and foremost, we need to know the truth. We *always* need to know the truth.'

At this point, Browning walked over and stood directly behind The Mayor, placing his hand on the older man's shoulder. 'It's no secret that my client was a politician in this city for nearly four decades. In my opinion, any politician who stays in the game that long and doesn't step on a few toes isn't worth his salt. Is that what is behind these scurrilous charges? Is some unknown person out to settle a score? If so, that person is playing some pretty dirty pool.' Browning walked over to his own chair. 'They're playing dirty pool and I don't think you should stand for it.' He hesitated, then as if on sheer impulse he turned back to the jury. 'No, let me rephrase that. I don't think *we* should stand for it. You know what you do with a person who plays dirty pool? You send him packing. So let us do that. Let us do it together.'

TWO

Prosecutor Grant called Debra Williams to the stand first. He began by asking her about her background, her education, what she did for a living. There was nothing remarkable about her history, and it seemed that Grant wanted to make that clear, especially in contrast to Browning's earlier hagiography of The Mayor.

Finally he approached her, leaving his notes behind. 'Assistant pro at Oak Creek?' he said to begin. 'Would it be inappropriate to ask why I'm hitting my iron shots so thin of late?

There was subdued laughter from the assembly.

'You're probably lifting your head,' Debra said. 'Keep your eye on the ball.'

'Indeed.' Grant nodded. 'We all should keep our eye on the ball.' He looked at the jury for a long moment, as if appreciating that it was about to begin for real. Until now, it had been shadow boxing and feinting. Now it was eight-ounce gloves. He turned to Debra. 'The summer of 1995. How old were you that summer?'

'Fourteen. I would be fifteen in September.'

'Where were you living?'

'In the town of Trowbridge.'

'With your family, of course?'

'Yes. Well, my mother and my brother.'

'Your father did not live with you?'

'No. He . . . he left.'

Grant nodded and made a point of looking at his notes; he wanted the mention of the absent father to linger.

'How did you first meet the defendant, Joseph Sanderson the third?' he asked then.

'He has a lake house, on the, um . . . on the lake up there.'

'Lake Sontag?'

'Yes.'

'And Trowbridge is on the eastern end of the lake?'

'Yes,' Debra said. 'After my father left, my mother used to

clean cottages for different people on the lake. For extra money. Sometimes I helped out when she got real busy. And that year she started doing the Sanderson place.'

'She was hired to clean the cottage owned by Joseph Sanderson the third,' Grant said. 'And you got to know Mr Sanderson?'

'Yes.'

'And his wife?'

'Not really. She gave me a pop once or twice. But he was always nice. The year before he lent me his fishing pole. He showed me how to put a worm on the hook, like, to thread it so it wouldn't fall off. He knew lots about fishing.'

'Tell us what happened on the afternoon of July eleventh, 1995.'

Debra dropped her eyes, inhaled deeply before looking up and directly at The Mayor. The move seemed rehearsed, something to trigger her resolve. 'We were cleaning the Sanderson place. There was nobody there. I was cleaning the kitchen and my mom finished the bedrooms and stuff and she said that she was gonna drive over to the Robsons' and start there. It was . . . I don't know . . . down the road a bit, out on the point. So she left and I was cleaning the kitchen, and then . . . he showed up.'

'Who showed up?' Grant asked.

'He did,' Debra said, looking at The Mayor again.

'The defendant?'

'Yes. And he started talking to me. About the pickerel hatch that year, I remember. And he was really talkative that day. Like he'd been drinking.'

'Objection.' Browning said the word with such casual indifference that there seemed some confusion at first as to where it came from. Judge Pemberton was not among those confused.

'Sustained,' he said. He looked at Debra. 'Stick to what you know. You cannot speculate as to things you don't.'

She nodded. 'He was talking a lot, like I said. He said he was there for the weekend and that Mrs Sanderson was driving up later. And he was asking me about school and stuff. He told me I was pretty. I remember he told me I looked like Michelle Pfeiffer. After a while he took his bag or luggage or whatever down the hall. And a couple minutes later he came, like, halfway back, and he asked me if the big bedroom had been cleaned.

And I said yeah. And he said he didn't think so. He asked me to have a look. So I went down to the room and as soon as I stepped inside—' Here she hesitated.

'It's all right,' Grant said. 'Take your time.'

'As soon as I stepped into the room, he tried to kiss me. And I, like, tried to make a joke, and I just pushed away. I said, I have to finish the kitchen. I think I said my mom's waiting for me. But then he grabbed me and he did kiss me, hard. And then he kicked the door closed and he . . . he threw me on the bed and pulled my shorts off. And he raped me.'

Grant nodded, working the moment. 'And what did he say?'

'After I walked into the bedroom, he didn't say anything. He just . . . did it.'

'Did he say anything afterwards?' Grant asked.

'Yeah. Well, he left and went into the bathroom, and I got dressed and I was crying but I went back to the kitchen and kept cleaning the sink. I didn't know what else to do. And after a while he came back, and he just started talking like nothing had happened.'

'He didn't refer to what had happened?' Grant asked. 'He didn't make mention of the fact that he had just assaulted you?'

'After a while, he . . . he started talking about my mom,' Debra said. 'He said he knew my mom didn't have much money, and that she needed cleaning jobs. He said that he knew everybody my mom worked for.'

'So he was telling you that if you didn't keep quiet, your mom would lose these jobs?' Grant asked.

'Objection,' Browning said in his quiet, bored voice. He was reading some notes on the table and did not so much as look up. Watching him, Kate thought of a father, absently reprimanding unruly children while reading the newspaper.

Grant turned to Judge Pemberton and held his hands up as if conceding. 'What was your reaction,' he asked Debra, 'to what he was telling you? What did you think he meant?'

'That if I told anybody, my mom would lose her cleaning jobs. And we wouldn't have any money.'

'What happened then?'

'I finished cleaning the kitchen and I got out of there. I went over to the Robson place.'

'Did you tell your mom what happened?' Grant asked.

'Yes.'

'What did your mom say?'

'She didn't say anything. She was on a ladder outside, washing the bay window, all those little squares, and she didn't say anything. After a while, she told me to go inside and vacuum.'

'And that was it?' Grant asked.

'No,' Debra said. 'That night, after supper, we were sitting outside. She was having a cigarette. I remember cuz she gave me a cigarette that night. First time she ever did that. And she asked me why I wasn't going into town to hang out with my friends, like I did most nights. And I told her I didn't want to see anybody because I was ashamed. And finally she told me there was nothing we could do about it. Because he was rich and we were poor.'

'Because he was rich and you were poor,' Grant repeated.

'That's what she said.'

Grant walked back to the table. Kate watched him as he once again went through the lawyerly pose of reading from his notes. It seemed he'd accomplished what he wanted to and he wanted the testimony to sink in.

When he finally turned back to Debra Williams, he backtracked, asked her about her schooling, her life before and after the rape, what her relationships as an adult had been like. He kept her on the stand until half past three, and then he thanked her for her testimony.

As Browning stood to begin his cross-examination Grant announced that he wished to meet with the judge and Browning in private, that there were matters of procedure that needed clarification. After some consultation at the bench, the judge called an adjournment until the following day.

'Matters of procedure, my ass,' Kate said. She and David were standing in the rear parking lot outside the courthouse. Kate and the others had been advised to use a side door which led to the lot. The media were gathered again by the front steps, waiting for Browning and The Mayor to emerge. A couple of reporters had approached when Kate and the other three women had exited the courthouse but they had been shooed away by a pair of cops who were there, Kate suspected, at Grant's behest.

'Why do you say that?' David asked.

'Grant called the old man a serial rapist in his opening statement and then he put a woman on the stand who backed it up. That's what he wants the jury to go home with. Not whatever Browning's going to have for Debra Williams.'

Glancing back, Kate saw Frances walk out the front door of the courthouse while Browning was conducting an interview with the press corps on the steps, The Mayor standing at his side. Frances was watching the old man and even from that distance Kate could see the contempt on her face. When Kate waved Frances started over. She was wearing a black t-shirt with a Fair Trade logo on the breast and tan cotton pants. Her dark hair was tied at the back of her neck. She hugged Kate.

'I didn't see you in there,' Kate said.

'I got here late and got stuck up in the balcony, with the proletariat,' Frances said.

'What did you think of Browning?' David asked.

'I think he's a windbag,' Frances said.

'But a professional windbag,' Kate said.

Frances nodded. 'And you can tell how much he loves the spotlight, how he loves to hear himself talk. Can you imagine living with a guy like that? Pontificating from dawn to dusk? Must be exhausting.'

Kate listened absently, thinking about Browning, how he'd moved about the courtroom, the confidence in his step and his voice. How relaxed he was, like an actor playing a role he'd played a thousand times before. 'Grant said that he'll be coming after us.'

Frances reached out to push Kate's hair away from her face. 'He's not God,' she said. 'He can babble away from here until doomsday but he can't alter the truth.'

'No,' Kate agreed.

'Still, what drives a guy like that?' Frances wondered. 'He has to know that he's defending a creep. What makes him want to do that?'

'The chance to strut his stuff?' Kate suggested.

'Story I heard, he's making a million flat for this,' David said.

'Flat or round, doesn't make it right,' Frances said.

THREE

Carl got a room at the Riverview Motel out on the highway. The motel had once been on the outskirts of Talbotville but now, with subdivisions spreading like moss, it would be considered part of the town proper. He unpacked his clothes and stowed his tools in the small closet and then took a shower. Shaving in front of the cloudy bathroom mirror, he took a long look at himself, something he never did. But he wondered what he might look like to her. If he would be what she remembered, or if she bothered to remember him at all.

He got dressed and lay down on the bed and turned the TV on. He watched the Tigers and the White Sox until Chicago scored five runs in the seventh inning to take a four-run lead. He flipped through the channels for a bit and then he shut the set off and left.

Archer's was still in business on Locke Street. The sign was the original, faded and shabby, a red and white plastic image of the name itself with an arrow running through it from left to right. Carl parked in the lot out back and walked around to enter through the front door.

He drew some looks, the stranger arriving. A few of recognition. Carl didn't stare but he didn't look away either. Willard Jones was pulling draft behind the bar. The last Carl had seen of him, back in Carl's serious drinking days, Willard had been pulling draft at the Queens Hotel across town. When he saw Carl he extended his hand.

'Lookit here,' Willard said. 'Where you been, man?'

'Over in Dundurn. I figured you'd retire at the Queens.'

'I bought half of this place eight years ago. Me and Chuck Donaldson.'

'Making any money?'

'Not that I've noticed. What are you drinking?'

'Draft will do.'

Carl looked around the room while Willard drew the beer.

Most of the people who had been staring earlier had gone back
to their drinks. There were two couples in the corner, though,
who were still watching him. One of the men – a stout, red-faced
guy with a stringy mustache – was enthusiastically telling the
other three a story. Carl had the feeling he was the subject of
the story.

'On the house,' Willard said.

'Thanks, Willard.'

'So what're you doing over in Dundurn?'

'Security systems. Mostly commercial stuff, video surveillance,
alarms.'

'Good future in that stuff,' Willard said.

'That's what they say.'

He and Willard talked a bit until Willard moved away to serve
someone else. The party in the corner was still quite interested
in his presence, it seemed. Carl was certain he knew the fat guy
with the mustache, the guy doing most of the talking. The ball
game was on the set above the bar. Since Carl had left the motel
the Tigers had scored a half dozen times and now led eight to
six. The White Sox manager looked as if he was inclined to break
something.

Carl drank two glasses of beer and talked on and off to
Willard, mostly about nothing. Strange, when two people don't
see each other for years, that they have nothing to talk about.
Carl thought it would be the other way around. He was just
about to leave when the front door opened and Rufus Canfield
shuffled in, wearing a tie and an ancient brown corduroy sports
coat and walking with a cane. He looked like shit, Carl thought,
but even when Rufus had been young and relatively healthy,
he'd looked like some thinly disguised version of shit.

Coming out of the sunlight, Rufus blinked a few times, looking
around irritably, as if he was entering the place against his will.
When he saw Carl, though, he smiled slowly and made his way
over. He switched the cane to his left hand and offered his right
before taking the stool beside Carl.

'I've been thinking I might see your face.'

'How are you, Rufus?'

'You have eyes, don't you, man? I'm about half crippled, getting
old, getting bloody cantankerous.' He got Willard's attention and

held up two fingers. 'It's the cantankerous part that surprises me. I was always a pretty cheerful fellow.'

'What happened to your leg?' Carl asked.

'I got hit by a car. You believe that? A fucking dog gets hit by a car. Broke my shinbone and destroyed my knee. Three operations later and the medical establishment says it has done all it can do for me. Still able to sit up and take nourishment though.' This he said as the beer arrived and he took a drink, the foam congregating in his bushy mustache. His reddish hair was still as thick and untamed as a bramble bush. His eyes were hound dog sad, though, and he had red veins on his cheeks and nose. He smiled at Carl again and nodded, as if agreeing about something.

'How's business?' Carl asked.

'Business,' Rufus said. 'I lost my mind a few years ago and bought the local newspaper, the weekly.'

'The Trib?'

'Yes, sir. You have the honor of drinking with the managing editor.' Rufus had more beer. 'You also have the honor of drinking with the copy boy. And the cub reporter. The janitor too.'

'Getting crowded in here,' Carl said. 'So you're not practicing?'

'I suppose I am,' Rufus said. 'To an extent. Wills and real estate, that's about it.'

'No criminal stuff?'

'Not really.' Rufus laughed. 'With the paper, I suspect there would be a conflict of interest if I was to report on a case I was trying. But the situation hasn't come up.'

Carl took a drink, looking at himself and Rufus in the mirror behind the bar. 'Did defending me hurt your reputation?'

'Getting disbarred for two years hurt my reputation,' Rufus said. 'Had nothing to do with you. Christ, it's not like I got you off.'

'Disbarred for what?'

'I had a pal who owned a funeral home, over in Chichester. He was taking pre-paids – money from people who pay in advance for funeral arrangements. Old people, mostly. The money's held in trust. My friend was living beyond his means and he began dipping into these accounts. Well, these people started to expire, as people do. And oops . . . there was no money to bury them. A good fellow, he just fucked up. I tried to help him out and in doing so, I too fucked up. He went to jail for a year and I got disbarred.'

'I never heard about it,' Carl said.

'Well, it wasn't much of a crime,' Rufus said. 'And until recently you probably didn't follow the Talbotville news anyway. Put it this way – Miles Browning wasn't in town for the trial. But he is now, and so are you.'

'Yup.'

'Have you spoken to her?'

'No.'

'But you intend to,' Rufus said. 'That's why you're here.'

'I suppose.'

'Were you at the courthouse today?'

'No. I stayed away.'

'Then why are you here?'

'I haven't quite figured that part out yet.'

Rufus gestured to their seedy surroundings. 'So you've come here to do your figuring?'

'Good a place as any. Is that why you're here, Rufus?'

'I'm about done figuring. I've lost faith in it, like so many things.'

Carl looked in the mirror again. 'Your past is the one thing in this life you can't change.'

'That's rather profound.'

'I stole it.'

Rufus drank again. The glass was nearly empty already. He looked down the bar where Willard was in conversation with a waitress. 'Maybe you should talk to Frances,' he said. 'I know the two of them are close.'

'Where would I find Frances?'

'She's running the family farm. I guess you wouldn't know that.'

'Frances is running the farm?' Carl repeated. 'Now that surprises me.'

'She's not just running it,' Rufus said. 'She's turned it into a growing concern, pardon the pun. *Vanguard* magazine did a profile on her last year, even put her on the cover, sitting on a tractor, looking somewhat sporty and earthy at the same time. Woman's gone green on us, Carl. Raises organic vegetables and free range chickens and, I don't know, all that wonderful stuff that's supposed to make us live longer. I'm inclined to agree with Mr Marx on that subject.'

'Karl?'

'Groucho. In his dotage, he was being fed steamed succotash or something and he said that he didn't know if such fare was going to make him live longer, but he knew it was going to seem longer.'

Carl laughed, and when he did he stumbled into eye contact with the fat man in the mustache again. The man was on his feet, making his way to the washrooms in the rear.

'Who is that guy?' Carl asked.

Rufus turned. 'Harold Sikes. Why?'

'I seem to hold some sort of fascination for him.'

Rufus finally caught Willard's eye. Carl put a ten on the bar. His round.

'He's a volunteer firefighter,' Rufus said. 'He's also a lazy lout who's been running his father's farm into the ground for years. But he would have been there that night. He would have been fifty or sixty pounds lighter then. No smarter.'

Rufus reached for the fresh beer and drank. Carl was falling behind but he wasn't going to try to drink with Rufus Canfield. After a moment Harold Sikes came out of the back and walked directly to the bar and took up a space maybe ten feet from them. Carl could see now that he was drunk, all puffed up in the process. He tapped a thick forefinger on the bar.

'Shot of Wild Turkey,' he demanded. He gave Carl a sideways glance as he waited for the bourbon. 'My buddy Red Walton drank Wild Turkey.'

Carl turned to Rufus, who was watching Sikes warily. Willard delivered the shot to the fat man.

'To Red Walton!' Sikes said. 'My buddy. He deserved better than he got.' He slammed back the drink and then swaggered past the two men where they sat at the bar, his shoulder just clipping Carl's back. He went back to his table and sat down, wearing the smug stupid grin of an eight-year-old who'd just jumped off a roof and landed unhurt. Carl could hear him telling the others what he'd just done, even though they had watched him do it.

'That'll give old Harold something to brag about for the next month or so,' Rufus said.

'Good for old Harold.' Carl put it out of his mind. 'You been following the trial, Rufus?'

'I have.'

'What do you think? Are they going to convict him?'

'You get what you pay for in this life, Carl,' Rufus said. 'Sometimes you get more than you bargain for, but you nearly always get what you pay for. The Mayor's paying Miles Browning a lot of money to get him an acquittal. Grant's a competent man from what I know of him, but he might be out of his depth on this one.'

'Will Browning put him on the stand?'

'The Mayor? Absolutely not.'

When Rufus switched to rye, Carl decided it was time to make a move. He wasn't interested in getting drunk and Harold Sikes was growing louder and braver by the minute. Carl didn't need any aggravation from that corner either.

It was still daylight when he walked outside and got into his truck. He drove through the main drag, saw that half the stores he knew as a kid were gone. There had been butcher shops, mercantiles, hardware stores. Some stood empty now, others housed dollar stores and bulk food shops.

He drove on, heading north, toward the old place. On the outskirts of town both sides of the highway were bordered by large box stores, the reason the downtown core was dying. Out here the parking lots were three-quarters full.

In the face of such progress he doubted the old house would still be there but it was, apparently still beyond the reach of the creeping commercial sprawl. But not for long, he knew. The place was a small brick bungalow, a hundred yards or so from the highway, the lot backing on to Millard's Creek. Carl slowed by the drive and then pulled over on to the shoulder of the road. There was a mini-van parked by the house, and an older Buick angled on the lawn, the grass grown up around the rockers. Someone had decided to paint the brick exterior of the house a dull purple. The vegetable garden out back was sprouting weeds three feet high. The woodshed where Carl had built his first Harley was gone.

The house looked too small for a family of five. Of course, it hadn't seemed that way when Carl was growing up. He and his older brother shared a bedroom in the basement, while his parents and his sister had the other two bedrooms on the main floor. Laurie was now living in Montreal and called him every Christmas. His brother stopped talking to him when Carl went to jail, but Carl knew from Laurie that he was living in Nashville, where he had tried to break into the music business and now was working as a school custodian.

The last time Carl had been at the house was the day of his father's funeral. The old man had retired a half year earlier, after working for the town for thirty-four years. It took him exactly six months to drink himself to death. He had actually begun the exercise two years before that, when Carl's mother was killed, but the act of going to work every day had delayed the inevitable.

Carl's mother had been hit by a drunk driver while walking home from town on a summer afternoon. The driver, who claimed the sun was in his eyes, was from Rose City, where he owned a large furniture and appliance store. The police charged him with impaired driving and motor manslaughter, and the case dragged on for nearly two years until a judge dismissed the charges, ruling that the man had been denied the right to a speedy trial. Carl's father died convinced that somebody had been paid off. Carl was inclined to believe it as well.

Carl himself went to jail a few months later. Other than a few random nights in the local lockup, he had somehow avoided the place during his younger years. He knew guys who did time back then and some of them wore it like a badge, like it was an accomplishment. The facility at Auburn had held none of that for Carl; the place was neither romantic nor scary, nor anything other than boring. He was in a unit with other guys roughly his age, away from the kids who were brawling every other day, and he passed his days playing cards, or ping-pong, or working whatever jobs became available, in the laundry or the wood shop or the kitchen. He kept his own counsel, and he kept out of trouble. When he got early release, he couldn't say that he had gained any great insight from being there. All that he knew was that he didn't plan to return.

With a last look at the house, he pulled out and continued on, toward the river in the distance. He drove across the bridge and followed the winding river south, past the abandoned saw mill, still standing but at a significant lean. There was a new church on a rise just past the mill. The sign read The Faith Jubilee Worship Center. The place was enormous, with a paved parking lot the size of a football field and impressive landscaping that climbed three tiers toward the back of the property, a cacophony of flowers and rocks and fountains suggesting the Promised Land itself. A stone Jesus was standing in the center of the garden, his arms outstretched to worshipers and financial contributors alike.

Carl wasn't sure what he was even doing there. Too much time had passed. And it had always been about time. Taking time. Making time. In Carl's case, serving time. Whoever said that time heals all wounds didn't know what they were talking about. Time does nothing of the sort; it merely dulls the memory. Until there's nothing left. Carl wouldn't call that healing.

The sun was setting on his right as he approached the farm. Looking ahead, he saw a blue Land Rover pulling out from the property. As it neared, the vehicle drifted across the center line toward him. Carl slowed down; he could see the driver behind the wheel, gawking over at the river as he drove. Glancing back to the road, he suddenly realized his error and jerked the wheel violently to the right. The vehicle fishtailed and then straightened. The man, who was bearded and wearing sunglasses, gave Carl an apologetic little wave as they met on the road.

A little farther along Carl spotted a woman walking and soon he saw that it was Frances, moving up from the river bank with a Border Collie at her heels. As he drew closer he could see she was dressed in khaki shorts and a light t-shirt. Her hair was long but pulled back at the neck and tucked beneath a felt hat, possibly a man's fedora. Her father had favored Biltmore snap brims. She wore wellies on her feet and her stride was long-legged and fluid as she came up the hill. She carried a bundle of flowers in her hand, and she pulled away its leaves, discarding them as she walked.

The farmhouse was on a rise, as were most along the river

valley. The place was of red brick, its construction dating back to the 1870s. There was a wooden veranda along the front and down the south side, the railings and spindles and newel posts freshly painted white. A solid bank barn was behind the house to the left, with a machine shed alongside. Beyond that, on a gravel drive, was a building of recent construction, a warehouse of red ribbed steel with a green roof. The barn was maybe eighty feet long and across the gable, in block letters, were the words RIVER VALLEY FARM.

He arrived at the driveway in advance of her and so he drove in, stopping there, the engine idling. She'd been watching his approach and now she came up on him, speaking sharply to the dog, which had begun to bark. She wasn't smiling as he rolled the window down, but she wasn't frowning either. If she was surprised to see him, she wasn't letting on.

'Just like a country preacher,' she said. 'Show up at supper time.'

'I already ate,' he told her.

'I don't see you in ten years and you start out by lying to me? Park up by the house.'

He did as he was told. When he got out the dog came at him barking again.

'He's all talk,' Frances said, and sure enough the dog settled down as it reached Carl. He put his hand out and it came to him at once, its whole rear quarters wagging promiscuously. As Carl patted the animal, it seemed to him that Frances was regarding him as she always had, with the slightest disdain. He couldn't be certain; she was a hard one to read and nothing at all like her sister. Frances had always played her cards close to her chest while Suzy had been all primary process; a blind man could see what was on her mind.

'Well,' Frances said, 'you look OK . . . for an old man. Don't tell me you're looking after yourself after all these years.'

'You already warned me against lying.'

She smiled at that, removing the hat and shaking her hair loose. She was still beautiful, there was no question about that. Carl would have been surprised to discover otherwise. Her dark brown hair was thick and unruly, her skin tanned and smooth. She would be forty-four or forty-five now, a few years younger than Suzy. She indicated the flowers, which were tiny and purple.

'I have to put these in water,' she said. 'Then I could use a beer. How about it?'

'I just left Archer's.'

'I didn't ask you where you just left. I asked you if you wanted a beer. Come around back.'

Following her, Carl spotted a man hoeing a row of cabbages in a field off the end of the barn. He was tall and thin, wearing a wide-brimmed hat. He looked up from his hoeing and watched Carl for a moment from the distance.

'That's Perry,' Frances said as she walked. 'He works for me. I call him the hired man when I'm feeling John Steinbecky. You'll meet him at dinner.'

'I'm not staying for dinner.'

'Chrissakes. You drive out here just to leave?'

She led him to a flagstone patio which ran along the rear wall of the original house. There were mismatched chairs and a round wooden table of scarred pine. A barbeque constructed from a steel drum was on the grass just off the flagstones.

'Sit,' Frances said, and she went into the house.

Carl sat in one of the chairs and looked out over the farm. It appeared the entire acreage had been planted in garden vegetables. Corn, tomatoes, cauliflower. Grapes along the fence row to the north, raspberries and strawberries on the south side of the grape vines. There were forty or fifty chickens scratching around in a large pen behind the old barn, and a red rooster standing one-legged on a manure pile, overseeing the brood.

The barn looked the same as it had more than thirty years earlier, when Carl used to wait there for Suzy, who was doing her own waiting in the house, marking time for her father to stumble up to bed after drinking a half bottle or so of rye. It would be eleven o'clock, sometimes midnight, when Suzy would enter the dark barn carrying the red wool Hudson's Bay blanket. They would make love in the hay, or sometimes escape down the gravel road to where Carl's Harley was parked, far enough away that John Rourke – drunk or sober – couldn't hear the bark of the mufflers. Summer nights they would ride to Fiddlers Bay, spread the blanket on the cool sand, fuck like horny teenagers, which is exactly what they were. How could that have been over thirty years ago?

Frances came back, carrying the flowers in water and two bottles of beer, a brand Carl had never seen. She gave one to him and had a long drink from the other, then set it on the table while she went over and lit the charcoal in the steel drum. She fanned the flames until she was satisfied with the effort, then returned and sat down.

'I've got some chicken marinating,' she said. 'I'll treat you to a River Valley Farm meal.'

'Rufus Canfield told me about you and this place,' Carl said.

'I'm sure he was mocking me,' she said. 'Man lives on rye and coke and deep fried chicken wings. I suppose he told you he's a newspaperman these days.'

Carl nodded and had a drink. The beer was peaty and sharp. 'He doesn't seem real happy about it.'

'I would think not, with newspapers going the way of the dodo.'

Carl gestured toward their surroundings. 'I thought that was true about small farms too. But here you are. I thought you loved Chicago. Shit, you even became a Cubs fan, didn't you?'

'I did like Chicago. I still do.' She took a drink. 'But life is a crooked road, Carl. Dad died in 2005, and then mom got sick about a year later. Ovarian cancer. It took her a long time to die. I came home to take care of her. While she was dying – and I guess this is typical – while she was dying, she decided she wanted all she could get out of living. That first spring she bought a bunch of organic seeds and planted them in her little garden by the shed. And things just took off from there.'

'When did she die?'

'May fifteenth, 2008,' Frances said. 'Planting season. By that time, we were into it whole hog. I never thought for a minute I would ever be a farmer. Then again, this isn't my father's farm anymore, Carl. This is a different animal.' She smiled at him. 'You remember my father, don't you?'

'The guy that wanted to shoot me?' Carl asked.

'You knocked up his eighteen-year-old daughter. Were you expecting a warm embrace?'

'You having fun, Frances?'

'Little bit,' she admitted. 'My father was big on chemical fertilizers and engineered seeds and all of it. But then my mother – well, it was strange – my mother never really started thinking about the earth until she knew she was about to depart it. And I got caught up in it. Watching your mother die while she is furiously making everything around her live does something to you.' She tipped the beer back and after drinking she smiled. 'So here I am, schlepping around in rubber boots and a dirty t-shirt, drinking beer with an ex-convict on the back patio. And I thought being a Cubs fan was hard on my self-esteem.' She kept smiling until he smiled back.

'Rufus told me you were a cover girl for some fancy magazine,' he said.

She scoffed. 'Me and my John Deere. The tractor looked better than I did. Those people were here all day and ended up using six pictures. Your average twelve-year-old with a cell phone could have done it in five minutes.'

Carl glanced around, taking in the plush fields teaming with produce, the chickens scratching in the yard. 'Looks as if you're doing OK, though.'

'You'd be surprised. We have a website, and we ship stuff all over North America. This is one of these things . . . not only does it make good sense health-wise, but it's extremely fashionable these days to boot. There's a pop singer – Nikki something, flavor of the month – well, she mentioned in an interview last year that she buys berries from us for the organic smoothies she drinks on tour. We got thousands of hits because of that one interview. We put her quote on the website and our online sales went crazy. Teenagers, right?' She laughed. 'Of course, six months later Nikki went into rehab. We didn't post that.'

'So you're making money and you're saving the planet,' Carl said. 'I remember you wearing mink coats and dating millionaires.'

'I never owned a mink coat in my life.' Frances stood and walked over to check the coals in the drum. Carl looked at her legs as she bent at the waist to blow on the embers. When she turned, she caught him. 'I don't want to burst your bubble, but I don't believe for a nanosecond that I'm saving anything. The people who are destroying the planet are too damn big and their actions just too fucking rampant for me and my free range chickens to take them on. All I can do is keep my own little corner clean. I'm no idealist, Carl.'

She sat down again. 'You know the ironic part about this business? It turns out that the way things were done a hundred years ago is the right way. When it comes to farming, progress is the problem, not the solution. Animals are supposed to eat grass, not corn. Manure sustains the soil, not chemicals. And ugly tomatoes taste better than the pretty ones from the hothouse, and they're better for you.'

Perry, the hired hand, was approaching now, trudging slowly across the expanse of lawn between the house and barn. Carl watched the mopey approach. He was around forty and he wore overalls and heavy black work boots. He'd removed the straw hat and was carrying it in his hand.

'So he's the field hand,' Carl said. 'What else?'

'You're a nosy bastard for somebody who hasn't been around for ten years,' Frances said. 'That's all he is. He's a sweet soul but a good sneeze would blow him off his moorings. I wouldn't inflict myself on a guy that sweet.'

'What about the guy in the Land Rover?' Carl asked.

'What about him?'

'He damn near ran me off the road. Looked as if he was just leaving here. What did you do to rattle him, Frances?'

She smiled. 'Maybe he was asking personal questions that were none of his business.'

Carl laughed. 'Hey, I can take a hint. Besides, I thought you were married.'

'I was. For about eight seconds. A real estate agent in Chicago who couldn't understand why I didn't want to spend my life having lunch with the girls.'

'You had to get married to figure that out?'

'I'm not too bright, I guess.'

'That's not the Frances I remember,' Carl said.

'What about you?' she asked. 'You ever get married again? You were so good at it the first time.'

Carl smiled and shook his head. He indicated Perry. 'The two of you run the whole show?'

'No. I've got a full-time and a part-time doing the online

orders. Grace and Joanne. That's the new building over there. Perry and I and Mike run the farm. But Mikey's on his way out. He missed the market run this morning for the second time in a month. He doesn't know it yet but he's gone. I'd call him on the phone but I'm looking forward to telling the little prick to his face when he shows for work Monday morning.'

'Now that's the Frances I remember.'

They ate on the patio. Frances pressed Carl into service to grill the chicken while she went into the house and put together a salad of greens and onions and tomatoes. She opened a bottle of red wine.

As they ate, they talked mostly about the farm and the marketing of everything. Perry was openly resentful of Carl's presence, and he took his meal in near complete silence, speaking only when asked a direct question. After reluctantly shaking hands, he never looked at Carl. He was bony and angular but he had a voracious appetite and used every means available to stuff food into his mouth, like a man in a pie-eating contest.

It was growing dark when they finished eating. Perry declined dessert and said he would be going. He told Frances he'd see her in the morning, then walked off into the night.

'He live in the forest?' Carl asked.

'He rents a little house, down the road about a mile. He enjoys the walk.'

'I don't think he enjoyed the company,' Carl said.

'He gets like that when I have visitors. Male visitors.'

'Like the bad driver in the Land Rover?'

'I thought we'd established that that was none of your fucking business.' She smiled.

They had dessert and then Frances brought a bottle of brandy out on the patio. They sat where they'd sat earlier. The night air had cooled and at some point Frances had changed into jeans and a v-neck sweater.

Carl had left Dundurn before dawn. With the beer and the meal, and now the brandy, he was growing tired. It felt good to be sitting on the patio, though, with this woman he'd always liked, but who had always been wary of him. There was something different about her now. She'd had a restlessness about her that Carl remembered, and that restlessness seemed to be gone. She was more comfortable now, not so much with herself – she'd always been that – but with everything around her. Maybe she realized that the place she'd avoided all those years was actually where she wanted to be. It had probably surprised the hell out of her. It would surprise the hell out of Carl.

'Tell me about Kate,' he said.

'I wondered when we'd get to that.' She raised the brandy snifter to her nose, inhaled as she considered what she would say. 'What do you want to know?'

'Shit, I don't know. What does she do?'

'She has a day job, working for an insurance company. Office work. Weekends, she tends bar at a place called Shoeless Joe's. Sports bar, it's got outdoor volleyball, that kind of stuff. She's a jock. Lord knows where that came from. Not from my side of the family, and you weren't an athlete, you were a juvenile delinquent.'

'So you keep telling me.'

Frances shrugged. 'She beat the odds, I think. I mean, it took her a long time to get it together but she's doing all right. She really knows who she is, and I know that sounds like New Age bullshit, but it's not. Look where she came from. She had Suzy for a mother. She had you for a father. There's two strikes right there.'

'Don't pull any punches, Frances,' Carl said.

She half smiled and took a drink of the brandy, holding it in her mouth for a time before swallowing. 'You two were a disaster together. Suzy was an addict in waiting from the day she was born. She used to eat sugar by the spoonful when she was four years old. And you were a serial hound dog. How long were you faithful to my sister after you two got married?'

'We need to talk about that?'

'You're right,' Frances said. 'I don't want to know.'

'I did want Kate to come live with me,' he said then. 'After Suzy died, I tried to get her to come live with me.'

'Christ, she didn't even know you! She's eight years old, her mother overdoses and she's supposed to go live with a stranger?'

'I was still her father. That didn't count for anything?'

'She was better off here, with my parents. And you damn well know it.'

'Yup.'

'Yup,' Frances repeated. 'Don't give me that cowpoke attitude. Tell me what you want from her now.'

'Nothing,' Carl said.

'But you intend to see her?'

'I'd like to.'

'You figure after all this time she's going to be any good at the father–daughter thing?'

'You think I am?'

'No, I don't,' she said. 'But for what it's worth, I'm glad you're here. You've scored some brownie points with me, showing up. Better late than never. And, just so you know, I don't believe you're harboring any ulterior motives. You were never like that, even when you were fucking up in spectacular fashion.'

'I appreciate that. Part of it, anyway.'

'You should.' Frances stood up. 'You can sleep in the spare room tonight. You've had too much to drink to be driving.'

Carl knew that she was right. There was a time when he would've argued the point. No, there was a time when he would just have left.

'You going to the courthouse?' Frances asked.

'I should talk to her first,' Carl said. 'I want to.'

'Wanting to is reason enough to go,' Frances said.

'All right.'

He fell asleep with the brandy still in his hand. Frances took it from him and then she cleaned up, carrying the dishes inside and loading the dishwasher. When she went back out to the patio the air had grown suddenly cooler. She pulled her chair close to the still warm barbeque and looked at the wild flowers on the table. She'd put them in an antique milk bottle, with Talbotville Dairy etched in the glass, that she'd found a couple years earlier on a dusty beam in the old barn. Martin had picked the flowers for her, down by the river flats, shortly before he'd climbed into his Land Rover and left for the airport.

She'd been seeing him for several months, after he'd shown up the previous fall with the magazine people to take pictures of both Frances and the farm for the profile. He worked free-lance and, after returning the following week to offer Frances some prints that the magazine wasn't going to use, he had asked her to a Sting concert. Frances, aware that she hadn't been on anything resembling a date in months, had accepted, even though she wasn't a fan of the singer. That opinion didn't change over the course of the evening but she and Martin started seeing quite a lot of each other afterwards.

He was a few years younger than Frances and very good-looking – almost too good-looking, she'd told herself early on, before she got to the point that she no longer noticed it. It was a strange thing about humans, she thought: first attractions were almost always based on physical appearances, which in time became the least important element of a relationship. Martin favored a slightly bohemian look: he wore his hair past his collar and had a full beard, giving him a rugged mien befitting his reputation as a man who'd photographed African plains and Swiss peaks and Australian deserts. In real life he was not the rugged type, not at all. He was soft-spoken and introspective and prone to quoting century-old poets Frances had never heard of.

They got along quite well, and even traveled together, once to Barcelona for a photography exhibit and once to New Mexico, for fun. Martin was educated in a good many disciplines, which drew Frances to him while at the same time reminding her that she no longer had a wide range of interests, unless one was to consider the many different ways to grow a tomato to be a renaissance art form. Frances did not.

The sex was good. As she might have expected of a man with an artistic bent, Martin was gentle and inventive, not to mention flexible and able, and he did not, as some men did these days, concern himself much with the subject of who finished first.

In spite of all that, his leaving today had been a little tense. He was off to South America on an assignment, actually two different assignments, and he'd been quite certain that Frances would be anxious to tag along, or at the very least to join him in Peru or Chile for a week or two. She'd been explaining to him for a month or more now that she couldn't do that but it hadn't been until today that he seemed to get the message, after assuring her over and over that 'Perry could handle things at the farm'. It was an absurd suggestion and one that Frances found somewhat patronizing. Why was his work more important than hers? Sensing her aggravation, he had climbed down the river bank and picked the flowers as an apology of sorts, she guessed. She had kissed him before he left, but it hadn't been much of a kiss. She was certain that he was unhappy with her, but he was, in general, passive in the face of any conflict. Maybe too passive, she thought. Once, in a restaurant in Spain, a waiter had brought him a different entrée from the one he'd ordered. Rather than correct the man, Martin had eaten the meal. Frances, on the other hand, was prone to speaking her mind, a trait that didn't always serve her well.

Now she sipped her brandy while looking at the man sleeping in the chair. He was, if anything, better-looking than he had been as a young man. He was a few pounds lighter than she recalled, yet he had filled out, grown into his looks. He was not pretty and never had been but he had a sexual quality about him, and a toughness that he didn't cultivate. The lines around his eyes and the gray in his hair made him a little older, but not much. There was a scar on the bridge of his nose that she remembered and one on his upper lip, only partially concealed by his mustache, that she did not. His hands were calloused and misshapen, the fingertips blunted and marked by years of pounding nails, shoveling dirt, carrying shingles and whatever else he'd been up to since she'd seen him last. He was a man who could do things. Or at least he was a man who could do things of a physical nature.

If there were traces of gray in his hair, there was nothing else about him that would qualify as such. He had always been someone who viewed things in black and white, even when he was on the wrong side of a situation. This had been particularly true with regard to the event that had landed him in prison. Frances remembered quite clearly how attracted she was to him as a teenager, and how infuriated she was with herself for being so. There was nothing about him at the time that she approved of, not a single redeeming feature. He was like a case study of bad behavior, a stereotype. He drove a Harley, he smoked and drank and fought, he worked blue-collar jobs, one after another. He impregnated Frances's sister when she was still a teenager. He was a picture postcard of everything Frances disapproved of. And yet there was something about him that had been attractive to the fifteen-year-old girl. It wasn't the image of the bad boy – Frances had never been interested in that particular cliché. He was honest, albeit in a frustrating way. The fact that he lacked any real sense of diplomacy often made that honesty hard to detect. But it was the thing that had attracted Frances to him, even if his lifestyle had not.

And now he was back. And the man who lived his life in black and white was now quite obviously in a gray area that he clearly didn't recognize. Frances had never seen him uncertain about anything before. Not that he was the first father in history to be estranged from his daughter but Frances could see that he was at a loss as to what to do about it. He was a man who could *do* things but this wasn't something he could fix with a hammer or a saw or an axe.

She watched him asleep in the chair. She had been of the opinion that she would never see him again. Indeed, she hadn't known where he was or even if he still *was*. It wasn't something she thought much about. He was ancient history, like a lot of people in her past. All that changed tonight. If nothing else, he happened to be the father of her niece.

Which had to count for something.

FOUR

The next morning Browning took down Debra Williams.
'The summer of 1995.' It was ten in the morning and
Browning was on his feet and talking as soon as Debra
was installed on the stand. He was like a dog that hadn't eaten
in a couple days and could barely wait for the food to be poured
into its bowl. He was talking to Debra but looking at the jury,
scanning the faces one by one. 'You were fourteen years old. Is
that what you said?'

'Yes,' Debra replied. Braced by Browning's hungry pit bull,
her body language was suddenly different. Her shoulders were
hunched, her eyes guarded. She glanced from time to time at
Grant, as if seeking refuge there.

'And you were in . . . what grade?' Browning asked, still
taking inventory of the jury. It seemed to Kate that, under his
scrutiny, some of the twelve looked every bit as uneasy as did
Debra Williams.

'I had just finished ten. Going into eleven.'

Now Browning turned to face her. 'Were you a virgin?'

'Objection,' Grant said, and he stood up.

It seemed that Judge Pemberton had been expecting this, or
perhaps something like it. He had his elbow on his desk, his chin
on his fist, as he looked from Grant to Browning, shifting his
eyes without actually moving his head. 'I'm going to allow it,'
he said after a moment. 'To a point.'

'Were you a virgin?' Browning asked again.

'No.'

'As of – what was the date of your claim – July eleventh,
1995? As of July eleventh, 1995, how many sexual partners had
you had?'

Debra stalled, and in that delay she lost something. She lost
it in a split second and she would not get it back. 'Two or three,'
she said finally.

'So you don't know,' Browning said. 'You were fourteen years old, you were sexually active but you really don't know how many partners you'd had? You don't know if it was two or three, so it could've been four or five or six?'

'No,' Debra said.

'What is the point in this?' Grant demanded.

Judge Pemberton looked at Browning. 'She answered your question, counselor.'

Browning bowed slightly toward the bench. He went back to his notes, spoke without looking up. 'Did you, Ms Williams, use drugs at this time?'

'No,' Debra said, but her voice trailed. 'What drugs?'

'Well, let's try to narrow it down, shall we?' Browning said. 'Did you smoke marijuana?'

'Yes. I tried it.'

'You tried it?' Browning said. 'You were arrested for possession of marijuana in April of 1995. Had you tried it at that point or were you just carrying it around for ballast?'

'Mr Browning,' Judge Pemberton warned.

Browning held up one hand, as if holding himself accountable. Kate looked at Grant. It was obvious that he had no knowledge of the arrest. He sat stone-faced at the big table, his jaw muscles tight.

'I tried it,' Debra said again. 'Those charges were thrown out.'

'They weren't exactly *thrown out*,' Browning told her. 'You were given a conditional discharge, due to your age, which means you were found guilty but do not have a record.' Browning looked over at Grant. 'Such information is sometimes hidden away in the catacombs of jurisprudence past.'

Grant smiled at the slight but his expression was that of a man in need of a laxative. Browning turned back to the stand.

'Did your mother know about the arrest?' Browning asked.

'No. I don't remember. I don't think so.'

'That's three answers to one question,' Browning said. 'Would you care to pick one and go with it?'

'She didn't know.'

Browning shook his head as he went back to the table. 'Now the record shows that the conditional discharge was granted in August of 1995. Is that correct?'

'I guess. If that's what it says.'

'That's what it says. Do you agree or not? We need to be accurate here. That's the one thing I must insist upon.'

'Yes.'

Browning took a moment with his notes. 'Do you know a Shelly Bosfield?' he asked then.

It took a moment for Debra to reply. 'Yes, I knew her.'

'How did you know her?'

'We went to high school together.'

'You also went to *court* together,' Browning reminded her. 'Ms Bosfield was also charged with marijuana possession. The same incident as you. Is that true?'

'Yes.'

'Is it true that you boasted to Ms Bosfield that you were very good friends with the family of the accused – Joseph Sanderson the third – and that you merely had to ask Mayor Sanderson to have the charges against you dismissed and it would be done?'

'No.'

'I would advise you to be careful now,' Browning said. 'You are under oath. Ms Bosfield will be testifying. Are you certain you never made any statements to that effect?'

'I don't remember ever saying that.'

'You don't *remember* saying it. That's a little different from denying you ever said it.'

Browning waited for a comment but did not seem concerned when none was made. 'While we're testing your memory, let's try this one. I suggest to you that sometime in July of 1995 – approximately the time you claim you were attacked by the defendant – you were indeed in the lake house alone with Mayor Sanderson. And at that time you did indeed ask him if he would intercede on your behalf with the courts with regard to your outstanding marijuana charges. Does any of this sound familiar?'

Kate looked over at The Mayor. He was watching neither Browning nor Debra Williams. He was staring at a spot on the wall above the jury box, his face in quiet repose, nodding slightly, as if he was listening to a concerto.

'That never happened,' Debra said. She was sitting forward in the witness box now. She held her left hand tightly with her right, as if the very act was holding her together.

'I suggest to you that it did happen,' Browning said then. 'I also suggest to you that Mayor Sanderson told you that he was sorry but he could not intervene on your behalf. Is that true?'

'No. I asked him for his advice,' Debra said. Kate saw the air go out of Prosecutor Grant. 'Nothing more than that.'

'His advice,' Browning repeated. 'Did you tell Shelly Bosfield of the mayor's refusal to help you?'

'Yes. I mean no. He didn't refuse to help me. I never asked for that.'

'That's right. You didn't ask for that,' Browning said. 'You just asked for – what was it? His *advice*. Did you tell Shelly Bosfield of the alleged attack on you?'

'No.'

'No?' Browning asked. He turned and walked toward the jury. 'Funny that you would mention one thing and not the other. Funny that you would neglect to tell her that you had been raped. Allegedly.'

'I never told anybody.'

'Just your mother, right?' Browning asked, still with his back to the stand. He was now regarding the jury as if they were all sharing in a private joke.

'Yes.'

'Will your mother be testifying as to that in this courtroom?'

'My mother is dead.'

'When did she die?'

'Two years ago.'

'When specifically?' Browning pressed, still facing the jury. 'If you don't mind.'

'Two years ago in March.'

Now Browning turned. 'And you brought these charges against my client two years ago in June. Isn't it odd that you waited until the one person who could in some small manner corroborate your story was no longer around? Isn't that odd?'

Debra stared back at him, then looked at the judge. 'Am I supposed to answer that?'

'Let's call it rhetorical and move on,' Browning said. 'Ms

Williams, have you ever been convicted of defrauding money from welfare services?'

Debra looked quickly over at Grant. 'I made a mistake once,' she said, offering her reply to him instead of Browning. 'I started a new job, and I wasn't going to get a check for two weeks, so I thought I could cash my assistance check.'

'Answer the question,' Browning said. 'Were you ever convicted of welfare fraud?'

'Yeah.'

Browning smiled. 'See? Wasn't that easy?' He walked to the table and had a look at his notes. 'Let us keep in mind that that is all in your past. You have since pulled yourself up by your bootstraps. Isn't that right?'

'I don't know what that means.'

'It means that you no longer seek to acquire money by dubious means.' Now Browning turned to her. 'Ms Williams, do you know a Lawrence Filsinger?'

'We've met.'

'What does Mr Filsinger do?'

'He's a lawyer.'

'He is indeed a lawyer,' Browning said. 'Is it true that he intends to launch a civil action on your behalf against my client if my client is convicted of these charges? A civil action that would presumably seek a sizable cash settlement?'

'I don't know what he's gonna do,' Debra said. 'Nothing's been agreed to. Not on my account anyway.'

'Have you discussed the matter with him?'

'I've discussed this case with people. Yeah.'

'I'm not interested in all of the fascinating conversations you've had regarding this matter,' Browning said. 'Just this one. Will you please answer the question? Have you talked with Mr Filsinger about mounting a civil action against my client?'

'We *talked* about it. Yeah. But nothing was agreed to.'

Kate was watching Grant again. He looked like a man at a poker table who was thinking forward to his next hand rather than the one just dealt him. Because he knew the one he was holding was a loser.

'You talked about it,' Browning said then. 'And in talking about it, I'm sure Mr Filsinger informed you that without a conviction in this court, you have no civil case against my client. Without a conviction, there will be no pot of gold at the end of the rainbow for you.'

'Objection,' Grant said half-heartedly.

'I withdraw the remark,' Browning said. He looked up at Judge Pemberton. 'I have nothing more for this witness.'

FIVE

C arl woke early and took a moment to remember he was in the guest bedroom at the farmhouse. The room was fancier than he was accustomed to – a lot of pillows, lacy curtains with floral patterns, a settee with red upholstery in the corner. It was just dawn as he got out of bed and dressed. There was a bathroom next to the bedroom. Washing his hands after relieving himself, he noticed a man's razor on the vanity, along with a can of shaving cream. He assumed that the items belonged to Mr Land Rover. He made it downstairs and out the door without seeing anyone. He got into his truck and headed for town.

In a diner on Main Street he ordered ham and eggs and toast, then drank coffee while he waited for the food, realizing he'd had quite a bit to drink the night before. The booze, like everything else of late, had seemed to come at him in a rush.

Forty-eight hours earlier he'd been at work at NuTech Industries in Dundurn. After work most of the crew was heading to Shooter McGraw's for beer and wings and to play some eight ball. Carl considered going home to catch the six o'clock news but the apprentice Billy Curtis kept pressing him to go for a beer. A recent hire, the kid had for some reason decided that Carl was his mentor. Carl had no idea why, but he gave in, thinking he could watch the news at the bar.

Shooter McGraw had played twelve years in the NHL, mostly with the Maple Leafs, with a couple of quick stops in Philadelphia and Chicago at the end of his career. How he'd acquired his nickname was a topic of conversation in the bar from time to time. Since he'd never scored more than ten goals in a single season in the majors, any notion that he was a sniper was invalid, and even ridiculous. He was a lousy pool player, so it seemed unlikely he'd earned his name on the felt. Billy, who was rarely short of theories, was of the opinion that McGraw was so named because of his propensity for downing large numbers of shooters.

That fact that Shooter was a colossal drunk gave credence to that particular thesis. He'd purchased the bar seven years earlier, and promptly renamed it in his own honor. There were twenty TV sets in the place, everything from a sixty-inch flat screen against the back wall to smaller plasma units mounted over the bar. Shooter carried all the pay-per-view events, and he threw large, artery-clogging parties for Super Bowl, the UFC championships, various NASCAR races and virtually anything else that drew a crowd. Most mornings he opened the place at eleven and most nights he was so drunk by eight o'clock that he had to be driven home by one of the staff. Early on, given the unruly element in a place that catered to pay-per-view sports and young drinkers, Shooter had taken on the role of bouncer. He'd proven in the NHL that he fought about as well as he scored, and a man who couldn't fight when he was sober was unlikely to improve his skills after he'd had a couple dozen beers. It took only two or three shit-kickings in the parking lot to convince Shooter of this. Nowadays, he allowed his wait staff to handle the roughnecks.

Billy Curtis and Carl arrived this Thursday at the same time, having left NuTech's parking lot one behind the other. Julie was working the bar, wearing a skirt that showed her excellent legs and a red Shooter's t-shirt. Her blond hair was in a ponytail, revealing a neck that was every bit as fetching as the legs. She wore dangling silver earrings that looked like fishing lures. Carl and Billy sat at the bar and ordered draft beer.

'Any chance you could put the Rose City news on that set?' Carl asked.

Julie was probably the only one in the town who knew why Carl would prefer to watch the news rather than first round coverage of the PGA Colonial Classic from Ohio. Before drawing the beer she found the remote and changed the channel.

'Woman's got an awesome body for her age,' Billy said, watching her.

Her age, Carl knew, was forty-two. He also knew that she had a terrific body for any age.

'Why don't you take a run at her?' Billy asked.

'Why don't you?'

'I tried. She called me a pup and told me to pound salt.'

'So she's got a good body *and* good judgment?'

'Fuck you.'

Julie brought the beer and Carl paid, tipping her too much. She gave him a look of reprimand and then moved off to serve someone else.

'She likes you,' Billy said. 'She's always checking you out, dude, when you're shooting pool or whatever. She looks at you like . . . I don't know, but she looks at you. You could fuck her, easy.'

Carl had fucked Julie, off and on, for almost two years. And during that period she had fucked him right back. If it was up to him he would still be fucking Julie, but she had put an end to it last winter. She'd told him that he was missing something and when he asked what it was she said that she wasn't sure but if she figured it out she would tell him because he – more than she – would benefit from the information.

Their relationship hadn't changed that much. They still flirted, they still talked about things that they probably didn't talk about with other people. They just didn't go to bed together anymore. Which was taking a key ingredient out of the mix, as far as Carl was concerned. That could change, if one of them could figure out what it was he was lacking. But he wasn't counting on that happening any time soon.

'Pick up your motor yet?' Billy asked now. He asked the question every Thursday. He and Carl had been working together five days a week since Billy hired on three months ago, while Carl taught him how to rough wire the alarms and video equipment, then how to hook up the systems. Yet Billy only asked about the Harley engine one day a week. Thursdays at Shooter McGraw's. It was as if he'd decided early on that this was the way to wear Carl down. He was a confident kid. In a general sense he really didn't know his ass from his elbow, but he had the confidence of someone who was willing to learn. Carl liked him.

'No.'

'Why don't you just sell me the goddamn bike?'

'It's not for sale.' Carl was watching the screen, where the news was starting.

'It's gonna sit in your back yard until it rusts into the ground. You're too old to have a Harley anyway.'

'Yeah? What's the cut-off age on a thing like that?'

'How old are you?' Billy asked.

'Fifty-two.'

'Then it's fifty. Time to sell. Thing's just gonna sit in your back yard.'

'I'm going to put it together this summer,' Carl said. On the screen the lead story was about a shooting in west Rose City. Two people dead. The cops were not releasing any information other than to say that the deceased were 'persons of interest' to the police. Cop talk.

'It's fucking July already,' Billy said. 'You're not gonna put it together.'

Julie had served the newcomers and now she was standing a few feet away, watching the newscast.

'There are lots of Harleys for sale,' Carl said. 'Why do you have to have mine?'

'Cuz it's a '72 hardtail,' Billy said. 'And that's what I want.'

'You never heard of a '72 hardtail 'til I told you what it was,' Carl said. Footage of the Rose City courthouse flashed on the screen. Carl pushed some coins toward Billy. 'Put us up, will you? Before everybody gets here.'

Billy scooped the money into his hand and stood. 'You're gonna sell me that bike,' he said, before heading toward the coin-operated eight ball tables in the back.

Julie picked up the remote again and increased the volume on the set. The place was not busy yet and as such not as loud as it would be in an hour or so, when hearing the TV would be almost impossible. On the screen, a young reporter was standing in front of the courthouse, microphone in hand. The reporter was female, and she looked like a model or an actress playing a reporter in a movie. But they all looked like that nowadays. She was responding to a prompt from the anchor.

'. . . as Miles Browning showed in his opening remarks why he's considered one of the country's pre-eminent defense lawyers. Browning had his way with the prosecution's case, suggesting that the accusers were planning a big money civil suit against former Mayor Sanderson should he be convicted. Prosecutor Thomas Grant will need a strong showing if he's hoping for that to happen.'

Julie turned to Carl. 'Had his way with them? Did she actually say that?'

But Carl was still looking at the screen. The anchor had just asked the reporter to describe Sanderson's demeanor during the testimony. Behind the reporter Prosecutor Grant could be seen, speaking with other media, and behind him four women were walking out of the courtroom. Last in the line was Kate.

'. . . very composed and, like yesterday, completely unfazed by the rather sensational nature of the testimony. Of course, over his years in office The Mayor earned a reputation for stoicism and grace under fire. Back to you, Phil.'

Carl watched Kate as she moved out of the frame. She held her head high and it seemed that she glanced with disdain toward the camera for just a second. Her dark hair was long and she was lovely, not just in the way she looked but in the way she carried herself, the confidence in her walk. Watching her, Carl felt a pang in his chest he didn't recognize.

'That's her, isn't it?' Julie said then. 'That's Kate.'

Carl nodded. The newscast moved on to another story and Julie switched back to the golf. She lowered the volume and turned to him.

'How long has it been since you've seen her?'

'Twelve years.'

'You look like you've seen a ghost. She's not a ghost, Carl.'

Carl took a drink of beer. 'I went to see her when I got out of jail. For about five minutes.'

'Why just five minutes?'

'Way she wanted it,' Carl said. He put the glass on the bar. 'I bought her a puppy. I thought . . . shit, I don't know what I thought. She didn't want the puppy. Not if it was from me. She was a smart kid.'

'The puppy probably wasn't a real good idea,' Julie said.

'I guess not.' Carl looked up at the TV, where a commercial was now showing. 'Did it seem to you that the reporter was kind of biased toward The Mayor?'

'It seemed to me that the reporter is a fucking idiot,' Julie said.

Carl nodded. He told himself that the reporter's mental inadequacies really didn't mean anything. What went on outside the courtroom had no bearing on what happened inside. He drank from his glass, aware that Julie was watching him closely.

And then she said, 'Your past is the one thing in this life you can't change.'

Carl turned to her and then Billy came back. 'We're up next. We gonna order some wings?'

'You go ahead,' Carl told him.

'Gimme a large extra-hot, beautiful,' Billy said to Julie. 'And another round. You know, I'm thinking I might just take you home with me tonight, Julie. What do you think?'

'I think . . . why would I pour you a second beer when the first one obviously scrambled your brains?' She moved off to get the beer.

'I think I'm getting to her,' Billy said.

'Oh yeah,' Carl told him. 'You're doing great.'

Julie brought the draft and Billy paid. She looked at Carl for a long moment.

'Sarge is the puppy,' she said. 'Isn't he?'

'Yeah,' Carl said. 'Sarge is the puppy.'

After a while someone organized the pool tournament. There were twelve players, five bucks a man, double knock-out. Carl and Billy teamed up. They were beaten in the finals by Big Ed Houston, who wired the boards for the new systems, and a girl named Sherri, who'd started at NuTech the previous week. Big Ed couldn't, in Billy's words, 'sink a rock in the ocean' but the new girl could shoot. She had pierced eyebrows and tattoos on her arms and her own three-piece cue. Billy took an immediate shine to her, rolling up the sleeves on his t-shirt to show off his own ink work. Sherri played him like a bass fiddle while she shot lights out and took all the money. Enamored, Billy played like a man who couldn't sink a rock in the ocean.

Not that Carl was much better. His mind wasn't on the game and twice he sank a high ball when he was supposed to be shooting lows. It didn't help that every time he looked over toward the bar it seemed that Julie was watching him. Watching him for what? He smiled at her once and when she finally smiled back – it took longer than it should have – her expression was maternal, sad even. Carl didn't need anyone to be feeling sad over him, not tonight. Not ever. After losing at pool, he waited until she went into the kitchen for something and then he left. He wasn't in the mood to talk.

It was still daylight when he got home. He'd drunk four draft at the bar and, although he was far from drunk, he could feel the effects as he passed through the quiet streets. It seemed to have cooled off, if only slightly, and he drove with the windows down, the oldies station playing loudly. 'Fortunate Son' by Creedence was blaring as he pulled in the drive. He saw Sarge on the porch, stretched out in his usual spot in the shade. Carl got out of the truck and went up the steps.

'Hey buddy,' he said, as he looked in the mailbox and pulled out a couple of letters and some flyers. 'Come on, I'll cut you up some steak.'

He opened the screen door and stood there, opening the hydro bill as he waited for the dog to come inside. He glanced at the amount before opening the flyer from Home Hardware. 'Sarge, come on.'

And he came to the slow realization that Sarge wasn't getting up.

He buried the dog in the back yard and afterward he sat on the deck and drank beer and at one point he put his hands to his face and was surprised to find that he had been crying. The wind came up and it seemed as if a storm was approaching, but then the moon appeared, sneaking from behind the clouds like a timid actor venturing out from the wings for the first time. Soon the stars were shining like diamonds above the treetops.

Around eleven o'clock he called down to Shooter McGraw's and asked for Billy Curtis. He told Billy he would sell him the hardtail for a thousand dollars and that he should give the money to Mary-Ann in payroll. She could send it to him with his last check.

He packed his bags before he went to bed. He set his alarm for six but he was awake and up before then. He loaded the truck and made a cup of coffee from instant.

The sun was just showing as he hit the highway and headed for home.

SIX

S aturday morning Frances was down at the warehouse before the sun cleared the barn roof to the east. She and Perry loaded the truck themselves. Mike was supposed to help but he never showed and he never called either. It was the second time in a month it had happened. And both times a market day.

Everything was early this year so they had lots to load – berries, potatoes, corn, peas, beans. This week Frances even had the first tomatoes of the season, heirlooms she'd started in the greenhouse in March and planted outside on the first day of May, covering them with burlap on the nights when frost threatened. Along with the jams and jellies and maple syrup it took them the better part of an hour to load the GMC stake truck. Frances had wanted to be at the market for six and that wasn't going to happen now.

'It would have, if he'd showed up,' Perry said, meaning Mike.

'Well, that's twice,' Frances said. 'I wonder if little Mikey is hip to the three strike rule.'

They were on the road by then, Frances at the wheel and Perry in the passenger seat, drinking tea from a plastic thermos he'd owned since he'd shown up looking for work six years earlier and probably for twenty years before that. Frances had a cup of coffee in the plastic holder on the dash.

It was still early enough that the traffic heading into the city was light and it took them less than thirty minutes to get to the market. The first thing Frances saw when she went down the ramp to the market stalls was the yellow seven-ton van with Parnelli Farms on the side. The truck was parked carelessly on an angle, with the front end extended into the space reserved for Frances's stall.

'Lookit this,' she said, and she stopped and got out.

Two kids, teenagers probably, both in dirty shorts and tank tops, were unloading the Parnelli Farms truck, carrying boxes of vegetables to the tables, while another guy was filling six quart baskets and setting up the displays. This man was stocky, of medium height, maybe in his forties. He wore a denim smock with the name Arnie stitched on the breast pocket, and a cheap straw hat that a farmer might wear, or at least a man pretending to be a farmer.

'Excuse me,' she said, approaching. 'You're blocking my spot.'

The man Arnie was arranging tomatoes in quart baskets now, the tomatoes large and very red, perfectly shaped. 'Just unloading here. Be five minutes.'

'Then I'm five minutes later getting set up,' Frances said. 'You're in my way, Arnie. It is Arnie, right? Or did you borrow that shirt the way you borrowed my spot?'

'We'll just be a few minutes,' Arnie said impatiently. 'Go get a cup of coffee or something.'

One of the grungy kids walked over with a crate of cantaloupes. Frances looked at the boxes on the pavement. The crates were unmarked but she knew the stuff was from the south – Florida or California for the most part. The kid gave her a smile that was somehow flirtatious and mocking at the same time and then went back for more. Frances turned to Arnie.

'Maybe if your guys parked in your own spot to begin with, I wouldn't have to stand around watching you polish your plastic tomatoes while they unload.'

'What did you say about my tomatoes?' As if that was the problem.

'Move the fucking truck,' she told him, and she went back to the GMC.

They didn't move it, at least not until they finished unloading. Frances sat fuming behind the wheel. Perry had more tea and said that he had half a notion to report Parnelli Farms to the market board.

'The board doesn't give a shit or they wouldn't let these guys in here,' Frances told him. 'There was an agreement.'

By the time that Frances was finally set up, Arnie had already made a half dozen sales. He ran the stall by himself; the two vegetable toters had disappeared as soon as the unloading was done. Frances saw them later, sleeping in the back of the big truck. She relaxed somewhat once she started doing business, but she was still pissed off, and it wasn't entirely to do with the parking situation.

'So where is Parnelli Farms anyway?' she asked Arnie. There was a lull in business and she had walked over to his stall.

'Toronto.' He was stacking ears of California corn and replied without looking at her.

'Really? What do you have – a couple hundred acres down at Yonge and Bloor?'

He glanced over and smiled as if to say, fuck you, lady. They both knew there was no such thing as Parnelli Farms, unless a warehouse somewhere could qualify as such. Just as Frances knew that her organic produce wasn't quite as pretty to look at as that offered by Arnie the urban farmer. But that was the reality of the situation. She didn't mind competing with area farmers – real farmers who grew their own product, whether it was organic or not. They were local farmers supporting the local farmers' market.

At noon she left Perry in charge and went over to Wenger's Deli for a sandwich. Perry had packed his standard lunch, white bread and a couple of tins of sardines and an orange soda. The sardines would linger on his breath for the rest of the day. Frances had prepared a lunch too but in the rush to get loaded that morning, she'd left it on the kitchen counter back home. She was going to blame that on Mike too, if he managed to get his lazy ass to work Monday morning. She bought a smoked turkey on whole wheat and sat on a folding chair at the back of the stall, eating and talking to Stan Wenger when he wasn't serving customers.

'I thought city was going to put a limit on these guys,' Stan said when she told him about her run-in with Arnie from Parnelli Farms.

'They did,' Frances replied. 'But nobody enforces it. I figure somebody's getting paid off. Problem is, the market's not full. So these guys show up with their five tons of hothouse vegetables and they get a stall. I don't know how, but they get it.'

'There's somebody you could ask,' he said.

She turned in the chair to follow his eyes. Bud Stephens was standing across the market square, talking with a tall man in a white western shirt. Bud, wearing a beige suit, was gesturing dramatically with both hands, holding forth on something.

'Bud the slug,' Frances said. 'What's he doing here? This isn't his ward.'

'Produce shopping?'

'I doubt it. Look who he's talking to.'

'Who is that guy?'

'That's Hank Hofferman.'

'That's Hofferman?' Stan said. 'OK, that makes sense now. See that butcher's stall just past them? They're brand new, calling themselves H and H Pork and Sausage. Gotta be his pork.'

'If you want to call it that,' Frances said.

'How would he know Bud?'

'City mouse, country mouse.' Frances shrugged. 'There was a rumor that Bud helped Hank out with permits on the new rendering plant out on the highway. It's not Bud's ward either but I heard he had his nose in there. Bud's got his nose in every-thing, since The Mayor's untimely resignation.'

'Aren't they related?'

'Bud's the favorite nephew,' Frances said. 'How do you think he got elected? Which means he is *not* close with the new mayor. On the outside looking in these days.' She looked across the market again. 'This might not be Bud's turf, but I'd still like to know what he thinks about these assholes ruining our market.'

Hank Hofferman saw her approaching. He was a galoot, a hulking cowboy who had never ridden a horse. Gas-guzzling Hummers were more his line. He wore his jeans high, cinched in place with a belt featuring a big silver buckle. She watched him smile and say something to Bud, who was laughing as he turned toward her. Bud's blond hair was artfully messed up, spiked here and there and held in place with product of some kind, a look that might have worked for a twenty-five-year-old but seemed a tad desperate for a man twice that age. He was sporting a goatee Frances had not seen before. Not only that, but he wore a lot of jewelry – rings, bracelets, chains around his neck. In general, he was pretty much a poster boy for everything Frances did not care for in a man. Approaching, she was feeling a little contrary, and being laughed at didn't help.

'What's so funny, boys? A little old lady get hit by a truck?'

'Hugged any trees lately?' Hofferman asked.

'Really?' Frances asked. 'Is that the best you got?'

'Don't tell me you've given up on saving the planet, Frances.'

'Don't tell me you've given up on fucking it over, Hank.'

Frances turned to Bud. 'I thought council passed a motion to stop these phony farmers from parachuting in here. Am I wrong about that?'

Bud had a take-out coffee in his hand and he took a drink and then belched into his fist before replying. 'What phony farmers would you be talking about?'

Frances gestured across the lot. 'Parnelli Farms. This market is supposed to support local growers. We don't mind American produce coming in during the winter but it's July, for Chrissakes. And if these guys are farmers, I'm Mary Magdalene.'

'They make the market a bigger place of business,' Bud said. 'They provide more product, and more variety. It actually helps you in the end because it draws more people past your little stall.'

'My little stall?' Frances said. 'That's bullshit. These guys undercut our prices. Don't start with that nonsense that it brings more people in. We keep books – these guys hurt our bottom line.'

'I'll look into it,' Bud said, but his tone made it abundantly clear that he wouldn't.

'Maybe I'll look into it,' Frances said. 'Somebody's getting paid off here or these guys would never get a stall.'

'That sounds like a threat,' Bud said. He looked at Hofferman. 'Do tree huggers make threats? Isn't that against their code or something?'

'I want to know how they don't get splinters,' Hofferman said. He grinned, sticking with his aw shucks persona, the dumb country boy in his western shirt and his Wrangler jeans and pointed cowboy boots.

'I hear you've been buying farmland again, Hank,' she said. 'You're not building more pig barns, are you? I thought the bottom was falling out of the pig market. At least, the kind of pigs you produce.'

'What's wrong with my pigs?' Hofferman asked.

'Cramming three thousand sows in a barn and pumping them full of chemicals doesn't exactly produce a hog fit for eating, Hank. I hear even the manure is toxic. The local farmers won't spread it on their fields. I'm talking about the real farmers now.'

Hofferman smiled. 'Well, I'm still making a dollar or two. Same as you, Frances.'

'You don't do anything the same as me,' Frances told him.

'Gal's a little wound up today,' Hofferman said, smiling at Bud.

'It's all an act,' Bud said. 'Straight out of the Green Party play book.'

'Come on, Bud,' Frances said. 'You're wearing a store-bought tan and more jewelry than a Kardashian and you're calling me an act?'

Driving home later, Frances decided that her best move would be to start a petition and to have it signed by all the legitimate farmers who used the market. At least they would be on record as saying they opposed the interlopers. It would be up to the council to do something about it, and Frances didn't have a lot of faith in that happening. There was nothing she could do about that.

'That man was just plain rude,' Perry said, referring to Arnie from Parnelli Farms. 'Maybe next time I'll punch him in the nose.'

Frances, behind the wheel, looked over at him. The first time she'd ever met him he'd been wearing a cloth cap and overalls, looking for all the world like Hank Fonda in *The Grapes of Wrath*. He was built like the character too – gangly arms and legs, a prominent Adam's apple. But she'd learned that the resemblance ended rather abruptly right there. Perry was no Tom Joad. And Frances was quite certain he'd never punched anyone in the nose in his life.

She also knew that, with his loyal servitude and his slow proficiency and his sardine breath, he was half in love with her. That was something else she couldn't do anything about.

SEVEN

After Debra Williams's testimony Grant sidetracked and spent two days building the technical side of the prosecution's case, calling all of the investigating officers to the stand and having them describe just how the force came into possession of the information which led to the charges against The Mayor.

Grant next called Dr Kenneth Strong to the stand. Strong was a psychologist who specialized in trauma cases. He spoke to the mental states of the four women, the lingering effects of the attacks, and under Grant's questioning he tackled the tricky, speculative subject of what might have been, compared to what was. The testimony was risky business, but Grant had to chance it. There existed no physical medical evidence, usually key in rape cases.

Kate knew what Grant was doing, but still she chafed under the doctor's suggestion that she had somehow been diminished by what had happened to her all those years ago. She was in the courtroom to demonstrate that the opposite was true. The Mayor had not damaged her. She was a victim of nothing, particularly of him.

Browning had little in the way of cross-examination for the cops who testified. In his dismissive manner he suggested that the officers had been rather naively led down a garden path 'festooned with falsehoods' and that for him to revisit that path would only lend credence to the lies. He also suggested, somewhat cryptically, that a more competent police force would never have listened to the outrageous fabrications which now formed the foundation of the case against his client. He did make a point of telling the jury that they were basically just repeating whatever stories they'd heard from the accusers. Watching, Kate got the impression that Browning was saving his best stuff for the women themselves.

Browning was not so magnanimous with Dr Strong, particularly with regard to Strong's suggestions that the four women had been robbed of more fruitful lives as a result of being attacked at such an early age.

'Interesting that you can opine on such matters,' Browning said to the doctor. 'I have your accreditations here, and they are impressive. Medical doctor, doctor of psychology, fellowship at Harvard. Yet I have to ask – is this list complete?'

'It is,' Strong replied warily.

Browning stroked his chin as he studied the paper in his hand. 'For you to tell the court what these women *could* have been means that you have powers far beyond that of a doctor of medicine, or even a psychologist. Yet I see nothing on your résumé that says you have a degree in the metaphysical. Do you hold, for instance, a Bachelor of Clairvoyance?'

Grant stood. 'My colleague is making light of a serious matter.'

'I withdraw the remark,' Browning said. 'Nothing more for the witness.' Walking back to the defense table, though, he stopped and turned toward the doctor. 'Although, if you really *were* clairvoyant, you'd have seen it coming.' Most of the jurors laughed and Judge Pemberton called it a day.

The next morning Grant put Maria Secord on the stand.

The witness wore a long brown skirt and a black sweater, another turtleneck that did not quite hide the lunging panther which ran along her neck nearly to her earlobe. Grant took her through the standard route – where she was born, schools attended and the rest. Maria's voice, forged by late nights and cigarettes and hard liquor, was not unpleasant to the ear. She looked directly at the jury often as she spoke. She glanced from time to time at The Mayor too, but he never returned the favor, maintaining his pose of being apart from the proceedings at hand. 'The summer of 1997,' Grant said, getting to it. 'You were sixteen. How did you come to know Joseph Sanderson the third?'

'My mother knew Mrs Sanderson,' Maria said. 'My mother's active in the church and that's how they met.'

'Just to clarify – when you say Mrs Sanderson, you mean the accused's wife?' Grant asked.

'Yeah. That's who I mean.'

'And which church?'

'St Patrick's. One time they were doing this fundraiser for some charity thing in Africa someplace. And Mrs Sanderson's church got involved. She goes to St Stephen's. Or did anyway, back then. So they had, like, bake sales and rummage sales, you know, stuff like that. And I guess they became friends.'

'Who did?'

'My mother and Mrs Sanderson.' Maria's tone was slightly impatient, as if she was prepared to tell her story if Grant would stay out of the way. 'I was looking for a summer job and Mrs Sanderson got me an interview for work at city hall.'

'What kind of work?'

'Intern.'

'In the mayor's office?'

'Yeah. Well, it was, like, not just in his office. City hall. Running errands for a bunch of different people.' She waited for Grant to say something and when he didn't she continued. 'So I got the job. And my first day there, I was real nervous. Cuz nobody really told me what I was supposed to do. I remember being worried that I was gonna have to type something and my typing wasn't that good. But the first morning I was just, like, photocopying shit . . . oops, sorry.' She glanced at the judge. 'I was just photocopying stuff, and delivering papers here and there.'

'Had you met Mayor Sanderson before that day?'

'No. I met him for the first time when I got there that morning. I remember he shook my hand and kept on walking. I didn't think he even noticed me.'

'What happened later?'

'He went for lunch, like, pretty early, I remember. Like maybe eleven thirty or so. He came back a couple hours later – he was smiling then, and talking a lot. He sent his secretary to lunch and she told me to stay in his outer office and answer the phone, just take down messages and whatever. But after she left, he came out and told me to come into his office. As soon as I walked in he closed the door and kissed me. He didn't say anything. He stuck his tongue in my mouth. He smelled like whisky. I tried to grab the door handle but he pushed me down on the carpet. He kept trying to kiss me while he was pulling my dress up. He ripped my panties and he was trying to get at me. In me. And I was crawling backwards, and suddenly he . . . he finished.'

'He ejaculated?'

'Yeah. I could feel it on my legs.'

'Then what happened?' Grant asked.

'He stood up and he zipped his pants. He looked at me and then he gave me forty dollars and told me to buy a new dress. Cuz he came on my dress too. It was a new dress.'

'That's all he said?'

'No,' Maria said. She looked at The Mayor. 'He told me to go back to the outer office. He told me that if anybody called to tell them he was in a meeting.'

'That was it?'

Maria continued to stare at The Mayor, who was posed perfectly in profile, his thumb beneath his chin and his forefinger on the tip of his nose, his own gaze fixed on the far wall of the courtroom. 'No,' she said. 'He told me not to say anything about what happened because nobody would believe me anyway. He told me I would look like a fool.'

'And did you tell anybody?' Grant asked.

'Nobody.'

'Because of what he told you?'

'I don't know,' Maria said. She hesitated. 'I was pretty messed up. I was sixteen years old and I'd just been raped by the mayor of the city. I didn't know what to do. I had no idea . . . what to do.'

'But wouldn't you tell your mother?' Grant pressed.

'No,' Maria said. 'My mother was – she was going through a hard time. I wasn't gonna lay this on her.'

'When you say she was going through a hard time, what do you mean?'

'A bunch of stuff. My old man left when I was little but he kept coming back, you know, for a month, or two months or whatever. He was always drunk, and he was always mad. He would beat my mother up. Like, for no reason.'

'A moment, your honor,' Browning said as he stood up. 'Is there some connection between this drunken wife-beater and the charges filed against my client? Because otherwise – I don't know where the prosecution is going with this.'

Judge Pemberton looked at Grant.

'If we can allow the witness to finish,' Grant said.

'Go ahead,' the judge said after a moment.

Maria Secord watched Browning with loathing as he sat down. 'Anyway,' she said after a moment, 'my mom was going through tough times. She worked at the canning factory for minimum wage, and then she was always laid off in the winter. It seemed like being friends with Mrs Sanderson was important to her, for some reason. I guess cuz she was, like, from the other side of the tracks or whatever. That whole trip. So after her being smacked around by my old man and everything, I didn't want to come home after my first day at work and tell her that her friend's husband raped me.'

The courtroom was very quiet. Grant took advantage of the moment, walking back to the table and taking an inordinate amount of time to look over his notes. Kate kept her eyes on Maria Secord. There was something in her expression. Victory maybe. She had finally told her story, and she had told it in front of the man who had raped her. Whatever else happened, they weren't going to take that away from her.

After several moments, Grant approached the witness again. 'So you kept quiet for more than ten years. What made you come forward finally?'

'There were always rumors floating around about the guy, you know—' Maria began, but she was interrupted at once by Browning.

'Objection,' he said, reverting to his bored tone. 'Has my colleague called this witness to the stand to discuss rumors?'

'The witness will stick to what she knows to be fact,' Judge Pemberton said.

Maria nodded. 'I heard . . . from a friend . . . that he was being investigated,' she said.

'By "he" you mean the accused?' Grant said.

'Yeah. So I decided that I should tell what I know. What he did. So I got hold of a cop I knew, and he hooked me up with the cops doing the investigating.'

Grant glanced over at Browning. 'Call it intuition but I have a feeling that the attorney for the defense will question your motives for coming forward at this late date. So I'll do him this kindness – why are you doing this?'

Maria Secord was waiting for the question. 'Because I've

always been ashamed of what happened. How screwed up is that? *I* was ashamed and he *wasn't*. And that never made any sense to me but it's the way it was. I don't know why. Maybe because he was rich and we were poor, or he was this powerful guy. I don't know. But he should be the one who's ashamed. And I guess if that's ever gonna happen, this is the place it's gonna happen.'

Browning began his cross-examination after lunch. First he sat at the table for a long time, staring at Maria Secord while tapping a pencil lightly against his double chin, measuring her up. At one point he shook his head, as if he despaired of trying to decide just what would possess a woman to tell such an outrageous tale. Finally he stood, approaching her with his hands plunged deep in his pants pockets, his eyes cast to the floor.

'Just out of interest,' Browning asked, to begin, 'where were you a week ago Saturday, Ms Secord?'

'I was . . . I don't know . . . at home probably.'

'What time did you have lunch?'

'What?'

'What time did you have lunch, a week ago Saturday?' Browning asked again.

'I don't know. Noon, I guess. One o'clock.'

'So, it could have been noon, it could have been one.' Browning turned toward the jury. 'And yet you *know* – you have actually testified under oath here that you *know* that Joseph Sanderson went for lunch at eleven thirty on a summer's day back in 1997. Funny how specific you can be about that. Of course, little details like that can be very effective when attempting to sell a story.'

'Objection,' Grant said.

'Counselor,' Judge Pemberton warned.

Browning smiled contritely, then glanced toward the jury, again as if sharing a private joke with them. He let the smile drop and turned back to the stand. 'What do you do for a living, Ms Secord?'

'I'm a waitress.'

'Where?'

'Actually, I'm between jobs right now. I last worked at the Power Plant.'

'I guess we can assume that the Power Plant is a restaurant

and not a hydro-electric facility. Have you always been a waitress?'

'No.'

'What else have you done?'

'I've had a few jobs. I worked at Sears. I worked at Home Depot.'

'Were you ever an exotic dancer?' Browning asked. 'A stripper?'

Maria's contempt for Browning was palpable. 'Yeah.'

Browning raised his eyebrows slightly, as if he was actually surprised at the revelation. 'At the time that my client allegedly . . . pushed you to the floor . . . were you a stripper?'

'I was sixteen years old.'

'Answer the question.'

'No.'

'So it was later on that you made that particular career choice.'

'Is that a question?'

'An observation,' Browning said. 'After the alleged attack, you claim you told no one.'

'That's right.'

'I assume, however, that you immediately quit your job at city hall?'

'No.'

'No?' Browning's eyes widened as he moved toward the jury again. 'Are we to believe that a sixteen-year-old girl was sexually assaulted by her employer on her first day of employment and yet continued to come to work every day?'

'I didn't know what else to do.'

'You could've quit,' Browning said. 'As a matter of fact, there were a number of things you could have done. You could've screamed. Apparently you did not. You could have called the police. You chose not to. You could have told your mother, your friends, your priest. You did none of these things. Is that correct? You told nobody?'

'I'm telling you now,' Maria said. She was staring at Browning's back, challenging him.

'You're telling me now,' Browning repeated, turning. 'Yes, you are. I hear you've also told Lawrence Filsinger. Do you know Lawrence Filsinger?'

'I don't know him. I met him. Once.'

'During that one meeting, did Mr Filsinger broach the subject of a civil suit against my client?'

'Yeah.'

'And were you agreeable to that possibility?' Browning asked.

'I wasn't one way or the other,' Maria said. 'If you're trying to say this is about money, you're wrong.'

'Oh, come now,' Browning admonished. 'Let me tell you what I think. I think that I'm seeing a young woman who's looking for a score. A young woman who heard that the police were pursuing trumped-up charges against my client and decided – based on a very brief period of employment at city hall nearly two decades ago – that there was some free cream to be had, and that she might as well dip her spoon in that cream while she could.'

'I'm lactose intolerant.'

'That's very good,' Browning said. 'When you're finished joking, are you going to tell this court that you've never considered the possibility that there's some money to be made from this?'

Maria shrugged. 'I hear you're making a nice chunk.'

There was a murmur of laughter throughout the room. Browning was taken aback. 'But I'm not telling lies to make it,' he snapped. He caught himself immediately. 'But you will admit there's money to be made. Thank you, finally, for your candor. I think it helps us to understand better why you might come forward with an unlikely story like this, after all the intervening years.'

'I never—' Maria began, but he cut her off.

'Or perhaps you're financially set,' Browning said. 'Tell me – do you still work as a stripper?'

'No. Why – you got a birthday coming up?'

There was more than a murmur of laughter in the room this time. Grant dropped his head and pinched the bridge of his nose with his thumb and forefinger.

'No. My birthday has passed, thank you,' Browning said. He turned toward the jury, nodding his head as if agreeing to some obvious truth. 'I don't think I have anything else for this witness. In fact, I think she has told us all that we need to know.'

EIGHT

Kate was working the afternoon shift at Shoeless Joe's on Saturday. There was a volleyball tournament in the adjacent sandlot scheduled for four o'clock and Kate got there an hour beforehand to set up the outside bar. Sasha, the manager, was leaving as Kate arrived, heading for a wedding somewhere, and as she left she told Kate that a new kid, Nathan, would be helping her. The kid slouched in minutes later, texting somebody as he came through the door. When Kate introduced herself, he nodded without looking up from his phone.

The two of them went to work, carrying the liquor and the beer kegs and the glasses and condiments outside. The bar itself was simply two rough pine planks atop a couple of aged whisky barrels, beneath a bright Stella Artois awning. There were shelves built to the rear, against the outer wall of the building.

Kate found working with Nathan to be almost exactly like working by herself. When she told him to do something he went about it reluctantly, and when she didn't he sat on one of the bar stools and played with his phone. By the time they were ready to serve drinks some of the players had begun to arrive and Kate had yet to make up the tournament schedule. Nathan assured her that he could handle the bar so she took the sign-up sheets inside, out of the wind, and drew up the brackets on sheets of Bristol board.

When she walked back outside with the schedule, she stopped short. Carl was there, sitting at the end of the rough bar, drinking a draft beer that was more foam than beer, courtesy of Nathan's expertise as a bartender. He was sideways to her, looking up at the baseball game on the big screen above the bar, and didn't see her at first. Watching his profile she was reminded of a hawk, the distinctive sharp nose, the slightly feral aura about him. He was thinner than she remembered, wearing brown pants and a black t-shirt. His hair was scattershot with gray and longer than the current style, falling to his collar. He had a mustache that was somewhat out of fashion too, reaching past the corners of his mouth. He looked fit, though, healthier than when she'd seen him last.

She had an urge to walk back inside before he turned and spotted her. But there was nowhere to run to and, even if there was, she had a feeling he already knew she was there. After watching him a moment longer, she went over and took the glass of beer from him. She dumped the foamy mix into the sink before turning to Nathan.

'Watch.'

She drew a fresh draft, tilting the glass so there was a half inch of head. Pouring, she glanced over at her father, who was watching her in turn. He was the same but different somehow. There was something worn about him, as if some of the sharp edges had been filed off, but only slightly. She has always thought of him as a coiled spring, but now it seemed as if that spring had lost a little of its temper. That happened with springs over time. Did it happen with people? Maybe it was just that he had lived longer. As simple as that.

'Hello, Kate,' he said when she set the beer in front of him. His voice cracked when he said her name and he coughed, clearing his throat.

'Hello, Carl.'

He indicated the draft. 'Thanks.'

'Got a rookie on the tap.'

'I figured that.'

'I'm surprised to see you, Carl,' she said.

'Thought I'd stop and say hello.'

'Yeah. That's the part I'm surprised about. Is there something I can do for you?'

'No,' he said. 'There's nothing you can do for me. I just . . . stopped by. I've been following the trial.'

'Frances told me.'

'I thought she might fill you in.'

'She didn't fill me in, just said that she talked to you.'

'I guess there wasn't much filling to be done.'

Kate thought about that, what it meant. 'You still live in the city, then?' she asked.

'No. I've been over in Dundurn, last ten years or so. I've been following the trial though and I've been thinking about you. I thought I would . . . well, I don't know. I guess I've just been wondering how you've been.'

'I've been fine.' She wasn't sure why she was so intent upon giving him nothing, but that's what she was doing.

He took a drink and wiped his mouth with the back of his hand. 'Frances said you have a boyfriend?'

'Yeah, I do.'

'Well, that's good.' He drank again. It seemed like a stalling tactic while he pondered how to keep the conversation moving. Not that she was helping in that regard. 'What does he do?'

'David?' she asked. 'He works at a recycling place.'

'That would be a good thing to get into,' Carl said. 'Nowadays.'

'Seems to be.'

Kate glanced down the bar, where Nathan was again texting on his phone. Denny was coming in at four, she knew. He could help with the bar and then Nathan could go off and do whatever he considered to be gainful labor. She turned back to her father. 'So you thought you would stop by and what – offer me some moral support? Is that it?'

'I guess that's it.'

'No offense, but you're a little late in that regard, Carl.'

He exhaled heavily and looked around. Some of the volley-ballers were putting up the nets now, uncoiling the anchor ropes, stretching them out.

'Frances told you I worked here?'

'Depends,' he said. 'Is she in trouble if she did?'

Kate paused, then shook her head. 'No.'

He smiled. 'Good.' The smile changed him, made him younger. His craggy brows lifted and she could see the startling blue of his eyes. She remembered that blue very well.

One of the players walked over to ask Nathan where the mallet was to pound the stakes into the sand. He might as well have asked Nathan for directions to Jupiter. But it gave Kate an excuse to go back to work.

'We got this tournament going on,' she said.

Carl nodded and she walked away. She was aware of him watching as she provided the players with what they needed and then went about pinning the sheets with the brackets to the fence.

Under his gaze, she kept on the move, as if to show how busy she was. Denny arrived and Kate asked him to take over the bar while she went inside. There was a round window there, an old porthole, in fact, that someone had salvaged from a wrecked ship at the bottom of the lake. Kate stood just to the side of it and watched Carl as he sat at the bar, drinking the beer, staring straight ahead. She didn't know what to feel. Of course, he hadn't taken her completely by surprise; Frances had told her he'd been around. But that didn't mean she was comfortable with his showing up. Hell, she wasn't even comfortable about the thought of him. It had been too long, and it had become too easy not to consider him. She saw him drink off the beer and, after glancing at the door to the bar, get to his feet to leave. On an impulse, she decided she would walk him out to the parking lot.

She picked his truck out long before they got to it. Among the Hondas and Jeeps and Chryslers was an older Ford pickup, with no hubcaps and red primer over the rear wheel wells. If her father was a vehicle, Kate thought, this is what he would look like.

'Well,' she said when they reached the truck, and that was all she said.

'I'd like to . . . I don't know . . . buy you dinner or something,' he said.

'I've got a lot going on right now,' she said. 'I work two jobs, and the trial and everything. So I don't know when I'd have time.'

He opened the truck door. 'OK.'

'Listen, Carl. Whatever happens, I'm not going after a settlement. That's not why I'm doing this. OK? There's not going to be any money.'

The instant the words were out of her mouth she knew she'd made a mistake. She told Frances later that she couldn't have hurt him more if she had plunged a knife into his chest. He never spoke a word. He got into the truck and drove out of the parking lot and was gone.

Bud stood naked in front of the mirror in the en suite bathroom. He had showered and just finished drying himself off. Ignoring the clothes hamper three feet away, he tossed the towel into the corner, then stood there looking at himself, something he did infrequently of late. His belly was quite a bit larger than he would have guessed it to be, even though he was well aware that he'd gone from a thirty-four to thirty-six inch waist when buying pants recently. He pulled his stomach in and turned sideways, throwing his shoulders back. That was better. He found, however, that he couldn't hold the pose for very long. Turning toward the mirror again, he stepped closer to examine his face. He'd grown the goatee a couple of months earlier in an effort to hide his double chin. It had worked well enough, he thought, but now he could see a lot of gray in the whiskers. Was it there before? Surely he hadn't gone gray over the course of a couple months. Whatever the case, he didn't want a gray beard. Either he would have to start coloring it, as he did his hair, or he would have to lose some weight. Dyeing his goatee held about as much appeal as did dieting.

Bud had been down this road before, albeit thirty years earlier. In high school he was a fat kid who wasn't good at sports. Back then he was still known as Delmar, the name his father had burdened him with before taking a powder when Bud was four. He had no memory of his father and his mother claimed that she couldn't remember where the name had come from. To her knowledge, nobody in Bud's father's family had a name like that. They were all Joe or John or Ralph. Whatever its origin, the name Delmar was bound to attract some ridicule in high school, particularly when the kid wearing it was fifty pounds overweight and couldn't throw a baseball across a room. And it did attract ridicule, in fairly large amounts.

Bud eventually took his nickname from an uncle on his mother's side, a loud, fast-talking ladies' man who never seemed involved in any kind of employment. Bud didn't adopt the new name or drop the weight until he was finished high school, and working a dirty job in a pulp mill along the canal. The work was hot and involved heavy lifting. Bud hated it but he had decided he was sick of being the fat kid named Delmar and over the course of a year he gained a new name and lost nearly sixty pounds. He never had a girlfriend in high school; in fact, he rarely had a conversation with a girl in high school but now, with money in his pocket and new clothes on his back, he found that women were attracted to him. He made up for lost time and, in spite of marrying Deanna in a weak moment after she'd led him to believe that her father was the owner of a Chrysler dealership and not just the fucking head salesman, he'd been making up for it ever since. But now, having turned fifty-one a month earlier, he was looking at a physique that was beginning to remind him of the fat kid Delmar. And the high-school years.

Bud couldn't go back to that. He had to take charge and he had to do it in a manner that didn't involve going to work again in a pulp mill.

From the front room of the condo he heard Deanna come in and a few moments later she walked into the bedroom, removed her shoes and joined him in the bathroom, where she hoisted her skirt and sat down on the toilet to go. She didn't comment on him, standing there naked in the bathroom in front of the mirror.

'Where you been?' he asked.

'We had dinner at Brady's.'

'We?'

'Me and Selma and Lily.' He could hear the dribble of her urine in the bowl.

'I gotta lose some weight,' he told her.

'Then do it.'

He turned to face her. 'Look at my gut. It's fucking huge. All the extra weight is concentrated right there. Everything's out of proportion.'

'Talk to a nutritionist,' she told him. 'Get on a plan.'

'My belly makes my penis look smaller than it really is. Look.'

She didn't look but reached for the toilet paper.

'Look at my penis,' he said. 'It's the same size as it always was but it looks smaller. It's relativity. You know that?'

'Yeah.'

'Look at little Bud. Look at him.'

'I've seen him. Seventeen years now.'

She stood up, tugged her skirt back down and walked to the sink to wash her hands. Bud stepped behind her and put his hands on her hips.

'You know,' he said. 'As my darling wife, you should be willing to help boost my self-esteem.'

'How would I do that?' Now she was looking at herself in the mirror, top lip pulled back to examine her teeth.

'You can make little Bud bigger,' Bud said. 'You have the power.'

'No thanks,' she said. 'Shit, I have fucking parsley or something between my teeth. Why wouldn't someone tell me?'

'We don't have to fuck,' Bud said. 'A blow job would be nice.'

'I said no thanks.'

She squeezed a line of toothpaste on a brush and began to clean her teeth. Watching her work the foamy toothbrush vigorously in and out made him grow hornier. Strange, he'd never considered it an erotic act before.

'It will only take a couple of minutes,' he predicted.

She spit and rinsed, then spit again. 'I'm too tired,' she said.

'Not too tired to go out for dinner five fucking nights a week.'

'Girl's got to eat,' she said, turning to him. She kissed him lightly on the lips. 'A week from now we'll be in Portugal. I'll suck your cock in Portugal.'

She walked out of the bathroom and into the bedroom, where she turned on the TV before starting to get undressed. Bud followed. As he watched her, still aroused in spite of her rejection, his cell phone began to ring. He found it in his pants, on the chair. Hank Hofferman was on the other end.

'Got a gitch in the plans,' Hank said.

'You mean glitch?' Bud asked.

'Yeah. Glitch. We gotta meet.'

By the time Bud got off the phone, Deanna had changed into baggy pajamas and was back in the bathroom, smearing some sort of cream on her face. There would be no action tonight, for either of the Buds.

They met the next morning in a truck stop called Brannigan's, on the highway at the north end of town. Hofferman was sitting in a booth, drinking coffee, when Bud walked in. Bud asked the waitress for a Hires root beer and when he was told they didn't have any he ordered tea instead.

'What's going on?' Bud asked.

'John McIntosh,' Hofferman said. He announced the name like it would mean something to Bud.

'Who's that?'

'Farmer out on the Irish Line. He called me up, wanted to know what I was doing with the concession.'

'What's it to him? I thought you had the whole thing bought up,' Bud said.

'I do. But he's across the road. His family has been there for something like a hundred and fifty years. There's this rumor out there I'm gonna put in more sow barns. You heard Frances Rourke the other day.'

'What does he care?'

'All these old-timers are against intensive livestock operations.'

Bud's tea arrived, just the bag in a cup of hot water. Bud dunked the bag a few times and took it out. 'Why are these old-timers against intensive livestock operations?'

Hofferman made a face like he was experiencing gas. 'Old people, they don't like progress. I had a hell of a time putting those first barns in, years back. These people got together – called themselves Hogwatch – and they petitioned to stop me. Dug up all these stories off the internet, about manure lagoons overflowing, steroids in the feed, shit like that. Tree huggers. Council backed me in the end, though. They had no choice, I met all the zoning requirements. When I was building my first barn, though, one of these Hogwatch guys put a torch to it one night. A fireman was killed fighting the fire. Guy went to jail for it. Guy named Carl Burns.'

'An arsonist named Burns?' Bud said. 'That's a hoot.'

'The dead fireman didn't think so,' Hofferman said.

'A dead fireman wouldn't think anything, would he?' Bud asked. 'So what'd you tell the old guy?'

'Told him that's not what I'm doing.'

'You tell him about the landfill?' Bud asked.

'No. I didn't know if I should or not. Nothing's been made public. He's a pretty sharp old bird. And there's some influence there too.'

'What kind of influence? I thought he was a farmer.'

'His brother's a senator. The family's old-time Liberals.'

'For Chrissakes,' Bud said.

'Yeah. You keep telling me we might have to go through an environmental assessment. I been hearing all it takes to shit-can an assessment is for somebody in the capitol to whisper in some-body else's ear.'

'Well, that can't happen,' Bud said. 'I've already leaked the Michigan pull-out to my guy at the *Times*. This has to be a slam dunk. It goes like this – one day the city admits that there's no place that'll take our garbage, and the next day Bud Stephens delivers the Talbotville plan. Game, set and match.'

'I'm just saying there might be a problem,' Hofferman said.

Bud sipped the hot tea while he thought about it. 'You say you talked to him on the phone? Not in person?'

'Yeah, on the phone,' Hofferman said. 'I figured maybe you should talk to him.'

Bud nodded and drank his tea. 'All right, then.'

Not that Bud had any appreciation for such things, but the McIntosh farm on the Irish Line was immaculate. A wide curved lane shaded by ancient white oaks led to a fieldstone house, behind which stood a number of barns and outbuildings painted green with white trim. The front yard was enormous and there was a pond along one side, the grass around the edges meticu-lously trimmed. The level of water in the pond was low due to the heatwave and the drought, and as Bud drove his Escalade into the driveway an old man in overalls was standing by the water's edge cutting lily pads with a scythe-like blade on the end of a long pole. The old man wore a cap with a Massey Ferguson logo on the front. Bud was pretty sure that his name was John McIntosh.

They sat on the porch and talked. The old man lived alone, he said, having lost his wife two years earlier. He was eighty-one years old. They discussed the weather for a bit. Bud knew that people who lived in the country were obsessed with the subject, probably because they had nothing else to talk about. He kept expecting the old man to ask him why he was there, but he never did. He was a sly old bastard; he was going to make Bud come out with it.

'What's in the pond?' Bud asked.

'Nothing. Oh, some frogs and maybe some little catfish.'

'What's it good for?'

'I don't know that it's good for anything,' John McIntosh said.

'I had it dug when my kids were little. I built a raft for them. And they used to sail their toy boats in it too. Nowadays I just try to keep the cattails and lily pads from taking over.'

'Why don't you just fill it in?' Bud asked.

'I don't think I will.'

Bud told him then that he was a councilor from Rose City, and after a moment he added that he was a lifelong Liberal, which wasn't even remotely true. The old man nodded upon hearing the information, although he seemed to be little impressed with either claim. When Bud told him that the city was possibly thinking of putting in a landfill on the concession across the road, the old man nearly spit up a lung.

'That's preposterous,' he sputtered. 'That's good farmland. What kind of idiot would do a thing like that?'

'The surveyors have done their work,' Bud said. 'They tell us it's a good spot for a landfill.'

'That land drains into the river,' the old man said. 'How are you going to contain the run-off? Who will guarantee that?'

'Well, now, the engineers have assured me that would not be a problem,' Bud lied. 'With modern methods, we can pretty much assure, um . . . what they call safe containment.'

The old man sat silently for a time, but his eyes were narrow and his mouth was working, even though no sound came out. After a long while he nodded his head. 'I guess we're going to have to see about this,' he said.

Bud glanced at his Escalade, parked in the drive. 'It's progress, Mr McIntosh,' he tried then. 'We're a disposable society, that's the sad truth. We can turn a blind eye to it, or we can meet the problem head on. It's up to leaders like me to see that our trash is disposed of properly.'

'You figure you're a leader?'

'Yes, I do.'

'I'd say you're a nincompoop, running with a bunch of other nincompoops.'

Bud blinked a couple times. The comment actually hurt. He'd been called any number of names since entering public life but never a nincompoop. 'You can think what you want,' he replied after a moment.

'We'll have to see about this,' the old man said again. 'I was born in this house. I don't figure on getting up every morning and looking at a goddamn dump across the road.'

Bud thought about that line as he drove back to the city. The fucking arrogance of it. How one man decided he would stand in the path of progress. It infuriated Bud.

Like most selfish people, Bud had little time for other selfish people.

Bud and Deanna Stephens were invited to Saturday dinner at the Sandersons'. Louise and The Mayor had people over almost every Saturday, although Bud and Deanna were rarely included. This night there were just the four of them. The Mayor cooked a prime rib roast on a spit in the stainless steel gas barbeque he'd bought that afternoon at Hackett's Hardware. The unit was five-feet long and, along with the rotisserie, it had six burners, a warmer and a steamer for vegetables or seafood.

'What did that set you back?' Bud asked.

'More than my first car,' The Mayor replied.

'It probably has more options than your first car.' They were drinking manhattans on the patio, with The Mayor raising the stainless-steel lid from time to time to make sure the beef was still turning.

'I'm glad Aunt Louise called,' Bud said. 'I need to talk to you but I wasn't sure about the timing. I assume you've had a rough week.'

'Don't call her Aunt Louise.'

'I've been calling her that since I started to talk.'

'It's time to stop.'

Bud shook his head in apology.

'I've had a good week,' The Mayor said. His tone was clipped. He had another look at the roast before continuing. 'I'm seven days closer to exoneration.'

Bud, still back on his heels, took a drink. 'I intended to make it down to the courthouse one day but I've been tied up. The landfill. And Hofferman.'

'What's going on?'

'First of all, Michigan is officially out of it,' Bud said. 'It hasn't been announced yet but as of the end of next year, they won't be taking any more of our trash.'

'And you thought I didn't know that?' The Mayor asked. 'What's with Hofferman?'

Bud told him about the old farmer John McIntosh with the brother in the senate and the vow to throw a monkey wrench into the works. The Mayor waved the old farmer away like he was swatting a fly.

'Influence,' he snorted. 'Politics doesn't drive this. Money does. Our current and temporary mayor is going to suggest we send our trash north. We want to send it out to Talbotville, an hour away. Anybody with enough brains to check out the price of fuel will know which is the better plan. Does this Hofferman have the land sewed up?'

'Says he does,' Bud replied. 'He'd better have.'

'You don't believe him?'

'This guy is as dumb as dirt,' Bud said. 'I don't know how he manages, but he does. That land still needs to be re-zoned. You don't think people aren't going to be screaming for an environmental assessment?'

'Let them scream. There's not going to be an assessment.'

'Why not?'

The Mayor gave Bud a look that suggested that he was asking stupid questions. Bud fell silent under the stare. The Mayor ignored the pout, emptied his glass and then poured another drink from a pitcher. He added ice cubes before offering the pitcher to Bud, who had a refill and changed the subject.

'So how was Miles Browning in action? The *Times* referenced Clarence Darrow. The *Gazette* compared him to Johnny Cochran.'

The Mayor smiled. 'So who does that make me . . . John Scopes or O.J. Simpson?'

'They both got off,' Bud reminded him.

The Mayor had a drink. 'Watching Browning at work is like watching a Cy Young winner on the mound. He never rattles, never throws the wrong pitch. I'll tell you something about him. When I hired him, he asked me if I might consider making a deal with the Crown, some sort of plea bargain to avoid the publicity of a trial. I told him absolutely not. And then he told me that if I had said yes, he would not have represented me. That's a winner.'

The sky was threatening rain so they ate inside. Louise had

prepared roasted potatoes and asparagus. Deanna brought her Waldorf salad, known for being almost inedible. Louise opened two bottles of Chilean red. The meat turned out well.

'What did you expect?' The Mayor asked. 'A forty-dollar roast cooked on a five-thousand-dollar barbecue.'

The conversation rested for an inordinate amount of time on the Stephenses' upcoming trip to Portugal, with Deanna describing sights they had yet to see, meals they had yet to ingest, wines not tasted.

'Are you two getting away this summer?' Bud asked during a lull in the blathering.

The Mayor nodded. 'We're going to Patagonia next month. Trout fishing. I've hired the guide that Tom Brokaw uses.'

'I thought, with the trial and all . . .' Bud said.

'This trial will be over very quickly,' The Mayor assured him.

'We don't have to discuss it tonight,' Deanna said.

'We can discuss it,' The Mayor said. 'It's not some secret. In a few days, it will be over. And *then* we'll have no need to discuss it again.'

'But that's not true,' Louise said.

'What's not true?'

'After the acquittal, we will definitely be talking about it,' she said. 'In earnest. These women didn't just decide to start telling lies on a whim. Somebody has an agenda here, and we're going to find out who.'

'You don't think McBride was involved?' Bud asked.

'Maybe not him,' Louise said. 'Maybe one of his guys, without his knowledge even. A Karl Rove. Face it – McBride would never have been elected without this.'

The Mayor smiled, said nothing as he poured more wine for himself.

'This has been a terrible thing,' Deanna said.

'OK, let's leave it for now,' Louise said, watching The Mayor's expression. 'Deanna, where do you fly into? Lisbon?'

'No, we actually—'

'Enough about Portugal,' Bud said. 'Louise is right about this. Somebody has to be held accountable. And you know who can tell us? These four women.'

'No,' The Mayor said sharply. 'I will not pursue this. I will clear my name and that will be the end of it. I'm seventy-two years old. I have no desire to run these women to ground. They have all suffered circumstances which we can only imagine. Broken families, drugs, you name it. I have nothing but sympathy for them.'

And that was the end of it.

NINE

Amanda Long was slated to testify on Monday morning. That changed abruptly when she showed up at the courtroom an hour late, and drunk. She denied being intoxicated at first but finally broke down and admitted to Grant that she'd gone off the wagon over the weekend. She hadn't fallen off; the prospect of testifying had pushed her. Grant sensed that wasn't quite the case. It was the notion of facing Browning that had done it. She'd been sober for three years and now she wasn't and if he felt bad for her, he felt worse for himself.

Kate was standing in the hallway outside Grant's office when he came out and told her.

'So she's not going to testify today,' Kate said.

'She's not going to testify at all,' Grant said.

A half-hour later Kate was on the stand. Grant, rattled by the abdication of Amanda Long, was off his game. He made a couple of false starts and as he stumbled through the standard background questions, Kate glanced over at the defense table. The Mayor was sticking with his Sunday-in-the-park pose, continuing for the most part to watch a spot on the wall above the jury. Browning, as well, appeared profoundly disinterested in the proceedings, at one point even turning in his chair to look over the spectators behind him.

Following his eyes, Kate saw that Carl was in the gallery, sitting beside Frances. David was at work. He wouldn't have known that Kate would be testifying today. None of them did.

Kate had to wonder if Carl had shown up and sat alongside Frances uninvited. She and Frances had rarely talked about him, but she'd always sensed that Frances had little use for her father. Maybe that wasn't true. It didn't matter much to Kate, one way or the other.

He had surprised her though, showing up at the bar on Saturday when he did. Not only that, but he'd handled himself that day a lot better than she had. She could say that being surprised was the reason for her behavior but she knew that wasn't true. She had wanted to dismiss him. And maybe even to hurt him. She had gotten used to not thinking about him. There was no up side to thinking about him. There was particularly no up side to that on a day like this, when she was supposed to be listening to Grant.

'Where did you grow up?' he was asking now.

'I lived in Talbotville. A couple different places.'

'With your parents?' Grant, working the broken home angle again.

'With my mother mostly,' she said. 'My parents split up when I was three years old.' She pressed on, helping things along. 'My mother died when I was eight and I went to live with my grandparents.'

'In the town of Talbotville?'

'No. They had a farm a few miles outside of town.'

Grant was still struggling to find his rhythm. He stood at the table for a time, going over his notes. Kate wished he would get out of the way, let her tell it. 'How did you first meet Joseph Sanderson the third?' he asked finally.

'We did a field trip to city hall in Rose City. Grade ten English. The teacher picked three of us to interview him in the mayor's office. It was short, five minutes or something like that.' Kate rattled the information off as if by rote.

'Tell the court what happened after that day.'

'He phoned the school a week or two later and asked my teacher if he could see the pieces we'd written. She sent them to him and then he called me a couple days later. At my grandparents'.'

'How did he get the number?'

'I have no idea.'

'Did he call the other two students?'

'No.'

'How can you be so sure?'

'Because I asked them.'

'All right,' Grant said. 'He called you at home. What did he say?'

'He complimented me on my writing. He said he'd been editor of his school paper in university. He said he wanted to be a writer but he wasn't good enough. He told me I was a better writer than he was.'

'And what did you think about this?'

'I was flattered.'

'When did you actually see him again?'

'He called me a couple times, to talk about writing. He had suggestions, what I should write about. He told me about a story he'd written about this old trapper's cabin near his property on Lake Sontag. He said the cabin had all this history, something about a murder in the nineteenth century, a murder that was never solved. He said he would give me the story if I wanted it. Maybe I could investigate it. Write about it myself.'

'What did you say?'

'I said I'd like to see it. He told me it was with all his university papers at his lake house there. One day he called and said he had to run up there for something, and he asked if I wanted to come along to get the story and have a look at the cabin. I was . . . I guess I was pretty excited. I wanted to tell my English teacher about it, but he told me not to. He said it would look like he was giving me preferential treatment over the other kids that had interviewed him. So I didn't.'

'Go on.'

'He picked me up after school. He said it was sort of on the way to the lake. It was snowing, I remember. I was thinking we might not go, because of the snow.'

'And when was this?'

'February twenty-fourth, 1998. The lake was frozen, and the road that he said went to this old cabin was snowed in. He said it was too far to walk, so we would just get the papers from the house. I was disappointed. I wanted to see the cabin.'

'Go on.'

'We went to the lake house.' Kate stopped. Browning was watching her now. The Mayor was once again cleaning his glasses. 'We went inside. He said his papers were in a cabinet in the living room.' She looked at The Mayor, vigorously rubbing the lenses with a tissue. 'He raped me there on the living-room floor, on a rough carpet. He didn't even take his coat off. I remember it stank of tobacco. His coat, I mean. I was crying and begging him to stop. He said he was teaching me. I was his student. He said I would learn to love it. When it was over he told me to get dressed and he drove me back to town. Before I got out of the car, he told me not to tell anybody because no one would ever believe me.'

Grant went back to his notes, picking up the papers and moving toward the jury as he studied them. The courtroom was quiet. He kept his eyes on the jury as he spoke.

'Were you a virgin at the time of the attack?'

'Yes.'

Grant regarded the jury a moment longer, then turned to walk briskly back to Kate.

'Did you tell anyone?'

'No.'

'Why not?'

'Because I believed him.'

'What about the papers he promised you? Did he give them to you?'

'No. I don't think there were any.'

'Did he ever call you again?'

'No.'

'Did you ever see him again?'

'Not in person.'

'What do you mean?'

'He was always on the news, or in the papers. I saw him there.'

Grant went to the table and picked up a ledger. He looked at the judge. 'At this point, I would like to introduce into the record the minutes of the Rose City council meeting for February twenty-fourth, 1998. It shows that Mayor Joseph Sanderson was in council for the morning session that day, but that he was absent in the afternoon. This in spite of the fact that council voted on three separate issues that afternoon. Issues that should have warranted his presence at the session.'

Grant provided copies to the court clerk and then walked across the room toward The Mayor, still ensconced behind his beatific smile.

'Kate Burns,' Grant said, 'you waited seventeen years to tell this story. Why are you telling it now?'

'Because I thought it was over and I was wrong,' Kate said. 'I told myself that it didn't matter. It was just something that happened, and it didn't mean anything, it didn't affect who I am.

But I was wrong. He's a rapist. He's a man who raped young girls and got away with it. I don't think he should get away with it any longer.'

Kate was on the stand until two o'clock, as Grant went over how she first heard of the investigation, her statements to the police and other logistical matters. When he concluded, Miles Browning stood and approached the witness stand. He looked Kate in the eye for a long moment, as if gauging her resolve. Then he turned to Judge Pemberton and requested an adjournment until the next day.

Kate took the stand again at five past ten the following morning. Browning had her wait while he stood at the defense table and made a production of arranging his notes. He was wearing a tan-colored suit today, with a white shirt and a navy blue tie. Kate realized that he'd never worn the same suit twice since the trial had begun.

Finally he approached her, carrying a single page. 'I'd like to go over the chronology here briefly. We know from the high-school records that the field trip to city hall that you mentioned took place on January seventh, 1998. And it was on this trip that you first met my client. You and several others. Correct?'

'Yes.'

'And you interviewed him?'

'Yes.'

'And you say that he called you at your grandparents' home a couple of weeks later?'

'Yes.'

'What was the date?'

'I don't remember. It was two or maybe three weeks after the field trip.'

'I see. Then he called again? And a third time?'

'That's right.'

'Do you recall the dates of the subsequent phone calls?'

'No.'

'It's difficult,' Browning said, turning to the jury. 'It's difficult, I suppose, to recall specific dates, especially from seventeen years past. My wife tells me that I can't remember what happened last week.'

A ripple passed through the courtroom.

'Wouldn't you agree?' Browning asked, turning back to Kate.

'With what your wife thinks?' Kate asked.

'Aha,' Browning said. 'Wouldn't you agree that it's difficult to remember specific dates of occurrences from seventeen years ago?'

'I suppose.'

'And yet you are certain of the date you were allegedly attacked? We have your sworn testimony that this occurred on February twenty-fourth, 1998. How can you be so certain of that specific date when you have admitted that you have no recall of these others?'

'There are moments in your life you tend to remember,' Kate said. 'I suppose being raped would be one of them.'

The reply set Browning back. 'Significant enough to remember, yet not significant enough to report to the police?' he shot back. 'Remind the court – why didn't you report this alleged incident to the police?'

'I did. Last year.'

'It had a long gestation period, this remembering act of yours,' Browning said. 'Getting back to your high-school field trip to the big city. Is it not true that you developed an infatuation for my client after that little excursion?'

'No.'

'Come now. You testified earlier that you were flattered that he complimented your creative efforts.'

'I was flattered, sure. I was in grade ten. He told me I wrote well.'

'Did you ever phone the mayor's office?'

Kate hesitated. 'Once. He'd mentioned the story about the trapper's cabin and I wanted to follow up on it.'

'Just once?'

'Yeah.'

'I'm not so sure about that,' Browning said. 'I just might be able to provide evidence, through my client's former secretary, that you in fact called there more than once. Would you like to reconsider your reply?'

'It was once.'

'We'll get back to that,' Browning said, as he walked back

to his notes. 'Ms Burns, how many abortions did you have as a teenager?'

Grant was on his feet. 'Your honor. What is the purpose of this?'

Browning strode quickly to the bench. 'My colleague has gone to great lengths to paint a chaste portrait of these young ladies. In the face of that, I think the jury is entitled to certain truths. This is not opinion, your honor, nor am I passing judgment. These are facts.'

Pemberton glanced at Grant before turning his attention to Browning. Kate thought she detected the slightest cast of contempt in his eye. But it could have been the light, it could have been her desire to have him on her side. It could have been nothing at all. Pemberton nodded his head almost imperceptibly.

Browning looked at Kate. 'Could you answer the question? If your memory fails you once again – well, we do have the hospital records.'

'Three.'

'Three abortions,' Browning said, turning to the jury again. 'While you were a teenager.'

Kate stared at his back but said nothing.

'I'm sort of out of my element here,' Browning said. 'Would that be the average for girls of your peer group; did all of your friends have multiple abortions in their teen years? Or would you be considered an over-achiever in this area?'

'That's enough, Mr Browning,' Judge Pemberton snapped. He looked at Kate. 'Disregard the question.' He turned back to Browning. 'You're not running this courtroom, counselor.'

Browning made a show of acquiescing, backing away with his hands raised. It didn't matter, Kate thought. Whether it was in the transcript or not, he'd made the point. Browning glanced at his notes a moment and came back at her, quickly, like a boxer who had found his range.

'Do you remember the date when you had your first abortion?'

'The exact date? No.'

'The second?'

'No.'

'Let's go for the hat-trick,' Browning said. 'Do you remember the third?'

'No.'

'Isn't it strange?' Browning said, smiling. 'Isn't it strange – that of all the momentous events of your teenage years, you can recall the specific date of just one? You can recall the date that my client allegedly attacked you, a date that conveniently – and a cynical person might say miraculously – coincides with a day when he was not in council, a little fact that I'm sure was provided to you by the people investigating this case.'

'Objection,' Grant snapped.

'Mr Browning, you are dangerously close to calling the integrity of this court into question,' Judge Pemberton said. 'I'm not advising you to refrain from such insinuation, I'm telling you.'

'My apologies to the court,' Browning said. He turned to Kate. 'Help me out here. I'm having difficulty understanding these memory lapses. What you want us to believe is that you put this traumatic event out of your mind for seventeen years, fairly struck it from your memory, and then suddenly – when all these other false accusations begin to surface – your memory starts to clear. And then, when the media suggest that civil suits involving large sums of money could be involved, everything comes into focus. Is that accurate?'

'I have no interest in civil suits,' Kate said. 'I don't want his money.'

Browning continued as if he never heard her. 'Suddenly, everything is crystal clear regarding that fateful day. You remember that the lake was frozen, the smell of an overcoat, the texture of a carpet.' Browning's voice rose now. 'But more importantly you're able to provide us with a definitive date when all this allegedly occurred, even though it's the *only* date from your teenage years that you can bring to mind!'

'I remember the date because it was my birthday,' Kate shot back. 'Joseph Sanderson raped me on my fifteenth birthday.'

It would be the only time throughout the trial that Browning was stopped cold. Even in this, though, he was imperturbable. He hesitated briefly and then returned to the defense table and his notes. Kate wondered how he would counteract what she'd said. And then she realized that he wouldn't because he couldn't.

What he would do was change the subject.

'Have you ever been arrested?' he asked, turning back to her.

'Yes.'

'For what?'

'Impaired driving.'

'Convicted?'

'Yes.'

'When was this?'

'2006.'

Browning nodded, looked over at the jury. 'And what have you done since 2006 to combat your drinking problem?'

'I don't have a drinking problem,' Kate said. 'I made a mistake once.'

Shaking his head, Browning sighed dramatically. 'If I had a nickel for every person I've ever encountered with a drinking problem who claimed they didn't have a drinking problem, I'd be a very wealthy man.'

'I thought you already were a very wealthy man,' she said.

Laughter followed this and Browning forced a smile. 'Well, we're not here to discuss my financial situation. Perhaps we'll find time for that after we have determined just why you would falsely accuse an innocent man of sexual assault. However – getting back to your history of drunken driving – you were convicted just the one time?'

'I told you it was once,' Kate said. 'There is no history.'

'Ah, but one time does indeed constitute a history.'

Grant stood. 'Is this going somewhere?'

Judge Pemberton looked askance toward Browning, who took a moment before shaking his head again, as if considering some great sadness.

'I'm getting tired, I guess,' he said. He looked at Kate. 'I'm just plain weary of this parade of witnesses put forth by the prosecution.' He gestured to The Mayor. 'On this side of the ledger you have a civil servant who has served Rose City for four decades in the most exemplary manner imaginable, a man who performed his civic duties over that vast period of time without even the whiff of impropriety.' He turned toward Kate. 'And over here . . . *over here*, we have a succession of witnesses that includes, quite frankly, some rather questionable characters. Drug abusers, strippers, drunken drivers, welfare frauds. It's all in the transcripts. It has been suggested to me that these women are lying. Tell me, Ms Burns, is it unreasonable for me to give credence to that suggestion? Now I'm not a psychologist but . . . is it unreasonable for me to entertain the notion that drug abusers and strippers and drunken drivers might also be capable of lying in order to line their own pockets in a potential civil suit?'

Browning was standing directly in front of Kate now, so close she could read the initials on his tie clip, she could smell the faint aroma of his cologne. His body language was relaxed but his eyes were cold.

She shrugged. 'Maybe girls who are raped at an early age are more likely to stray from the straight and narrow later on. Did you ever consider that?'

She could see that Browning was incensed at her tone. He turned away from her, smiling derisively toward the jury as he walked back to the table, a smile that suggested that Kate's remark was not worthy of commentary. He found a sheet of paper and turned back to her.

'Do you know a Lawrence Filsinger?'

'No,' Kate said, and she beat him to the punch. 'He contacted me about filing a civil suit and I told him no.'

'So now you're answering questions before I even ask them?' Browning said. 'You'll make me obsolete, Ms Burns. So you said no to Mr Filsinger? That's admirable. I'm sure that the jury will find that admirable too. We see before us a woman of integrity. Assuming we disregard the multiple abortions, the convenient lapses of memory, the drunken driving. Of course, if my client was to be convicted, you would then be free to change your mind with regard to Mr Filsinger and his money-making schemes. Isn't this just a pose?'

'I'm not going to change my mind,' Kate said. 'And I am not posing.'

'You are posing,' Browning said. 'And you are lying under oath.' He looked at Judge Pemberton. 'Nothing more for this witness. I've quite had my fill.'

Carl and Frances walked out of the courthouse together. Both their vehicles were parked in a lot across the street but they lingered out front for a while. The media were clustered together on the tiny patch of lawn between the courthouse and the street, waiting for one or other of the principals to emerge. Moments later, The Mayor exited through the front door and went down the steps without breaking stride, his wife on his arm as they headed for the waiting Buick at the curb. As they walked, The Mayor fielded some of the softer queries from the reporters.

'Very happy,' he said when asked about his feelings on the cross-examination.

'Did the Redbirds win again?' he inquired of one reporter.

'I've always had faith that the truth will win out,' he said as he ducked into the car.

Kate walked out of a side entrance a few minutes later, flanked by two cops in uniform who kept between her and the few reporters who hadn't flocked to The Mayor out front. Kate didn't respond to their queries. David was waiting for her. He hugged her when she came out and held on to her for a moment, as if further protecting her from the press. Seconds later Browning walked out on to the front steps and the media pack moved toward him.

Kate and David started for the rear parking lot, but Kate saw Frances standing on the front walkway with Carl. She hesitated a moment before walking over. Frances embraced her before stepping back to brush Kate's hair from her face.

'How's that for good old courtroom drama?' Kate asked.

'I'm proud of you,' Frances said.

Kate looked at Carl and nodded. He was hanging back, by the corner of the building. He smiled at her, and as he did she turned away.

'You guys want to grab a drink somewhere?' Frances asked.

Kate started to reply but stopped as a man approached along the walkway. He was carrying a tape recorder and had press credentials hanging around his neck. Pale and thin, he looked like one of the guys who wandered into Shoeless Joe's by accident every once in a while. They sat alone and drank Coors Light while reading stuff from their laptops.

'Ms Burns, you got a minute?' he asked. 'Peter Dunmore from the *Times*.'

'The *Times*?' Frances repeated. 'Shouldn't you be over there on the steps, kissing Browning's ring?'

'No, I should not,' Dunmore replied defensively. He gave Frances a long look before turning back to Kate.

'I don't have much to say,' she told him.

'You had lots to say on the stand,' he said, smiling.

Kate shrugged and shook her head.

'Did Grant tell you not to talk to the press?'

'No,' Kate said. 'He never said that. But I think he would prefer we didn't, especially while the trial's on.' She glanced at David. 'What do you think?'

'Up to you,' David said. He pointed his chin toward Browning across the way. 'But it looks like they're telling their side.'

'How about this?' Dunmore persisted. 'Let's have a conversation off the record. While everything is fresh in both our minds. I thought you were impressive today. I want to do a feature when this thing's over. I won't use anything you say without your permission.'

Kate, still uncertain, looked to Frances for guidance.

'Off the record is off the record,' Frances said. 'He can't go back on that. Can you, Mr Dunmore?'

'Did I do something to offend you?' Dunmore asked.

Frances smiled. 'Not yet.' She said to Carl, 'We going for a drink?'

He nodded and Frances turned to David and Kate. 'You guys want to catch up? We'll go to Salinger's.'

'We'll see how it goes,' Kate said.

Salinger's was a couple blocks away, an upscale place where the lawyers and clerks and others from the courthouse gathered after work. Carl and Frances took a table that overlooked the street. The place was relatively empty when they arrived but began to fill up almost immediately. Carl had a beer and Frances a rye and water.

'You were a little rough on that reporter,' Carl mentioned.

'Was I?'

'Seemed like it to me,' Carl said. He smiled. 'I'm pretty sure it seemed like it to him.'

Frances had a drink of rye. 'The *Times* has been in The Mayor's corner from the get-go on this. They were in the habit of endorsing him in every election he ever entered so maybe they're trying to save face now. You know, the venerable *Times* would never endorse a rapist, that type of thing. Whatever the thinking over there, the coverage has been slanted.' She had another drink before smiling at Carl. 'You know what, I'm going to cancel my subscription. That'll teach 'em.'

Carl drank from his beer and looked about the place. There were men in suits and ties, women in tailored outfits. They were regulars, it seemed, greeting each other with overblown familiarity, the guys doing fist bumps or mocking each other like playground kids. Carl knew the types. In a couple of hours they'd be three-quarters drunk, each attempting to outdo the other, awarding themselves with phantom promotions and bonuses, and one-upping each other with dirty jokes.

'I guess that was the worst of it,' he said.

'I hope so,' Frances said. 'That wasn't easy, what she did today.'

'Is it enough to convict him?'

'I don't know the answer to that.'

Her eyes widened and Carl turned to see Miles Browning and one of the young lawyers from his team walk into the place. They went directly to the bar, where the bartender greeted them like royalty.

'If not, there's the reason why,' Frances said. 'It's a shitty thing, what he's doing. And he's doing it for a shitty reason. Money. He's got this reputation as the top criminal lawyer in the country and he's nothing but a dirty little prick. A fucking high-priced character assassin.'

Carl watched Browning joking with the bartender. 'Were you surprised when The Mayor resigned?'

'I don't think he had any choice. It was an election year and he couldn't run with this hanging over him. But if he manages to get off, the story is he's going to run again. He loves being mayor. Nice image for a city, having elected officials who are scum.' Frances looked out the window to the street as she took a drink. 'I hope Kate comes by.'

'She won't,' Carl said.

'You don't know that.'

Carl had a drink. 'She seems to think I'm after something.'

'She told me what she said to you at the bar,' Frances said. 'She knows she shouldn't have. If it's any consolation, she feels like shit about it.'

'Her feeling that way is no consolation. I don't want her to feel like shit.'

He was still looking at Browning. Frances chuckled and he turned to her.

'What?'

'Look at you,' she said. 'Twenty years ago, you'd be across this room right now, punching Browning's lights out. And I know goddamn well you still *want* to do it. You're fantasizing about it right this minute. But you won't do it.' She smiled. 'Of all people to become civilized.'

'Should I apologize for that?'

'Hell, no,' she said. 'For one thing, I suspect that you're just marginally civilized anyway.'

'You sure know a lot about me.'

'Not about you,' she said. 'I'm a student of human behavior. You're older and wiser. Probably being in jail helped. You do remember prison?'

'Very clearly.'

Frances took a drink of the rye. 'Sometimes you have to have faith in the system. And not because it always works, but because it *sometimes* works. Even if it doesn't, Kate had enough guts to sit up there and stare down that lying fucking pervert and his million-dollar lawyer. She told the truth. Maybe this is one of those times when the truth is enough.'

Carl didn't look at her then. He passed a few moments pushing his beer glass back and forth in the little pool of condensation it had formed on the table top. 'She didn't tell the truth about everything.'

'What are you talking about?'

Now Carl looked at her. 'She said that she didn't tell anyone about the rape when it happened.'

'Yeah?'

'She told me. At least she tried to.'

'Jesus Christ,' Frances said. 'What did she say?'

'Not a lot. Because I wasn't listening to her. I wasn't listening to anybody back then.'

Kate talked to Peter Dunmore on the lawn in the shadow of the courthouse. David, giving them some space, waited in the parking lot by the car. The lot was thinning out quickly; it was quitting time and people were eager to get away. Even the media had largely dispersed, with the star player Browning gone.

'So what's with this Filsinger guy?' Dunmore wanted to know. 'Browning's beating that like a drum.'

'I'd never heard of the man until a few months ago,' Kate said. 'He called me at home one night.'

'How did he get your number? I couldn't find it.'

'I don't know,' Kate said. 'I don't know how any of this works.'

'Would you say he's an ambulance chaser?' Dunmore asked.

'Browning seems to think so,' Kate said. 'But if Filsinger's an ambulance chaser, what's Browning? All I know is that he called and said he wanted to represent me in a civil suit against Sanderson. And the city.'

Dunmore was writing in his notebook and now he looked up. 'The city?'

'That's what he said. He claimed that Sanderson used his position as mayor to, I don't know, gain our trust before he . . . did what he did. And with Maria Secord, it happened right in his office at city hall. And so the city's responsible. At least that's what he's saying.'

Dunmore thought about it. 'And that's where the real money is, if you're talking about a settlement.'

'I guess.'

'You told him you weren't interested.'

'Christ,' Kate said. 'It can't be about the money. You were in there. We're having a tough enough time as it is, getting people to believe us. They decide we're all just chasing a payday and nobody will.'

'And what about afterwards?'

'What about it?'

'If Sanderson is convicted,' Dunmore said. 'Will you go after the money then?'

'No,' Kate said, frustrated now. 'You don't get it, do you?'

'Maybe I do,' he said. 'But I had to ask the question. And now I have to ask another one. Why *did* you wait so long to come forward? Not just you – all of the accusers. You realize that's going to be a major stumbling block for the jury, don't you?'

'I guess it might be,' Kate admitted. 'I can't answer the question because I don't know the answer. It's like when you're sick and you put off going to the doctor. Why do you do that? Maybe I needed to know there were others, that it wasn't just me. Or maybe I'm afraid of him. Maybe it's a lot easier to pretend that it didn't happen than to admit that it did.' She smiled without much humor. 'Gee, I said I didn't have an answer and there's three. Take your pick, buddy.'

'They might all be true,' Dunmore said. 'Are you still afraid of him?'

'No,' Kate said. She hesitated. 'Yes. I am.'

'Are you afraid he's going to walk on the charges?'

'Yes, I am.'

'We going to Salinger's?' David asked when Kate joined him at the car. The reporter Dunmore was still standing alongside the courthouse, writing in his notebook. Kate didn't know if talking to him had accomplished anything. He did seem sympathetic to her, even if the newspaper that employed him did not. There was a good chance that nothing would come of it. She was OK with that too. She really didn't care what the *Rose City Times* thought of her.

Kate thought about it. 'I'd rather just head home.'

'Frances is kind of expecting us.'

'She'll understand.'

David hesitated. 'You don't want to talk to your father?'

'I really don't have anything to talk to him about,' Kate said. 'I'm not trying to shut him out but he really doesn't seem like my father. He's basically a stranger, David. How do you have a conversation with a stranger and pretend he's not a stranger?'

'I was watching him inside,' David said. 'It was hard for him to hear.' He paused. 'It was hard for me to hear.'

Kate put her arms around his neck and held him for a moment. 'Let's go home,' she said.

They picked up some Vietnamese take-out on their way and ate in the living room. Kate changed into shorts and a t-shirt and sat cross-legged on the floor while she picked at the food. David, on the couch with a fork in one hand and the remote in the other, flipped through the sports channels, looking for baseball scores. Finally settling on ESPN, he muted the sound and got up to get himself another beer.

'How's yours?' he asked.

Kate glanced at her bottle. 'I'm good.'

He came back and flopped on the couch, watching Kate as she picked at the noodles on her plate. 'I feel like we should celebrate,' he said.

'Celebrate what?'

'You did it,' he said. 'After all these years, you told your story. And that bastard had to sit there while you told it. In a way, it doesn't matter what happens now, Kate. Browning's going to try and twist everything around, you know that. You knew that going in. Thing is, you told the truth. And a thousand Brownings can't make a lie out of the truth.'

'But what if it accomplishes nothing?'

'You can't think about that,' David said. 'That's out of your hands. You did your job.'

'That's very Zen-like of you,' she said.

'It is what it is.'

'That's less Zen-like.' Kate pushed her plate away and got to her feet. She found the remote and turned the TV off, then moved to sit astride him on the couch. 'Thank you,' she said.

'You're welcome,' he replied. 'Um . . . for what?'

'For making me feel like a normal human being,' she said. 'I don't want to be a sideshow. That's why I couldn't decide whether or not to talk to the reporter. I don't want to be "the girl who got raped". You make me normal.'

'Gee,' he said. 'I had no idea I was such a saint.'

'Well, you are,' she said. She leaned forward to give him a lingering kiss. After a moment, she straightened. 'I'll tell you something else. Something I've been wanting to tell you. If I hadn't met you, I don't think I could have done this. Not on my own. So yes . . . we should go someplace to celebrate.'

'OK,' he said. 'Where do you want to go?'

She kissed him again, longer this time. 'I'm thinking . . . someplace warm.'

'Someplace warm?'

'Yeah.' She kissed him a third time. 'Do you have any suggestions?'

'Not really.'

'For a saint, you're a little obtuse.' She smiled.

'Give me a hint.'

Kate pulled her t-shirt over her head and tossed it aside. She wasn't wearing a bra.

David smiled.

TEN

Frances was up early the next morning. In fact, she'd been up most of the night, thinking about Kate and the trial. She'd been thinking about Kate for weeks now, leading up to things, but now she was forced to throw Carl in the mix too. She was uneasy about him. On the surface he appeared calm and in control of himself. But she hadn't been joking yesterday when she'd suggested that he'd become just marginally civilized. She wasn't at all sure what might happen if The Mayor was acquitted. Things could get interesting then, and not in a good way.

She sat out on the patio as the sun showed above the tree line to the east, drinking coffee and reading the *Rose City Times* while she waited for Perry to arrive. She wanted to run the cultivator through the tomatoes before heading in to the courthouse.

It was a busy news week in the city. The trial of former mayor Joseph Sanderson III was all over the front page. The *Times* had a handful of reporters covering it, providing exaggerated details of the lurid testimony and courtroom theatrics. The paper, continuing its biased reporting, seemed inordinately impressed by lawyer Browning. There was nothing in the edition by the reporter Dunmore, Frances noticed, before moving on to other news. Apparently EnviroFill, the Michigan-based company that had been taking virtually all of the city's trash for the past decade, was pulling out, two years before its contract expired. City councilor Bud Stephens was riding – at least in his eyes – to the city's rescue, announcing a plan to contract Hank Hofferman to receive the city's garbage at a new landfill on a large parcel of land near the town of Talbotville. The land in question was no more than three or four miles from where Frances sat with her coffee. The news did nothing to improve her mood. Reading that the Rose City Redbirds ran their winning streak to a record-setting sixteen games didn't help much either.

She almost missed the tiny item on page four. There had been a house fire on the Irish Line, some thirty miles south of Rose City.

That the fire was reported at all was probably due to the fact that the place had belonged to John McIntosh and had been built in 1847 by John's great-grandfather, an early governor of the area. The cause of the fire was believed to be faulty wiring, the result of aged circuitry overloaded by a faulty air-conditioning unit. So the fire, in effect, was a consequence of the heatwave. Whoever had written the report in all likelihood didn't know what Frances did – that the McIntosh property was directly across from that of the proposed landfill.

Miles Browning presented his defense of Joseph Sanderson III like a man who had left his car running in front of the courthouse. He had a roster of witnesses prepared to contradict virtually every aspect of each of the accusers' stories, and it was apparent that Browning had instructed them to be as concise as possible. The jury was treated to two days of rapid fire testimony designed not to create doubt of, but rather disbelief in, the prosecution's case. Browning himself was in full strut throughout, displaying the confidence of a man selling sunscreen at the gates of hell.

Louise Sanderson testified, stating that she had never known Maria Secord's mother, even in passing, not through her involvement with the church or anywhere else, making it impossible for her to have played a role in Maria's hiring at city hall. Grant's effort to challenge her under cross was tepid at best. The woman was revered in the city, mainly due to her charitable activities. Calling her a liar in open court wasn't going to help his case in the least.

An investigator from welfare services elaborated on Debra Williams's admitted gaffe in collecting social assistance. It turned out that she'd defrauded the agency five times, not once, and that the agency, in its mercy, had agreed to pursue just one of the charges.

Ninety-three-year-old Norma Stevens appeared. She had been The Mayor's secretary for most of his early tenure at city hall, and she testified that Kate Burns had repeatedly phoned the office during the winter of 1998, asking to speak to The Mayor. The old woman's memory of these calls was remarkably clear in spite of the fact that, during the course of her testimony, she referred to the accused twice as 'Mayor Sanders' and at one point mistook Judge Pemberton for her late husband, calling him 'Herb, dear'.

Even though Amanda Long did not testify, her statement had been read into the transcript. Browning called to the stand two case workers from separate rehabilitation centers who outlined her many failed attempts to beat her alcohol addiction, the testimony focusing on her propensity for lying.

Finally, Browning called Marvin Tallman. Tallman had worked for the Department of Lands and Forests for forty-seven years, all of his service having passed in the area surrounding Lake Sontag. He testified that there had never in that time been a trapper's cabin on the south shore of the lake, and that furthermore he had never heard of any tale involving an unsolved murder in the lake's history.

When Browning's revolving door of rebuttal witnesses had concluded, he turned to his summation. He was wearing a black suit – the first time he had worn black – with a dazzling white shirt and a scarlet tie. He spoke without notes, and his manner remained perfunctory, his demeanor suggesting that an acquittal, at this point, was a foregone conclusion, and that the jury would be doing justice and everybody else a favor by coming to that conclusion quickly.

'I was sitting in my room last night and I had this sudden feeling that I should apologize to you,' he said to the members of the jury. 'I felt as if your time – your precious time – had been wasted on these frivolous charges, hurled at my client. But then I realized that I was wrong. There's no apology required, because your time has not been wasted. In fact, you have been given an opportunity to accomplish something that few people get to do in this life. I began practicing law thirty-two years ago and over that period I have heard too many times that our judicial system is flawed. It is aged and rusty. It allows killers to run free, crooks to prosper, drug dealers to threaten our children. Well, ladies and gentlemen, I have long disagreed with that assessment. It does work, and you have the occasion here, in this courtroom, to display to those naysayers just how well it works.'

Browning paused and smiled at the jury, as if welcoming them into his brotherhood of believers. Then he turned and approached the table where the four women sat.

'Perhaps your job would be made more difficult if just one of the stories told by the four accusers held up. If just one of these women had presented a credible, reliable account of these allegations, then perhaps we would be given pause. But that didn't happen. They say that close only counts in horseshoes and hand grenades, but this wasn't even close.'

Browning walked back to his desk and picked up several sheets of paper.

'Maria Secord claimed that her mother was friends with Louise Sanderson. That proved to be untrue. You heard Louise Sanderson's testimony on the subject. She is perhaps the most respected woman in this city. Her character is beyond reproach. Maria Secord lied.

'Debra Williams said she defrauded welfare services one time, purely by accident. She defrauded welfare services five times, and five times is not accidental. Five times is criminal. Debra Williams lied.

'Amanda Long chose not to testify, so we will never know what her claims were, other than a statement which bears no value in this courtroom because it cannot be cross-examined. We know that she is, sadly, a woman embattled by alcoholism. However, by recording her statement at the onset of this trial, she was saying she would testify before you. She did not follow up on that promise. Amanda Long lied.

'Kate Burns – she of the quick wit and the sharp tongue – Kate Burns tells tales of cabins that never existed, of murders which never occurred. She denies making numerous phone calls to my client. His secretary, a woman with no ulterior motives, with no lucrative civil suit lurking in the background, says otherwise. Kate Burns lied.'

Browning brandished the papers above his shoulder as he walked toward the jury again. 'I must warn you that you are *not* here to judge these four women. Whatever circumstances have conspired to deliver them here to this courtroom, to inspire these outrageous tales, it is not for us to ponder. We have here four victims of broken homes, four women who have suffered from alcohol abuse, drug use, alienation from society in general. Furthermore, we have heard there are seedy elements on the periphery of this matter, whispering promises of financial gain in the event of a conviction. Who among us, having fallen on hard times, would not at least listen to those whispers? And who, in a moment of weakness, might not decide to tailor a story to fit certain accusations? No, you are not here to judge these women.'

Browning went back to the table, tossed the papers down, then pointed at The Mayor.

'You are here to judge this man. You know of his record as a civil servant, you know of his character. Has there been a single sliver of credible evidence presented in this courtroom to question that character? There has not. There has *not*. It's your duty to acquit Joseph Sanderson the third. It's your duty to demonstrate in the most clear and emphatic manner possible that our system does work. And when you walk out of this courtroom for the last time, you'll feel good about yourself. Your heart will soar. Trust me – I know that feeling. It is your duty to acquit this man.'

It seemed to Kate that Prosecutor Grant had, over the course of the trial, been diminishing before her eyes. Not in any physical sense but in some strange spiritual way she couldn't quite define. There just seemed to be less of him, day by day.

In summation, Grant restated the prosecution's case, and he went to great lengths to convince the jury that whatever the events in the lives of the four women after the attacks, those events had no bearing on the veracity of the testimony regarding the rapes in question. That the four had not led exemplary lives since could hardly be surprising. A sexual assault was a traumatizing experience. To suffer it as a teenager would multiply that trauma tenfold.

He questioned the testimony of the elderly and uncertain Norma Stevens, but casting aspersions on someone her age was a tricky proposition. He told the jury that there was no evidence of a cabin on Lake Sontag because The Mayor had, quite simply, made it up in order to lure Kate to the lake house. He had no chance, however, of impugning Louise Sanderson's testimony, and he did not try. She was, if anything, held in higher regard than The Mayor himself.

In the end Grant told the jury that they must decide who was telling the truth and who was not. It was as simple as that. He told them that he too had a belief in the system, and that he too was depending upon them to prove him right.

The jury was out for less than two hours. Joseph Sanderson III was acquitted on all counts.

*   *   *

Miles Browning held forth for some time on the front steps of the courthouse after the verdict, The Mayor himself standing alongside; a pair of media hounds reluctant to leave the stage. The four accusers were given the option of facing the media but they all declined and were escorted from the courthouse through the side entrance.

Frances went home with Kate but Carl decided to stay behind. He stood on the sidewalk outside of the media throng for a time, then gradually made his way through the crush until he was on the concrete steps below where Browning and The Mayor stood.

'You're innocent,' a reporter shouted to The Mayor. 'How does it feel?'

'I was always innocent. Should I feel different now?'

'Will you try to claim back the mayor's office?'

'I'm heading to South America. I'm going to try to claim a big trout or two.'

'Mr Browning! Why did they lie?'

'I have no idea,' Browning said. He smiled. 'I fear I'm not nearly as clever as you try to make out. Besides, my job was merely to demonstrate that they lied, not to establish why.'

'Why didn't your client testify?'

'There was no need,' Browning said. 'This trial should never have seen the light of day.'

'Mayor Sanderson! Will you be pressing charges against these women?'

'Absolutely not,' The Mayor replied. 'I have no desire to add to their woes.'

'We have sympathy for these women,' Browning interjected. 'People need to know that. They were coerced to lie. The question you – as the Fourth Estate – should be asking is *by whom*. As for the women themselves, leave them be. I myself have a teenage daughter. I have nothing but sympathy for these women.'

Now Carl pushed his way forward to step directly in front of Browning. 'This daughter of yours,' he said. 'Would you leave her alone with your client?'

Browning's face turned red. Carl stared at him before turning toward The Mayor. The old man looked at him for a moment. And then he smiled.

ELEVEN

K ate went back to work after the trial and waited for her life to return to her. The verdict had knocked her on her heels, but in the following weeks she reconciled herself to the fact that she had spent a lot of years living with the notion that The Mayor had gotten away with what he had done. This was just a matter of him getting away with it again. Apparently there was a part of her mental make-up that had been capable of accepting that fact. If she had lived with it before, she could live with it again.

As long as she didn't think about it too much.

So she went back to her life, to weekends working at the bar, to slow pitch, to movies and dinners with David. She returned to the insurance office, to a job that she tolerated but had no passion for. Who could? The politics there were a little strange when she returned and it was obvious why. After all, she had accused a senior citizen of a certain social status in the city of raping her. Probably half the policyholders were senior citizens of a certain social status. They looked at her differently now, at least some of them anyway, and she noticed that there was less harmless flirting. Were they afraid that she would accuse them of something, or were they pissed at her for taking The Mayor to court? She decided that she didn't care if either was true. She wouldn't allow herself any regret over what she had done. Things slowly returned to what she could loosely refer to as normal. She put the trial behind her. She wasn't sure she was moving forward, but she didn't feel that she was sliding back either.

Things changed in September.

The slow pitch finals were held on the last weekend of the month. Shoeless Joe's made it to the semis, and there Kate blew her knee out Saturday trying to score from second base on a bloop single. Her cleat caught on the bag as she rounded third and she felt the knee twist violently. She limped home but was out by twenty feet. Half an hour later she was in the hospital, and on Monday morning she had surgery.

The surgeon told her she would be off work for six weeks. Physiotherapy would begin once the swelling went down. He gave her a script for painkillers and told her to take it slow.

'Shit,' she said that night, lying back on the couch, her leg propped on cushions. 'I don't need a lot of down time right now.'

'Well, you got it,' David told her. 'Catch up on your reading. Watch some movies.'

So she caught up on her reading, and she rented some movies she'd been meaning to watch, and then some she had no desire to watch. And she went to physio, and she cleaned the house, hopping around on one leg.

And she grew bored. Boredom had a capricious nature. Sometimes it was a breeding ground for good things.

And sometimes it wasn't.

Autumn, when it came, slipped in through a side door and suddenly was just there, like a guest who'd arrived early for a party. It wasn't that the interloper was unwelcome, it was just that Frances wasn't ready for it yet. The farm was having its best year yet, which meant that Frances was busier than she'd ever been in her life, up at daybreak seven days a week, working in the warehouse or the fields for ten or twelve hours and usually falling asleep in a chair before ten o'clock. Her nails looked as if she worked on a chain gang. She hadn't had her hair cut since Martin had left for South America.

He was in touch regularly, e-mails and the occasional phone call, although most of the time his cell didn't work, especially when he was in the mountains. He continued to pester her to join him, suggesting that she fly into Santa Cruz one week and then, when she'd declined, Lima a couple of weeks later. He was depressed without her, he said. The work wasn't going well; he'd been sent to photograph some disappearing species that were proving to be, not all that surprisingly, difficult to locate. For some reason he didn't recall that his insistence that she drop everything to come running to his side was what had created tension between them to begin with. In any case, with fall approaching, there was no chance that she would be leaving the farm. And she kept telling him that.

Nevertheless, he continued to send pictures and e-mails and he called more frequently. During those conversations he invariably began to talk about how much Frances would love where he was at that particular moment, whether it was in a café in Bolivia or on a rock in the Galapagos. She noticed for the first time that he had a habit of telling her how great she would *look* there. As if she was an accessory. Other times he would even speculate on just how fabulous the two of them would look, standing on a peak in the Andes, or walking a Chilean beach. Maybe it was just the photographer in him, but it struck her as a strange thing, and quite likely not worth fretting over. More worrisome was the fact that he rarely asked her anything about the farm. And the less he asked about her work, the less she asked about his. It was sophomoric, she knew, and she told herself to stop. He was coming home soon, he said, whether he finished the assignment or not. The money was running out. Maybe then things would return to normal, although Frances couldn't recall just what normal felt like.

The drought had continued throughout the summer. In late August Frances hired Carl to overhaul the farm's irrigation system. The original set-up depended on a two-inch pipe that ran from an aged Beatty pump by the river to a pond behind the old barn. Frances's father had raised beef cattle and the pond had provided drinking water for the herd. But now the Herefords were gone, replaced by a hundred acres of thirsty vegetable plants. The old system wasn't up to the job.

After the trial Carl had hung around for a week, drinking at Archer's and dropping by the farm every couple of days, a man adrift. Frances had expected him to head back to Dundurn but it soon became evident that he wasn't going anywhere for a while. She wasn't sure why, and she suspected that he didn't know himself. She did know that whenever he'd been too long at the bar he would begin to talk darkly about The Mayor. Frances decided she would find something for him to do before he got himself into trouble. The new irrigation system was a fairly expensive proposition and one that she'd been putting off for a couple of years. But she needed water for the business, and she knew Carl to be someone who was very good at any number of things. Unfortunately one of those things was getting himself into trouble. So she hired him.

Carl, maybe knowing he was in need of diversion, took to the project like a hungry man to lunch. He found a pump powered by a six cylinder Cummins diesel engine at an auction sale near Kitchener, along with two thousand feet of four-inch aluminum piping. The engine was seized so Frances bought the entire system for a quarter of its value. Carl set up a shop in the old garage behind the house, stripped the motor down, freed and pulled the pistons, the crankshaft and the cam, then washed out the block with Varsol and honed the cylinders. He took the cylinder head to Krupp's in town to have the guides replaced and the valves re-seated. He bought main and rod bearings, rings, camshaft gears and a carburetor kit. Then, in the shade of the old machine shed, he reassembled everything. Frances happened to be walking by when he first started the engine; she stopped to watch him as he adjusted the mixture screws on the carburetor, his head cocked as he sought the sound he wanted from the idling engine. When he looked up and saw her standing there, he smiled. It wasn't the first smile she'd seen since his return, but it was the first one that seemed to come from somewhere inside of him.

Perry, who wasn't much of a smiler on his best day, became increasingly sour in the face of Carl's presence at the farm. When Frances had told him that she had hired Carl to install the new system, Perry had insisted that he could do it himself, although that wasn't true. Perry had more work than he could handle in the fields and besides, he couldn't have rebuilt the diesel engine in a month of Sundays. Perry had reacted by ignoring Carl outright, even to the point of not responding if Carl asked him where he might find a certain wrench or other tools. Frances could see what was happening but she decided she would let the two of them work it out on their own. She couldn't be concerned about a pissing contest between the two, even if Perry was the only one doing the pissing.

She had enough on her plate, having somehow allowed herself to be declared the president of a group called Halt All Landfills in Talbotville, a grassroots organization which quickly became known as HALT. Since Hank Hofferman had announced his landfill proposal for the Irish Line, several hundred citizens from the area had signed petitions against it. An initial meeting at the town hall had unexpectedly overfilled the place. Hofferman was the only one present in favor of the project and it was obvious he had seriously underestimated the public's resistance. Standing in front of the gathering, in his creased jeans and polished cowboy boots, he assured those present that he was on their side.

'I'm one of you,' he kept saying.

'You ain't one of me,' one old farmer told him. 'Not in them boots.'

When a second meeting was called ten days later, Hofferman was prepared. This time the gathering was at the auditorium of Talbotville High School, and even that venue was too small as several hundred people crowded inside, with the overflow listening from the hallways.

Hofferman arrived with an entourage this time. There were two engineers, one with a background in agriculture, the other in waste disposal. There was the local councilor from the riding. And there was Bud Stephens from Rose City. The six men were seated on plastic chairs across the stage in the front of the hall, beneath a picture of a very young Queen Elizabeth.

The moderator was to be Mayor Luanne Roper, but she was suddenly called out of town on an emergency and Rufus Canfield was summoned from the bar at Archer's to pinch hit. During the course of the evening it was suggested that Mayor Roper had been receiving sizable campaign donations from Hofferman for years in gratitude for her support on the contentious issue of factory hog farms. It was further suggested that the emergency that called her out of town may have been a premonition of her political future.

Rufus was sober enough to chair the meeting and yet drunk enough not to bother to conceal his disdain for the assembled experts on the stage. The engineers spoke first, one after the other, and they mouthed the anticipated assurances that the landfill would be completely safe.

'The soil in that area is clay-based, perfect for containment,' said the first of the two, a skinny man with rimless glasses and gelled hair. He had a slide show that displayed a number of landfills across the continent, all excavated in clay. If he expected that snapshots of various dumps would reassure the crowd of anything, he couldn't have been more wrong.

The second engineer was a local man, and it was known that he had worked on various projects for Hank Hofferman over the years, including the hotly debated sow barns. He spoke to the drainage concerns, describing to the assembly a series of ditches and lagoons that would safeguard the landfill in the event of heavy rains.

'But the land drains into the river,' Rufus objected.

'Not true,' the man said. 'It drains into a creek on the property.'

'Where does the creek drain?' Rufus asked.

The man looked at his map for a moment. 'Well, I guess that eventually it would drain into the river.'

Rufus gave the man a long look, raising his eyebrows theatrically. The local councilor was next up and he made a little speech about Hank Hofferman – local farmer made good, successful owner of several intensive livestock operations, a friend to the environment and to the common man. The speech was not meant to be funny and the councilor was dismayed when people laughed at it. He hurried on to talk about the benefits of the proposed landfill to the county, in terms of jobs and added tax income.

'Added tax income,' Rufus repeated. 'Does it mean that my taxes will actually go down, because the county is collecting additional monies from the landfill?'

'Well, no,' the councilor said slowly. 'It doesn't work like that. It would be a residual thing. Your taxes would not go up.'

'And when in the history of the world has that happened?' Rufus said.

'My point is,' the councilor said, getting testy now, 'more tax revenue for the county is a good thing. Not only that, but a project of this scope would be beneficial to Talbotville's image in general. There are investors out there who don't even know that Talbotville exists. This is going to raise our profile. This will put us on the map.'

Frances was standing along the wall. She was weary to the bone and had considered not even coming. Her distaste for Hank Hofferman had convinced her to drink a couple of cups of coffee and make the drive into town.

'Hold on,' she said now. 'Just so I'm clear on this – we're going to improve our image by accepting trash from the big city?'

'I didn't say that—' the councilor began, but Bud Stephens interrupted him.

'Then I'll say it,' Bud said, and he stood up.

Frances smiled. 'Speaking of trash,' she said.

Bud stared at her as if he was genuinely hurt. He had dressed down for the country crowd, wearing black jeans and a maroon t-shirt. His eyes weren't right, Frances thought. There was a chemical flash there she recognized from her partying days.

'Well, it's not organic cucumbers,' he said to her, 'but this *will* enhance this area's image. This project will mark Talbotville as a progressive community. Listen, people, I'll tell you what I tell my constituents in Rose City. You're either in the twenty-first century or you're not. We have a chance to build a state-of-the-art disposal facility in your area, something other communities are going to look at—'

'It's a goddamn dump and we don't want it!' someone shouted.

'Not in my back yard?' Bud said. 'Is that it?'

'We have our own garbage to deal with,' Frances said.

'Goodbye!' someone shouted.

'Look at it this way,' Bud said. 'One man's treasure can be another man's trash.'

Hofferman stood up and spoke softly to Bud.

'Turn that around,' Bud said quickly. 'One man's trash can be another man's treasure.'

The panel of so-called experts jumped through hoops and evaded questions from the audience for another half hour or so and the meeting broke up. Within a week, HALT was formed. Frances, by virtue of insulting Bud Stephens at the town meeting, was voted president. When would she learn to keep her mouth shut? Signs were printed, more petitions signed, late night internet searches on the dangers of landfills were launched by the dozen. A formidable grassroots organization was up and running. Whether it had anywhere to run to was another matter.

John McIntosh, who had lost his farmhouse to fire, volunteered to use his political connections to help fight the proposal, then died of a heart attack a few days later. It was presumed that the stress of losing the family home contributed to the coronary.

Whatever the case, he'd been looked upon by HALT as their ace in the hole. With both the local councilor and Bud Stephens on side with Hofferman, and Mayor Roper dodging the issue, the opponents had virtually no political leverage.

The house at River Valley Farm became the headquarters for HALT. Frances held little hope that they could stop the project, but she'd signed on to do what she could. There was a perception in the community that she was an expert in dealing with bureaucrats, apparently based on the fact that she had once lived in the big city of Chicago.

Carl had the new watering system up and running by the end of August, and as soon as he did it began to rain and didn't stop for a week. It didn't matter to Frances. It hadn't been the first drought since she'd taken over the farm and, with the climate changing, it wouldn't be the last. Next time, she'd be prepared.

She had gotten used to having Carl around, even if Perry was still in pout mode. There was more to Carl than met the eye but then Frances had always suspected that, even back when she hadn't particularly liked him, when he was being a bad husband to her sister. That was a long time ago and Frances needed to let it go. He was a good worker and he was fine company at dinnertime. Like Frances, he was of the opinion that the world was going to hell in a hand basket. Other than his relationship with his daughter, he could fix nearly anything. When she'd asked him to build an addition on to the River Valley Farm warehouse, he'd agreed.

The members of HALT met every Wednesday night at the farm, usually on the back patio, where they drank coffee and tea and volleyed back and forth terms like 'environmental assessments' and 'safe containment' and 'due diligence'. Before the first meeting Frances approached Carl as he was loading his tools in his truck at the end of the day. She explained what was going on.

'You inviting me to your meeting?' he asked.

'No.'

'You saying I should eat in town tonight?'

'Yes.'

'OK.'

'You know how people talk,' she explained.

Later that evening she discovered that people had already

talked. Perry was at the meeting, sitting silently all night as was his wont. He seemed to have no opinions about the landfill, or much of anything if the truth were known, which begged the question of why he was there. Frances, of course, knew why he was there. It was all about proximity. After everybody left he helped her carry the coffee cups inside and then he moped around the patio until she finally asked what was on his mind. He sat in a wicker chair, his bony hands clasped between his knees, waiting for Frances to sit beside him. She wanted to clean up and go to bed, but finally she sat. Perry went back to rubbing his knuckles.

'What?' she finally asked.

'I don't know,' he started. 'Seems like a lot of things are changing around here. Everything was going real good, and if everything is going real good, then it don't make sense to me to change things.'

'Are you talking about the meetings?'

'Not really.'

'What, then?'

'Well, just everything.'

Frances stood up. 'I'm going to bed.'

'Carl was in prison,' Perry said. He began to work his knuckles again.

'I know that,' she said.

'Oh.' Perry was put out. Apparently he had been counting on shocking her. 'Do you know he killed a man named Red Walton?'

'A man was killed. I know that too. Who told you this?'

'Guy I know. Harold Sikes. He was a friend of Red Walton's. He beat Carl up in Archer's bar a couple months ago.'

'Harold Sikes beat Carl up?' Frances repeated. 'Harold Sikes couldn't beat *me* up.' She looked at Perry for a moment and then she sighed. 'All right, if you're going to be listening to guys like Sikes, I guess I better tell you what happened. This all started when Hank Hofferman first applied to build these factory pig farms around here. Those sow barns are a disaster on a whole bunch of levels. The animals are penned so tight they can't even turn around. They're force-fed hormones and steroids and antibiotics. The manure is flushed into big lagoons which have a habit of overflowing from time to time, and they can flood creeks and ditches with this chemical-infested shit. There are airborne problems, dust and whatever, and on top of that these farms are putting the family farmer out of business. There was a group back then called Hogwatch Talbotville, kind of like this HALT thing we've got going. They tried to stop Hofferman. Asked for an environmental assessment, never got it, asked for a county-wide referendum, never got that either.'

'But you didn't live here then,' Perry said.

'No, but my parents did and they were part of Hogwatch. I told you – the real farmers are against these things.' She looked at his stubborn face a moment, wondering how much he was hearing. 'Carl was a member of Hogwatch.'

'Carl's not a farmer.'

'A lot of people belonged to Hogwatch. Anybody with a brain, basically. This was a health issue, you understand? Carl was against hog barns for his own reasons. I'm guessing because they represented big money. The pork goes to Beaver Lodge Foods, which is owned by the Montpelier family, old-time conservatives with big-time political connections. Which meant Hogwatch was never going to win the fight. They could take on Hank Hofferman, but not Beaver Lodge Foods. The county council issued all the necessary permits and Hofferman began to build the first barn, out on Ram's Head Road. When the barn was nearly finished, Carl drove out there one night and torched the place. There was nobody on the premises at the time. But a firefighter was killed trying to put it out. Fell off a ladder and landed in a pile of reinforcement bars. A bar went through him.'

'That was Red Walton,' Perry said.

'That's right. Volunteer firefighter. Carl was convicted of criminal negligence causing death. He spent two years in jail.'

'Then I don't think he should be working here. He's a criminal.'

Frances stood up. 'You don't get to decide who works here, Perry. Go on home. Tomorrow's another day.'

Perry took her advice. Following his protruding bottom lip, he trundled off into the night. Frances watched him, wondering if it was worth the aggravation, keeping him on. He was a good worker when given something to do that didn't require much logistical thinking. If Frances pointed to a spot and told him to dig a trench, he would keep digging until he got to Manitoba if she didn't tell him to quit. She was pretty sure, however, that there were plenty of guys around who could do the same, and without the slack-jawed fawning afterwards.

She went into the house and as she began to wash the coffee cups the phone rang. She glanced at the display and saw that it was Martin. She hesitated and then let it go to voicemail while she continued with the dishes.

Finishing, she pulled the plug from the sink and stood there a moment, watching the water swirl into the drain. On an impulse, she picked up the phone and called Carl's number in town. He answered on the second ring.

'Am I waking you?'

'No,' he said. 'Watching a movie about the Civil War.'

'I won't keep you from it.'

'I know how it turns out. The North wins.'

'Sure, spoil it for me,' Frances said. She looked at the coffee remaining in the pot and decided she didn't need any more caffeine before going to bed. Stretching the phone cord, she reached into a hutch along the wall and found a nearly empty bottle of brandy there. She poured the last couple of ounces into her coffee cup and sat down at the table.

'How was your meeting?' he asked.

'Like the road to hell.'

'How's that?'

'Paved with good intentions,' she said. 'I don't know. There's a lot of righteous indignation flying around but I really don't know what we can accomplish with it. According to Rufus, we could use some legal precedent. Apparently it trumps righteous indignation every time.' She sipped the brandy. 'Anyway, I didn't call you to bore you with that.'

'No?'

'I just wanted you to know that a guy named Harold Sikes has been shooting his mouth off about you.'

'I see old Harold from time to time over at Archer's. That guy must have a drinking problem . . . every time I walk in the place, there he is.'

'That's pretty funny.'

'It's an old joke,' Carl told her. 'So what's he been saying?'

'Oh, he told Perry that he beat you up a while back.'

'You'd think I'd remember a thing like that,' Carl said.

'You would think,' Frances agreed. 'Perry believed him. But Sikes could have told Perry you were the Marquis de Sade and he would have believed that too. Anyway, I just thought you should know you're a topic of conversation when these Mensa types get together.'

'OK.'

'I have a feeling you're not going to lose sleep over it.'

'Probably not.'

Frances took another drink. 'Well, I envy you that.'

'Not sleeping, Frances?'

'Not much.'

'This landfill thing?'

She hesitated. She hadn't called to unburden herself to him. They didn't have that kind of relationship. 'No,' she said. 'It's probably going to happen and we'll have to live with it. I'm just feeling . . . restless.'

'Why is that?' Carl asked. 'Things are going pretty good out there.'

'Maybe that's the problem,' Frances said. 'Everything's going great. To the point where it's predictable. I've been feeling lately as if I'm stuck in a rut, that old cliché. I realize it's a good rut, but it's still a rut.' She sipped from the cup. 'My problem is, I've always regarded complacency as a bad thing. I realize that's a conceit on my part. Most people would kill for a little complacency. People with real problems. Do you agree?'

'I don't know what most people would do, Frances. What they would kill for.'

She smiled. 'That might have been a poor choice of words,' she admitted. 'What about you, Carl? Are you complacent?'

'Not that I've noticed,' Carl said.

'I didn't think so,' she said. 'I don't know. I feel as if I've lost my capacity to be . . . surprised . . . by anything. Delighted by anything. Christ, I sound like a nut job. I must be boring you to tears.'

'Movies about the Civil War are predictable. You're not.'

'I feel like I am. I feel like I need to be surprised.'

'Surprises aren't always good.'

Frances had another drink. 'True. But they're never boring.' She paused. 'I want to ask you a question. When you're doing something, I don't know, work or whatever – do you ever think about how you look while you're doing it?'

There was nothing for a moment. 'I don't know what you mean,' he said, clearly confused.

Of course you don't, she realized. What was she thinking? 'Forget it.'

'Do I think about how I *look*?' he asked.

'It was a stupid question,' she told him. 'Really, forget it.'

'Do you think about how you look?' he asked.

She laughed. 'Actually, I don't. Hey, I need to apologize. You shouldn't have to listen to this. I'm going to bed and you go back to your movie.'

'It's all right,' Carl said.

'It's not,' she insisted. 'Good night, Carl.' And she hung up.

TWELVE

When Carl went to work for Frances he checked out of the motel and took a room at the Queens Hotel downtown. The room was large and overlooked the river, and it was cheap. There was a double bed and a couple dressers, with a little corner counter that had a bar fridge and a toaster oven. Frances had offered him a spare room at the farm but he'd declined. The hired hand Perry was turning out to be a bit of a problem and Carl suspected that his staying at the house wouldn't help. Lately Perry had moved on from ignoring Carl to telling Carl what to do, but only after Carl was already doing it. One day he told Carl to change the oil in the stake truck while Carl was beneath the vehicle, draining the pan. It seemed that he wanted to establish some sort of pecking order and Carl was fine with that, so long as Perry didn't peck too hard.

Carl phoned Kate once a week or so. Sometimes she came to the phone but most of the time she did not. He would leave a message on the voicemail or talk to the boyfriend David, whom Carl liked, based on the few short conversations they'd had. The plant where he worked was doing some innovative things with recycling, including shredding old tires to use in roadways and sports stadiums. Carl wished that Kate was as forthcoming as David. When she did come to the phone they would talk briefly and she would beg off, saying there was something she had to do, someplace she had to go. She never initiated a topic, never asked what he was doing, never inquired anything about his life at all.

In light of that, Carl was surprised when she agreed to have dinner with him on a Saturday night in late September. They arranged to meet at a restaurant in the city. Saturday morning Carl drove out to River Valley Farm and worked a few hours on the warehouse addition. Frances and Perry were at the farmers' market for the day so he was there by himself. Earlier in the week he had cemented in the posts for the addition, and strapped the posts with two-by-fours. The truss system had arrived on Thursday and it was in place. Now he was building lintels and framing in the windows.

He quit work at four and drove back into town to find a message from Kate on his hotel phone, saying that she had hurt her knee playing baseball and had to cancel. She gave no other details. He called her number and got her voicemail and hung up.

He showered and then paced around his room for a bit. He turned the TV on and turned it off. He thought about going to Archer's, but after his late-night conversation with Frances a few days earlier he wasn't in the mood to run into Harold Sikes, or anybody else laboring under the illusion that they had beaten Carl up. After a while he grabbed his jacket and truck keys and left. He picked up a six pack of beer and some ice and drove out to the farm. Frances and Perry were not back from the city yet. Fall was the busiest time for the market and often they didn't return until well after dark. Carl parked by the old garage and went inside. Earlier, he'd seen a fishing pole and a creel in a corner there. He put the beer in the creel alongside whatever tackle was there and packed some ice around it.

There was a Styrofoam coffee cup with a large black spider inside on the workbench. He dumped the spider out and carried a shovel to the cabbage patch where he dug some worms. He gathered his gear and crossed the road and walked down to the river bank.

A quarter mile upstream a creek ran into the river beneath the remains of a wooden bridge. Carl headed for the old pilings, walking through the ankle-high quack grass on the river bank. He sat on a timber that slanted down toward the creek and found a hook and sinker in the creel and baited up. He tossed the line out toward the swirl of the current where the creek entered the river and opened a beer.

He had a couple of nibbles right away and then nothing and when he pulled his line in his worm was gone. Catfish, he thought. He threaded the new worm lengthwise on the hook and then passed it back and forth over the barb a couple of times. He tossed into the creek and a few minutes later he had a bull-head on the line. It was no more than eight inches long, its belly bright yellow, whiskers twitching. He unhooked it, mindful of the fish's spikes, and tossed it into the shallow water along the shore.

He baited up again and didn't have another bite for the next half hour. The evening sun came through the trees and before long a succession of mud turtles slipped from the creek and aligned themselves on a fallen log across the stream. Red-winged blackbirds flitted from tree to tree, swooping down occasionally to pick something from the cattails along the river bank. The current in the creek was slow and from time to time a limb would drift past to enter the river.

Finally he reeled in and began to walk upstream. The creek meandered down from the northwest and about a thousand yards from the river it narrowed and tumbled through a rock cut, at the bottom of which was a deep pool. Carl stopped there and sat on the limestone ridge, dropping his bait into the water below. He opened another beer and thought about Kate, even though the whole idea in coming was to stop thinking about Kate. His mind went back a few weeks, to the day they'd spoken at the bar called Shoeless Joe's.

She had told him there was no money in it for him and walked away. Turned her back on him like the stranger he was and returned to her work, her shoulders squared, her expression as she turned suggesting she had already put him from her mind. Physically she had looked as he had expected, but then he had seen her on the news. Still, something about her – the way that she moved – had managed to surprise him. To Carl, she had always been beautiful, but this was something more than that. She had become substantial, he decided. She was a substantial woman and as such she knew what she did and didn't require. One of the things she didn't require was the stranger that was Carl. And she had no problem making that clear.

He wasn't sure what he had expected that day. He hadn't allowed himself a reunion scene in his mind. He hadn't debated on the merits of a hug over a handshake and it was just as well, because in the end there had been neither. He himself wasn't much of a hugger; he preferred to keep the world at arm's length, and a long arm at that. Still, it occurred to him that he had waited too long, that it was quite possible that she never thought of him at all anymore. It would be the natural progression of things, to think less and less of someone gone from your life as the years passed. But with Carl, the opposite had been true. She had always been in his thoughts.

He'd been looking forward all week to dinner. The last time he'd had a meal with her she had been ten years old. Coincidentally, he had taken her fishing that day and they'd caught a dozen or so lake perch off the pier. Carl had fried them up back at his place and the two of them sat at the picnic table in his back yard to eat. Afterward they had walked downtown for ice cream cones. It had been a good day together, just the two of them. They had talked about Madonna and school and boys. Things of that nature.

It had been a hundred years ago.

It seemed as if there would be no more conversations about Madonna or school or boys. Or anything else, for that matter. At some point he would have to consider throwing in the towel. In two months he had seen her twice, and not at all since the trial ended. Maybe it had been too late all along. Or maybe if the outcome of the trial had been different she would have been more willing to see him. He had no idea if that was true either. He'd had the chance to be a father at one time and he didn't do it. Some things, you only get one chance.

Frances had been right – he and Suzy had been a disaster together. If they had stayed together it would likely have meant the death of both of them. They split and Suzy didn't make it anyway, probably because she was slightly more crazy than Carl. Or maybe it was just the roll of the dice. When she'd overdosed Carl was still in Talbotville, living with a woman named Colleen and her two little boys. They were building the new highway to Rose City that summer and Carl worked on a paving crew. He'd been straight for over a year, other than beer and a little pot on the weekends. Suzy was living in town too, but they rarely saw each other. She was running with some wannabe biker types who frequented the Royal Hotel across from the train station. Carl found out later that Suzy had only started doing heroin a couple of months before she died. The last time he saw her had been at the Sunoco station at the west end of town. She was putting gas in a rusty Mustang convertible. The top was down and a skinny guy with greasy long hair was sleeping in the tiny back seat. Carl had filled his pickup and they talked for a couple minutes. She said she was heading for the city but she didn't say what for. She was thin and wasted, her pupils huge and her eyes restless, refusing to settle on him. She was dead within the week.

He'd shown up at the funeral home and John Rourke, mad in his grief, would have made a scene if it hadn't been for Frances stepping between her father and Carl. She'd told Carl he was welcome to stay, although there wasn't a lot of conviction in her voice when she said it. She was just doing what she could to stop a physical confrontation. John Rourke was a big man, and cruel to a point. Even though Carl and Suzy had been apart for five years, John had always blamed Carl for his daughter's drug use. Frances had never suggested anything of the sort. Suzy was always going to be Suzy, with or without Carl.

Carl didn't stay at the funeral home very long. He hadn't been part of Suzy's life when she died, and he'd never really been a part of the family, even when they had been together. He had talked to Kate that day, and the memory even now was as fresh as any he could lay claim to. She had been wearing a yellow dress, with a matching ribbon in her hair. She was sitting in a chair twenty feet or so from her mother's casket. Carl remembered that she was very composed. Her eyes were dry. He didn't feel as if he was her father and he wondered afterward if she felt that she was his daughter. He doubted it.

It was decided that Kate would live with her grandparents and Carl saw little of her after that. John was hostile to him on the odd occasion that he would stop at the farm. Carl was riding the hardtail at the time and the Harley itself seemed to raise the old man's ire. Carl ended up moving to Whistler for two years to build condos for a guy he'd gone to high school with, and from there to Montana with the same builder. By the time he made his way back to Talbotville, Kate was a teenager. They talked occasionally, usually when running into one another in town.

He'd been drunk the day she had tried to tell him about being attacked by Joseph Sanderson III. She never actually said she'd been raped, probably because she couldn't bring herself to say the word out loud. But she was trying to tell him something, and Carl had been hammered after shooting pool at Archer's all day. He wasn't listening to her and finally she just left.

And never came back.

Draining the second beer, he saw his line jump and he grabbed the pole. He pulled in a largemouth bass, maybe three pounds. He was surprised that there were largemouth in the creek. Fifteen minutes later he caught a fat, lolling carp, and then nothing else.

He decided to follow the creek further along. From the rock cut it swung back to the southwest and then straightened, flowing from the west. After a mile or so he came upon the town line, a gravel road with an aged concrete bridge under which the creek flowed. He kept going, into a hardwood bush, recently logged, the tops of the oak and ash and maple lying every which way on the forest floor. Good firewood going to rot if someone didn't cut it up and haul it out.

The sun was falling when he reached the next side road, the Irish Line. He could see the yellow variance signs posted from a fair distance up the creek and when he got closer he realized he was looking at the proposed site for the landfill.

It was good farmland, black loam mixed with the clay, and it was planted, at least the acreage in front of him, in soybeans. It would be the last crop ever on these fields, if Hank Hofferman got his way. The creek grew marshy here where it ran along the edge of the concession before angling off to the south. Looking toward the Irish Line, Carl could see the burnt-out shell of the McIntosh house in the distance. He had heard about the fire; the cops had been pretty quick to declare it an accident.

It would be dark in half an hour, he realized. As he turned to go, he saw a van pull up on the side road. After a minute a man wearing a tweed cap got out, carrying a paper in his hand. The man wore khaki pants and a leather coat and he was as thin as a sapling. He obviously had not seen Carl. He walked into the field across the road, and moved directly to an abandoned gas well along the creek bank.

Carl was headed that way and he kept going. Not wanting to startle the man, he made a point of coughing loudly when he was twenty yards away. The man turned.

'Hey,' Carl said.

'I'm not trespassing, am I?' the man asked. He was maybe seventy, Carl saw now. He wore brown horn-rimmed glasses and he had tufts of gray hair growing from his ears. His voice was a deep baritone, slow and measured.

'Not as far as I'm concerned,' Carl said.

'You one of them that's putting in the landfill?'

'No,' Carl said. He held up his pole. 'Just out fishing.'

'Lee Cumberland,' the man said. 'I drilled gas wells all over this area.'

'Carl Burns.' Carl shook the man's hand.

The man held out the paper. 'One of my old maps. There's a number of old wells on this land they're buying up. They put in a dump, all that goes to waste. Thought we had an energy crisis in this country.'

Carl glanced at the map, a faded foolscap with the roads and boundaries marked. He could see the line of the creek snaking through.

'Somebody ought to think about that,' the old man said.

'Somebody should do a lot of things,' Carl said.

'You got any idea how many old gas wells there is around here?'

'I don't,' Carl admitted.

'Neither do I. That's my point. Nobody does. This here's a county map, only goes back sixty years or so. There were no records before that. Hell, there might be fifty, even a hundred gas wells on this concession alone.'

'Does the county know about it?' Carl asked.

'Damn right they do,' the old man said. 'Because I went down there and told them. They didn't want to hear about it. They're a bunch of damn ostriches down there, they'll issue permits for anything. Same as when they put up those sow barns. County turned a blind eye and a couple years later one of their manure lagoons overflowed and contaminated a creek off the Fourth Concession. Were you around here when that happened?'

Carl was in jail when that happened. 'I heard about it,' he said.

'Well, they never learn, do they?' the old man said. 'Now they're going to let this landfill happen. Make any sense to you?'

'Not a bit,' Carl said.

'I'd like for somebody to tell me when it was that common sense became obsolete.'

Carl looked at the sun, falling below the tree line to the west, and he nodded to Lee Cumberland, an old man out reliving his well-drilling youth. 'Well, I'll see you.'

The old man, returning the nod, seemed a little put out that Carl wasn't more interested in what he had to say. But he held his tongue as Carl turned to follow the creek downstream, making his way in the failing daylight. After a time he heard the van start up and then pull away, tires crunching on the gravel road.

By the time he reached the river Carl was back to thinking about Kate. He didn't know what to do about her. Maybe there was nothing to do. Once the addition to the warehouse was finished, he knew he should head back to Dundurn. Back to installing security systems, back to pool at Shooter McGraw's. Back to Julie. Maybe in time he would figure out what it was he was missing and she would welcome him back into her bed.

Walking up the river bank, he could see the River Valley Farm produce truck parked down by the warehouse. The lights were on in the farmhouse and Frances would be inside. Perry would presumably have trudged home. Carl thought he would stop and say hello to Frances. If he couldn't delight her, he could at least mildly surprise her. As he approached, though, a familiar-looking blue Land Rover pulled into the driveway and parked. A man got out. About forty or so, he had longish hair and a beard and wore a leather bomber jacket and khaki pants. He was carrying a bottle of wine and as he got out of the car he popped a breath mint into his mouth. Watching, Carl realized why the vehicle was familiar. It had almost run him off the road a couple of months earlier, the first time he'd visited Frances at the farm. The bearded man was the driver that day too. Carl waited until the man walked around the house toward the patio out back. Then he crossed over to the machine shed, got into his truck and drove back into town.

THIRTEEN

Kate started spending time at Shoeless Joe's during the day. She'd stop in for lunch a couple of times a week, then stick around for an hour or two, hanging out at the bar, talking to whoever was on shift. She was still using crutches and her knee didn't feel much better than the day of the surgery, two weeks earlier. She was taking physiotherapy three times a week, but it only seemed to aggravate the joint. The lack of progress was discouraging.

On a rainy Wednesday she arrived around one o'clock and ordered the fish and chips special and a pint of Guinness. The place was quiet, the patio outside deserted due to the weather. Sasha was working the bar. She'd been all alone, reading the newspaper, when Kate walked in.

'So what's been happening?' Kate asked when she brought the draft.

'Summer's over and business is shit. Nothing's happening.'

'So make something up. I'm bored to tears.' Kate had a drink of the stout and looked at the bottles behind the bar, the glasses lined up, the limes and lemons and olives in their bowls. She liked working there, the order of things. 'You know I could help out here a few hours a week. I could work the bar.'

'I don't think you could,' Sasha said. 'With your insurance, I mean. I think either you're off work or you're not. They have people checking up on that.'

'So I'll do it under the radar. You won't even have to pay me.'

'And what happens if you injure yourself?' Sasha asked.

'Like if I pull a muscle lifting a shot glass?' Kate asked.

'Yeah.'

'Jesus. You're so anal.'

'Your fish is ready,' Sasha said, looking toward the kitchen.

As Kate was eating the front door opened and a guy came in out of the rain, his collar turned up and a leather laptop case beneath his arm. Kate glanced at him and went back to her haddock. Sasha carried a menu to the man, who took a seat by the front windows. Kate could hear her talking to the guy. When she came back to the bar, Kate pushed her plate away and asked for another Guinness. Sasha brought it and leaned close.

'You know that guy who just walked in?'

Kate didn't look over. 'Should I?'

'He was asking about you.'

The guy was Peter Dunmore. Wet as a drowned rat, his collar up, his face hadn't registered with Kate. Carrying her beer, she made her way on one crutch to his table and sat down across from him.

'Hi, Kate,' he said, closing the laptop.

'Peter, right?' she asked.

'Right.'

'Peter, who told me he was going to do a big piece in the newspaper after the trial. Right? Peter, who called me at home twice with follow-up questions.'

Dunmore exhaled heavily, said nothing.

'I have that wrong?' Kate asked.

'You've got it right,' Dunmore said. 'For what it's worth, I did write the piece. The paper decided not to run it.'

'Why not?'

Sasha arrived with a bottle of Coors Light for Dunmore. He ordered a club sandwich and Sasha took the menu and left.

'Why not?' Kate repeated.

'Because he was acquitted.' Dunmore shrugged. 'They said they would have run it if he was guilty.'

'He was guilty,' Kate said. 'Is guilty.'

'Not in the eyes of the court.'

'And not in the eyes of the *Times* either.'

Dunmore shrugged again. The gesture was already getting on Kate's nerves. 'My editor said we didn't want to give the impression that we were piling on after the fact. He'd already received a lot of negative publicity.'

'As opposed to the positive publicity that a serial rapist deserves,' Kate suggested.

'I didn't say that.' Dunmore took a drink of beer, barely a sip.

Kate glanced toward Sasha, watching from the bar, her curiosity running rampant, no doubt. 'You were asking about me?'

'Yeah. I saw you there. Thought it was you.'

Kate considered this. 'But you were aware that I worked here?'

'I did know that. Yes.'

'So this is not a coincidence. You being here.'

'I stopped for lunch,' Dunmore said. 'People need to eat.'

'Right,' Kate said. 'But not necessarily here. What do you want from me?'

'*From* you?' Dunmore asked, surprised. 'Nothing. I thought I owed you an apology. I mean, I told you I was going to write the piece.'

'But you did write it.'

'Well, yeah.'

'Then your paper owes me an apology. And I don't want it. So there you go.'

Dunmore sipped from his beer. 'I could buy you lunch.'

'I had lunch.'

'Well, I could buy you a beer.'

'That would make everything better.'

'I didn't mean that.'

'Then buy me a beer.'

He gestured to Sasha at the bar, indicating Kate's glass. He looked at the crutch, on the floor beside the table. 'What did you do to your leg?'

'Tore my meniscus.'

'Ouch. Did you need surgery?'

'Yeah.'

'I didn't know that.'

Of course you didn't, Kate thought. You don't know anything about me.

'It must be painful,' he said.

'Not as painful as some things,' she told him.

Sasha brought the fresh Guinness with the clubhouse. Kate finished one beer and started on the other while Dunmore began to eat. He kept glancing up at her while he did. After a time Kate quit looking at him. She wished she hadn't accepted the beer; now she was obliged to sit with him until it was gone.

'I'm going to hang on to my files,' he said, wiping his mouth. 'In case anything else comes up.'

'What does that mean?' Kate asked. 'What's going to come up?'

He backed off. 'I'm speaking hypothetically.'

'Are you really?' Kate asked. 'What's going to come up?'

Dunmore took a drink of beer and shook his head, as if chastising himself for saying too much. 'It's just . . . I heard something from a cop. Might be bullshit. You know what cops are like.'

'Tell me,' Kate said.

Kate drove directly to the courthouse from the bar. Prosecutor Grant was not there but as the receptionist was explaining to Kate that she wouldn't be able to see him without an appointment, he walked through the door. He told her to come into his office.

'Do you want coffee?' he asked.

Kate declined. She leaned her crutches inside the door and sat. Grant went behind his desk and glanced at a computer screen there, scrolling quickly through his e-mails.

'What did you do to your leg?' he asked while he read.

She told him, providing more detail than she had with Dunmore a half hour earlier. Grant, finished with his e-mail, leaned back from the monitor as she told it.

'Did you at least score the run?'

'Out by a country mile.'

Grant smiled. 'So how's it going?'

'You mean the knee?'

'No.'

'It's going all right.'

Grant nodded. He seemed to want to ask why she was there, but he wouldn't hurry her. 'We never really talked after the trial,' he said. 'That seems to be the way it goes when a case—' he hesitated – 'when a case is unsuccessful. But you should know that I thought you did a good job. Whatever the problems, they had nothing to do with you.'

'So what now?'

'What do you mean?'

'Are you still investigating him?'

'Are we still investigating The Mayor?' Grant repeated, as if asking himself the question. 'No,' he said slowly. 'I'm sorry, Kate. It's over.'

She watched him a moment. He was a decent man, she had

decided early on, and she still thought so. But he'd moved on, which meant he wasn't going to like what was coming next.

'I had a conversation today with a reporter who covered the trial,' she said. 'He says that a cop told him there were actually thirty-some women who were attacked over the years. Who came forward.'

Grant didn't say anything for a moment. 'Thirty-six,' he said.

'Thirty-six,' she repeated. 'So he'll be back in court?'

'No,' Grant said. 'It was decided that you four were the best we had. Our best chance for a conviction.'

'We were the best? Holy shit.'

'Some of the assaults were . . . less grievous, if there is such a thing. Grabbing women inappropriately in public, lewd suggestions, that sort of thing. Those women didn't necessarily want to take him to trial. The public exposure.'

'What about the rest?'

'The rest,' Grant said. 'We decided that they might not be up to it. Most of them hadn't done well since the incidents. Keep in mind, that's how he operated. He picked on the disenfranchised. You said it yourself. Is it any wonder that these women have fallen through the cracks?'

'But can't you build another case?' Kate asked. 'Put all thirty-six on the stand. A jury is not going to believe they're all lying.'

'It's not that easy. Believe me, you four were the cream of the crop. The others – well, three committed suicide, and let's just say the rest would not fare well in a court of law. You want me to subject them to Miles Browning?'

Kate got to her feet, her knee fragile beneath her. 'This really sucks.'

'I can't argue with that.' Grant stood as well.

She got her crutches beneath her and then stopped to look back at Grant. 'He's made getting away with rape an art form,' she said. 'Maybe he'll write a how-to book.'

'I'm sorry, Kate. We really did everything we could. And in the end he walked away. He paid his lawyer a million dollars and he walked away.'

'Can I have their names?'

'Pardon?'

'The other thirty-two women. Well, the twenty-nine survivors. Can I have their names?'

Grant's eyes narrowed as he looked at her, as if he had missed something earlier. 'No,' he said slowly. 'You can't have their names. What good would that do you?'

'I don't know,' Kate said, and she left.

She told David about it that night. They were sitting on the back deck, having a beer while chicken and egg plant cooked on the grill. Mister Jones was crouched along the fence at the back of the yard, whiskers flicking, ready to pounce on some prey, real or imagined.

'Thirty-six,' David said.

'That's how many came forward,' Kate said. 'How many didn't?'

'And Grant says it's over.'

'He got his ass kicked,' Kate said. 'He charged the mayor of the city with rape and didn't get a conviction. You can tell he doesn't want to go after him again. I would imagine even Grant has to answer to somebody. Either way, he's done with it.'

A dog barked then, the sound coming from beyond the fence. David jumped to his feet. 'It's Lex,' he said.

Lex was the neighbor's Dalmatian, a show dog with a pedigree that ran back to the nineteenth century and a propensity for killing cats whenever the opportunity arose. Mister Jones had had a number of narrow escapes. Even now, he was sprinting up to the deck, where he landed in Kate's lap.

'You're safe here, buddy,' Kate told him.

'I'll take a baseball bat to that fucking black and white mutt,' David said.

'But Patti says he's not chasing cats anymore,' Kate said sarcastically. 'I think she had a long talk with him. Taught him the error of his ways.'

'Bullshit,' David said. 'We had dogs like that on the farm. Once a cat-killer, always a cat-killer.'

The phrase passed Kate by as she got up to check on the chicken. But it came back to her at three in the morning. And she knew it was true.

'Sonofabitch,' she said out loud.

* * *

Bud slept until shortly after ten. Deanna was gone when he got up. There was a note on the kitchen counter saying she'd gone to Niagara with Sheryl. Bud had no idea who Sheryl was but then he really didn't know many of Deanna's friends. They were mostly dipshit shopping queens with too much time on their hands and too much money at their disposal.

He had been dieting for over a week and had actually lost two pounds already. It hadn't been easy: he'd cut out bread and pasta and pretty much anything deep fried. He would stick with it, he decided, after stepping on the scales that morning and discovering his success. If he could lose two pounds a week for three months, he would be happy. Under that positive frame of mind, he decided to reward himself for his efforts thus far. He put two frozen waffles in the toaster and ate them slathered with syrup, then had two more. The waffles were whole wheat, which made them a healthy choice. Finishing the second course, he remembered that he was meeting Hank Hofferman for lunch. He made coffee and drank it while watching *The Price Is Right*. He answered some e-mails. At eleven thirty he showered and got dressed. He got high and headed out.

Bud and Deanna's condo was in The Docks, in a building that overlooked the harbor. Twenty years earlier the area had been run down and forgotten, a dirty jumble of warehouses and depots and waterfront bars left over from the days when most of the city's goods came in by boat. Speculators had bought up most of the buildings and about ten years ago the area was revived. Many of the older places were bulldozed but a few – including the one where Bud now lived – had been gutted and renovated. Bud's building had once been the home of Gordon's Fresh Fish; it was now known as the Gordon Building. The neighborhood boasted more than a dozen pricey restaurants and four art galleries. Bud, on the stump, often made reference to his own contributions to the gentrification. In truth, his only involvement had been in buying his condo, and that only after the docks had become The Docks.

Bud walked to Spinnakers, three blocks away. It was a cool and sunny autumn day and Bud, under the coke, felt cool and sunny himself. A number of the people he met knew him by name and they spoke to him. Bud liked the feeling of being known, of being appreciated. He had always promoted himself as a man of the people and once in a while he felt that it was actually true.

Hofferman was late so Bud sat at the bar, drinking a root beer and talking with a waitress who was working her first shift. She told him she'd just arrived in the country from Sydney and Bud fell in love with her accent. She was thin, with straight dark hair and broad shoulders and a great rack – so great, in fact, that Bud suspected she'd had some work done in that area. The place wasn't busy yet and she hung around the bar, talking to him. Bud let it slip that he was a city councilor and a bit of a political force in the city. He began to fantasize about her breasts, whether they were real or not. Either way was all right with him. Her name was Gina.

'You know, one place I've always wanted to go is Scotland,' Bud told her.

'Me too,' Gina said.

'That's where you're from,' Bud reminded her.

'I'm an Aussie,' she said. 'From Sydney.'

'Oh, Sydney,' Bud repeated. He wasn't good with accents, or geography either for that matter. 'I thought you said – what's that city in Scotland, sounds like Sydney?'

'St Andrews?'

'Maybe.'

Further confusion was avoided when Hank Hofferman arrived. Coming in out of the bright sunlight, he stood in the doorway for a moment, looking for Bud. When Bud saw him, he turned to Gina.

'Lookit this hick,' he said. 'Guy's worth about five million dollars, dresses like he's going to the rodeo.'

'I like the hat though,' Gina said. 'Stetson, I'd say.'

'Right,' Bud said quickly. 'It's a cool hat.'

He and Hofferman sat at a table on the lower level, by the front windows. Bud chose that level because he knew that Gina was working the upper side. He didn't want her getting too cozy with Hofferman and his cool cowboy hat. If anybody was going to verify the authenticity of those Aussie breasts, it would be Bud.

They ordered drinks and lunch and while they waited Hofferman pulled another chair close enough to prop his size twelve boots on.

'That a Stetson?' Bud asked.

'Yeah,' Hofferman said.

'I thought so. Why do you wear a cowboy hat?'

'Keeps the rain off my head.'

'It's sunny out.'

'I like to be prepared.'

Bud didn't own a hat and wouldn't be caught dead wearing one. All these guys he would see on the street, from toddlers to senior citizens even, wearing baseball caps. It was the uniform of idiots. He looked away from Hofferman to see Gina serving customers up top. He liked the way she moved, hips swinging under the short skirt.

'We got some banking problems, Hank?' he asked, still watching her.

'Not that I know of.'

'Well, there was no deposit last week. The bank screw up?'

'It wasn't the bank,' Hofferman said. He removed the big hat and placed it carefully on the chair beside him. 'Way I understand this thing is that I'm paying for a service. Things were moving right along for a while there. Now they're not. Why would I pay for nothing?'

'What are you calling nothing?'

'I don't know if Rose City is gonna give me the contract or not. Isn't that where you come in?'

'That's where I come in,' Bud said. 'But I wasn't counting on certain things. For one – there's opposition at city hall because this is *my* project. We got some new blood over there and they're jealous of me because I get things done.'

'Or they don't like you because you're The Mayor's nephew,' Hofferman suggested.

'Yeah, yeah,' Bud said. 'Whatever. Thing is, they'll approve this eventually because it's cost-effective. I can look after my end, Hank. Question is – can you do the same?'

'What's that mean?'

'I've been hearing that the Ministry of the Environment has been getting bombarded with e-mails and petitions and shit from this group – what the fuck are they called – HALT?'

'Yeah. Some of the same bunch that tried to stop me from building the sow barns. How'd they make out then?'

Their drinks arrived, a beer for Hofferman and another root beer for Bud. The waiter was a pudgy kid with a serious acne problem. Bud wasn't thrilled about the prospect of him handling his lunch. He should've insisted they sit on Gina's side after all. Right now she was flirting with three guys in suits. They got the tits while Bud got the zits.

'Maybe they can't win it, but they can delay it with all their nonsense,' Bud said. 'They get babbling on about containment and we'll have a problem. Next thing they'll be hiring their own engineers, not those bootlickers you got on retainer. We don't need that, Hank.'

Hofferman took a drink of beer. 'I bought five hundred acres because you told me this was a go project. Now you're telling me it's not. Are you saying this HALT thing is in the way?'

'I'm telling you it might be.'

'Then what are we gonna do about it?'

'Who is this *we* you're talking about?' Bud asked. 'You got a mouse in your pocket?'

Hofferman looked over at him darkly, then had another drink. 'Where's The Mayor in all of this? I thought he was your guy.'

'He's behind this a hundred per cent. In a year, he'll be mayor again. But for now, he's not.' Bud looked around, then leaned close. 'Listen, he sees this as his way back in. He's of the opinion that the new mayor will fuck this issue up by supporting a plan to ship the trash out of here. But in the end, it's all about the bottom line. Our plan works based on fuel costs alone. Don't worry, this will go through.'

'Then let's get 'er done, son,' Hank said. 'But this opposition has gotta disappear. I thought this was your thing, Bud. Like old McIntosh. You made that go away.'

'Did I?'

'Oh, I forgot. The fire was an accident.'

'There was a fire?' Bud asked. 'That's a shame.'

The waiter arrived with the food, a steak sandwich for Hofferman and chicken quesadillas for Bud. Hofferman ordered another beer, then proceeded to devour nearly half the sandwich in one bite. Bud, watching in disgust, examined the food on his plate and concluded he wasn't hungry. He'd had waffles just a couple of hours ago and he really did need to stick to his diet.

He wondered how he looked to someone like Gina. Was he just another middle-aged guy with a big gut, hitting on a pretty young waitress? Hopefully she was smarter than that and could see him for what he was – a political force in the city. Women were attracted to power. Look at Bill Clinton, look at JFK. Those guys got more tail than movie stars. And, other than with a few feminist types, it never hurt their popularity. It was what men did. Real men anyway.

'I hear Frances Rourke is running this HALT thing,' he said. 'Did you know that?'

Hofferman, still chewing, shook his head. 'Hey, she's got a farmhouse,' he said around the mouthful.

Bud had a drink of root beer. 'I'm not sure that serial arson is the best plan of attack here, Hank. For one thing, it happens to be a crime. For another, it might seem a little coincidental after a while.'

'Wouldn't take a fire to scare her off anyway,' Hofferman said. 'She's just a woman, for Chrissakes. What makes you think she's the head of this thing?'

'The meetings are at her farm,' Bud said.

Hofferman shrugged and made ready to attack the sandwich again.

'Maybe you should talk to her.' Bud said.

'Why would I want to talk to a hippie?'

'She's not a hippie,' Bud said. 'That farm of hers is a fucking conglomerate. She does a huge online business. The woman sells lettuce on the internet. Can you believe that?'

'So what?'

'So she's a businesswoman,' Bud said. 'She might preach the party line out there in the boonies but deep down I have a feeling she's all about the money. Which means she's no different than you. That's how you need to approach her, Hank.'

The pimply faced waiter brought the beer. Bud glanced across the room and saw Gina at the bar, loading a tray with bottles of beer and drinks.

'Are you a breast man, Hank?' he asked.

'What?'

'Do you like tits?'

'Everybody likes tits. What the hell.'

'Lookit this waitress. Tell me if those tits are natural or augmented.'

Hofferman watched Gina as she crossed the floor. 'I don't know. They look pretty good to me.'

'But the question is,' Bud said, 'are they real or are they from Home Depot? I think I'm going to have to form an exploratory commission on this matter. I might even have to head it up myself.' He drank off the last of his root beer. 'But first we need to put a stop to HALT. Stopping HALT – isn't that like a double negative or something?'

'Goddamned if I know,' Hofferman said. 'I don't care about that shit.'

'Did you go to college, Hank?

'No, I didn't,' Hank said. 'But I'm betting you did. You want to compare bank accounts, asshole?'

'Easy now,' Bud said. The fact of the matter was that he hadn't gone to college. But he sometimes claimed that he had. It all depended on who he was talking to. 'We're on the same side, partner. Tell you what, Hank, talk to the woman. If she doesn't want to listen, maybe we'll have to take another tack. But talk to her, man.' Bud reached for his wallet. 'I'll buy lunch. But, speaking of bank accounts, you've got a deposit to make, right?'

FOURTEEN

Frances was loading hamper baskets of apples into the cube van when Hank Hofferman pulled in, behind the wheel of his black Humvee. The truck was diesel-powered and the engine rattled noisily until he shut it off. Frances gave him a short look, then went back inside for more apples. From behind the warehouse she could hear the whine of Carl's circular saw as he worked at the addition.

When she came out, Hofferman was standing by the open door of the van, looking at the cargo inside. He was wearing blue jeans with a crease ironed in them, and his usual black cowboy boots. A white western shirt with the logo HH stitched on the pocket. Self-advertising. He smelled as if he'd drenched himself in aftershave lotion. 'Nice-looking apples,' he said. 'Macs?'

'Heirlooms,' she told him.

'My grandfather had a little orchard over by Suttonville,' he said. 'He'd hire me and my brothers to pick for him when we were kids. Paid us a quarter a hamper. Cheap old bastard.'

Frances had no interest in his childhood tales. 'What can I do for you?' she asked.

'What can we do for each other, Frances?'

She put her knee beneath the hamper to hoist it on to the truck, then slid it further inside before turning to him. 'This ought to be good,' she said, taking her gloves off.

'I was thinking about how much we have in common,' he said.

'You weren't.'

'Well, I was. I'm somebody who sees the big picture and so are you. We're both in the business of supplying people with food.' As he spoke he walked over to look inside the warehouse, at the crates of squash and pumpkins and potatoes, ready for loading. Perry was in the back, pressing the inferior grade apples into cider. He glanced up, saw Hofferman, looked quickly away and continued to work.

'In a manner of speaking,' she told him. She really didn't want him in her warehouse.

He turned to her. 'This is smart, what you're doing here. You caught yourself a wave, didn't you? I've been thinking about doing some organic pork for a while now. Thing is, I'm not set up to market it the way you are. I mean, I could do it, but you've already got the customer base. Smart move would be for the two of us to throw in together.'

Frances smiled. 'Well, that sure came from left field.'

'Go big or go home, what I say. I sure as hell didn't get where I am by following the pack.'

'Then you don't need to follow me,' Frances said.

'I don't need you,' he agreed. 'You're right. But I'm making you an offer anyway. This would open up a whole new market for you. And not just pork. I been thinking of exotic meats – caribou, wild boar, elk. That stuff is real popular these days, especially in the urban areas. People in the city have no concept of money. Hell, you could sell 'em organic pork chops for twenty bucks apiece and they wouldn't bat an eye.'

'Those dumb city people,' Frances said. 'Hell, they'd probably even pay you to take away their trash.'

Hofferman showed his aw shucks smile.

'Because that's what this is about, right?' Frances went on. 'You're offering me a slice of pork pie in exchange for me changing my mind about the landfill.'

'I never said any such thing.'

'You didn't have to,' she said. 'So what if I was to agree to it? HALT has over a thousand members. You got a deal for everybody, Mr Hofferman? A pig in every pot and a Hummer in every garage?'

Without waiting for a reply, Frances went back into the warehouse for another hamper.

'Fighting the landfill is a waste of time,' Hofferman said, waiting for her to return. 'It's gonna go through in the end. You can muddy the waters and cost everybody a lot of money for lawyers but in the end it's gonna go through. Trash disposal is a necessity. You saying you don't produce garbage yourself? Come on, Frances. People will listen to you.'

'Not if I change my mind on this, they won't,' she said. She slid the hamper into the truck. 'And I'm not going to. So you can forget about you and me going into business together. As much as that breaks my heart.'

Hofferman, smiling, reached into the truck and helped himself to an apple. As he began to shine it on his shirt, Frances took it away from him and returned it to the hamper. The cologne, whatever it was, was overpowering. Frances remembered her father using something similar. It had been novel to her when she was five.

'I drove out here thinking I might ask you to dinner,' he said. He was getting testy now. 'But I see you for who you are now. For somebody running a glorified vegetable garden, you got a real high opinion of yourself. Where's that come from?'

'I was born with it,' she told him, and went back inside.

'You're nothing but a big frog in a little pond,' he said when she came back. 'Frogs get to croaking, they can make a lot of noise. But if they get in the way, they have a habit of getting squashed too.' He impulsively moved to block Frances from loading the hamper on to the truck. 'You listening?'

'That almost sounds like a threat,' Frances said.

'Let's call it good advice.'

'Sounded like a threat to me,' Carl said.

He was approaching along the side of the building, wearing his carpenter belt, a pencil behind his ear. He had a framing hammer in his right hand and as he approached he flipped the hammer end over end before catching it and sliding it into the loop on his belt.

'Lookit here,' Hofferman said. 'Killed any firemen lately?'

Carl walked up to Hofferman, who was a couple of inches taller than him and thirty pounds heavier. Hofferman was still blocking Frances from the truck. She could have stepped around him but she didn't.

'You're in the way,' Carl said.

'What's it to you?' Hofferman asked. 'You got a dog in this fight?'

'My dog died,' Carl told him.

Hofferman turned to Frances. 'Hear that? He's got no dog in this fight. Maybe there ain't much fight left in the dog.'

'Maybe not,' Carl said. 'We can discuss it. After you move out of her way.'

Hofferman looked at Carl, then glanced at Frances again, and this time his eyes showed a glimmer of self-doubt. She smiled and then he moved. Just a step, but he moved. Frances slid the basket into the truck before turning to Carl.

'Mr Hofferman has a business proposal for me,' she said.

'Yeah?' Carl said.

'Yeah. But I've instructed him to stick it up his ass so I think we're just about done here. Unless there was something else, Mr Hofferman? I assume that dinner invitation has passed me by?'

'I said this was a waste of time,' Hofferman said. He leaned in toward Frances. 'I'd remember today, though, if I were you. You might look back at it.'

'You're not all that memorable, Hank,' Frances told him. 'Go now.'

Hofferman shook his head, as if he pitied her, and he got in the Humvee and made a u-turn on the grass. When he was gone Frances took two apples from inside the truck and rubbed them both on her jacket and gave one to Carl.

'So somebody sent him,' Carl said as he took a bite.

'Why do you say that?'

'He said he told somebody it was a waste of time.'

'I don't know who that would be,' Frances said. 'He's the one with the most at stake. He's the one sitting on five hundred acres.'

Chewing on the apple, Carl thought about that. 'You know, I walked over there on Saturday. To the site. I was fishing the creek and I just kept walking. They can say what they want about containment. Water runs downhill. That property drains to the river.'

'I saw your truck by the shed when we came home from market,' Frances said. 'I wondered where you were. What time did you get back?'

'Just dark. You were entertaining your boyfriend.'

'Was I?'

'You were entertaining somebody.' Carl took another bite.

Frances started to say something, then thought better of it. Instead, she mimicked him, smiling and taking a bite from her own apple. He was watching her, smiling, but it was obvious he wasn't going to press her.

'Well, I'd better get these apples over to the market in Palmerton,' she said. 'I promised them for noon.'

'Perry not going?'

'He's cultivating that field in front of the bush,' Frances said. 'I'll leave him to it, before the rain starts.'

'Thanks for the apple,' Carl said. He began to walk away, then stopped and turned back to her. 'Somebody sent Hofferman, though,' he said. 'I wonder who.'

On the drive to Palmerton Frances thought back to Carl, munching on the apple while asking about her boyfriend. From a purely technical standpoint, she couldn't say whether the man that Carl had seen that night was her boyfriend or not, at least at the moment when Carl had seen him. In a general sense Frances wasn't all that comfortable with the term 'boyfriend', and she was even less at ease using the word 'technical' when describing any relationship, even just talking to herself.

Martin had called Thursday, having just arrived back in the country, and, after a few minutes catching up, had invited himself to dinner Saturday night. Getting off the phone, Frances reflected on the fact that she should have been the one doing the inviting, and wondered why she had not.

Having spent the day at the market, she'd been home for less than an hour when he arrived, carrying a bottle of wine and a gorgeous silk blouse he'd bought for her in Peru.

She threw together a salad and grilled a couple of steaks and they drank the wine. Afterward they sat at the dining room table while he showed her dozens of photos on his tablet, so many that after a while she lost track of which country was which. He said 'you would have loved it there' so many times she thought she might scream. Instead, she sat quietly and drank a lot of wine. Finally, in an effort to get away from the travelogue, she modeled the blouse for him and then he slipped it from her and they made love in the front room on the leather sofa.

They took a walk afterward. She wanted to show him the new warehouse addition, although he didn't show much interest in it when she did, preferring to tell her about the farms he'd seen on his trip, how beautiful they were, nestled in this valley or that, with an assortment of stupendous mountain ranges in the background. She pointedly mentioned Carl's name several times but he never asked about him, even though he hadn't been in the picture when Martin had left the country. He never inquired after Kate either, although he'd been aware of the trial. Thinking back, it occurred to Frances that in general he preferred not to know about certain things, especially things that didn't fit into his aesthetic view of the world.

Early in the evening he mentioned that she was off someplace else, and then joked about it a couple times afterward, including immediately after they'd had sex. She told him that it wasn't true, and she believed it when she said it, thinking that it was he who was acting differently. Still, when he told her he wasn't staying the night, citing work to be done in the morning, she didn't ask him to reconsider. It wasn't until an hour later, when she was in the kitchen cleaning up, that she realized what it was that had been nagging at her.

In the weeks that he'd been gone, she couldn't recall a time when she had missed him. Not even one.

Carl found Rufus Canfield sitting at the bar in Archer's later that evening. Rufus was finishing a plate of ribs when Carl walked in and joined him. Carl ordered a beer for himself, and another for Rufus. It was shortly past eight and the place was practically empty. There was a couple drinking Caesars farther down the bar and a few kids shooting pool in the back room. The bartender was a thin woman with jet black hair and a tattoo of a rose, also black, on her wrist. Carl paid for the beer and tipped her. She took Rufus's plate with her when she left.

Rufus made a half-hearted effort to remove rib sauce from his thick mustache before tossing the napkin on the bar. He wore his usual corduroy sports coat and a blue shirt. No tie. He picked up the newly arrived beer. 'Why, thank you, sir,' he said, as if speaking to the lager.

'What's new, Rufus?' Carl asked.

'Nothing is new under the sun,' Rufus replied. 'If we are to believe Mr Shakespeare.'

'I always thought that was the Bible.'

Rufus considered this. 'You might be right. And it could be

Shakespeare too. Which means he stole it. Did you come here to disillusion me, Carl?'

'I didn't think you needed any help in that department.'

Rufus smiled and saluted Carl with his beer glass before drinking again. 'Though I'm a little surprised to learn that you're a Bible scholar.'

'My mother sent me to Sunday school,' Carl said. 'I'm not sure that qualifies me as a scholar.'

'It just might, in these parts,' Rufus said. 'I do suspect you've come looking for me, though. Newspaperman's intuition. And I suspect it is not to question my literary references.'

'Hank Hofferman paid Frances a visit today.'

'Did he now?'

'Yeah.'

'And what did he have to say?'

'You want the short version?' Carl asked. 'He told her she'd be sorry if she kept fighting the landfill.'

Rufus thought about this as he took another drink, half emptying the glass. 'And what did Frances say?'

'You know Frances,' Carl said.

'Go fuck yourself, Hank Hofferman?'

'You got it.'

'Imagine my shock.'

'You know better than anybody my history with Hofferman and the pig barns, Rufus,' Carl said. 'But the truth is, I don't know much about the guy. Is he just a blowhard?'

'You're asking if he represents a genuine threat to Frances,' Rufus said. 'Do you mean in a physical sense?'

'I mean in any sense,' Carl said. 'He's got a lot of money tied up in that piece of property out there. Frances says he paid more than it's worth as farmland, mainly because most of the owners weren't looking to sell. If this thing falls through, then that's all it is – farmland. And he takes a bath. Sound right to you?'

'Inasmuch as very little to do with Hank Hofferman sounds right to me, yes,' Rufus said. He sat smoothing his mustache for a moment, like a cat in its grooming. 'I can tell you this. He's clumsy and inarticulate, but on a base level he's a rather clever fellow. He's never left his fingerprints on anything, as far as I know. Even these disgusting hog barns – he owns the business and markets the animals to Beaver Lodge, but the barns themselves are owned by various individual farmers. If there is ever any kind of liability issue, with the lagoons or airborne pollutants, whatever, the small owners are on the hook, not Hofferman.'

'Then what are you saying?'

'I'm saying he doesn't like to get his hands dirty. Does that help you?'

'I have no idea. I was hoping you'd tell me he was nothing but a loudmouth.'

'Would you have believed me if I had?'

'I guess not.' Carl turned on the stool as he took another drink. The pool shooters in the back were getting rowdy now. As Carl watched, a cue ball rocketed off one of the tables and hit the wall with a crack like a rifle shot.

'The question here, quite obviously,' Rufus said, 'is not to what extent you want to be involved. The question is – to what extent *can* you be involved? I notice you don't attend the meetings at the farm.'

'I can't go anywhere near it,' Carl said. 'All Hofferman has to say is, there's the guy who killed a man the last time you people went up against me.'

'Then again, you're working for Frances,' Rufus said. 'And I believe you're rather fond of her.'

'What the hell does that mean?'

Rufus laughed as he took another drink of beer, then held up two fingers to the rose-tattooed bartender, who was sitting down farther along the bar, leafing through a glossy magazine while ignoring the shenanigans in the back room. As Rufus waited for the beer, he looked thoughtfully at Carl, deciding something. When the draft arrived, he told the woman to put it on his tab and turned back to Carl.

'There's something I want to tell you,' he said. 'I very nearly told you this before but I was afraid you'd think I was trying to exonerate you in some way. Which is not the case. But it's something you should know.'

'I'm listening.'

'Red Walton was as drunk as the proverbial skunk the night he was killed. It was kept quiet for a long time after the fact.

But I got it firsthand a few years back from the coroner who did the autopsy, on a night when he himself was in his cups. Walton had a blood alcohol reading of point two five when he died. Three times the limit, Carl. Pie-eyed. Four sheets to the wind. Pissed to the gills. No way he should've been allowed at that fire, let alone up a ladder. Furthermore, Red Walton got drunk at the fire station that day. He was out of work and spent his days there drinking. I've even heard rumors that some of his fellow firefighters were trying to kick him off the department. But they closed ranks when he died.'

Carl sat quietly for a while. 'Doesn't matter,' he said finally. 'If I hadn't set the fire, he wouldn't have died. That's it.'

'Or maybe he would've gotten behind the wheel that night and killed a family in a car crash. The man was a bleeding fucking idiot, Carl. You can't predict anything in this life. So, while you were responsible for Red Walton's death, so was he.'

'But I was responsible,' Carl said. 'Hofferman will use it if he can.'

'True,' Rufus admitted. 'Which means you have to stay out of it.'

'That's what it means.'

Rufus finished one beer and pushed the glass carefully away, like a man making a move on a chess board. He reached for the full beer in the same deliberate fashion. 'He could very well have been running a bluff on Frances,' he said then.

'I thought of that,' Carl said. 'I guess we'll have to wait and see.'

Rufus took a long drink of beer. 'Have you seen your daughter?'

'No.'

'I assume you've tried.'

'Yeah.'

Rufus nodded and let it lay there. What Carl liked about the man was that he wouldn't ask questions that had no answers. Maybe that was the lawyer in him.

'I'm at a dead end, Rufus,' Carl said. 'A man reaches a certain age, he should know when to stop banging his head against the wall.'

Rufus Canfield smiled. 'William Blake said that you never know what is enough until you know what is more than enough.'

Carl picked up the full beer from the bar. 'You sure that's not from the Bible?'

'No,' Rufus replied. 'That one I got right.'

Bud Stephens, having boned up on Australian trivia via Google, invited Gina from Spinnakers to dinner Friday night. Before asking, he told her a heartbreaking and completely bogus tale of how he and his wife had recently separated and as a result he'd moved into the Four Seasons. They could have Thai food in his suite.

That afternoon he went to the opening of a new interior design store on Walnut Avenue. Walnut was a side street a few blocks from The Docks, a formerly depressed area that was becoming trendy due to that proximity. Secondhand stores and pawnshops were now boutiques and cafés. Clapboard houses slapped together during the Second World War were being renovated and quaint-ed up, their prices quadrupling in the process. The crackheads and junkies were being pushed toward Parkdale, where the dominoes had yet to fall. The crackheads and the junkies would have loved to stay in and around Walnut Avenue but they could no longer afford it.

Bud had managed to secure funds for new street lamps for the area, and for a few flower gardens where the old sidewalk meridians still existed. Mostly he had paid lip service to the neighborhood's transformation and as such was looked upon by certain locals – at least those who didn't examine things too closely – as being in some way responsible for it. Bud was not above encouraging such skewed perceptions.

The store was called Design Intervention. There was a ribbon cutting in the afternoon, followed by a wine and cheese reception. Bud wore his ivory linen suit, with a black t-shirt and the twenty carat chain around his neck. Upon arriving he was provided with a glass of warm white wine and he wandered around, shaking hands and talking about how exciting it was to see that particular area of the city undergoing a renaissance. The store smelled of paint and new carpeting and drywall dust.

He knew most of the people at the opening, if not by name then by face, and he was enjoying himself until the mayor showed up. Bud was holding forth on the landfill issue in an area in the back of the store where laminate flooring was on display when he heard the familiar voice. He turned to see Mayor McBride as he was stepping on to a small riser to speak. The mayor's comb-over was plastered in place and he wore what appeared to be a bush jacket of some sort. As it turned out, he was a cousin to one of the store's owners and he'd responded to the invitation on that account. Bud was required to listen to the speech and then make small talk with the man. He was even forced to pose for a picture with the mayor and the store's two owners. He left shortly afterward.

Bud ordered in food from Thai This, a new place in The Docks. When it came to more exotic fare he really didn't know good food from bad, so he reasoned that by saying he was trying the joint for the first time he was covered if Gina gave the meal a bad review.

She showed up just past seven, wearing a tank top and faded low cut jeans with boots of some sort of snakeskin. She usually wore her hair fastened back in the restaurant and tonight it was hanging loose to her shoulders. She had long dangling earrings of silver, and she wore a number of rings, also of silver. She smelled as good as she looked, and she looked great.

'Nice place, man,' she said in the cool accent when she walked in. Place sounded like plice.

Bud had stocked the bar earlier. He passed himself off in public as a teetotaler, although it was not remotely true. He explained to Gina now that he himself rarely indulged but he would make her anything she wanted.

'I'll just take a beer,' she said. Take sounded like tike.

'A true Aussie,' Bud said as he went into the fridge for a Stella. 'Do you know that Aussies drink more beer per capita than any other country?'

'I did know that,' Gina said. She was sitting on the leather couch, running her hands over the soft fabric. 'But Jesus, I hate to be a cliché, man. Maybe I'll chase it with a shot of tequila.' Chase sounded like chice.

Bud smiled. 'Maybe I'll join you.'

It was a warm night for October and they had their drinks on the balcony that overlooked the lake. Gina had a lot of questions about the harbor and its history. It turned out she had a degree in fine arts from the University of Melbourne. She intended on traveling for a year or maybe two before returning to get her teacher's certificate. She said she loved history.

'I had a prof back home who always said you can tell never tell what is until you understand what was,' she said. 'Makes you think.' Makes sounded like mikes.

Although Bud liked to brag that he knew every little mouse in every corner of his ward, his knowledge on the city's past was severely lacking. Bud wasn't very much interested in history, whether it was the city's or his own. So, to appease Gina's curiosity, he made a bunch of stuff up. It seemed unlikely she would check to see if Rose City actually was a major fur trading post at one time, or that the Battle of Rose City was a turning point in the War of 1812. And even if she did, by then Bud would have moved on.

They ate inside, on the glass-topped dining room table. Gina had been to Thailand, she said, and she declared the food from Thai This to be very authentic. To Bud, it was a little on the spicy side. Gina stuck to the beer throughout the meal, declining Bud's offer to open a bottle of wine.

'Don't be wasting that good stuff on me,' she said. 'I'm a simple girl.' Wasting sounded like wisting.

After they'd eaten, Bud asked if she would like coffee. He would call room service.

'Um, sure,' she said. Then she smiled. 'Unless you have Scotch?'

Bud did have Scotch. They went back to the living room and sat on the couch together this time.

'So how come you don't drink much?' Gina asked.

Bud gave her his standard speech on the subject, how he used to be a bad-ass back in the day, running with the wrong crowd, burning the candle at both ends. He threw in his line about living hard and dying young and leaving a good-looking corpse. The line was so old that it was becoming new again, especially to a woman of Gina's age, which Bud guessed to be mid-twenties. Then he did the turnaround, saying how he realized, upon entering public life, that he was responsible for a lot of people's lives, and that he could no longer be the wild man of his youth.

'I grew up,' he told her. 'That's the simple truth of it. So I decided to leave certain things behind.'

'You're very down to earth,' Gina said. 'You don't have the big ego.'

'I have no ego,' Bud agreed. 'That's the great thing about me.'

She laughed, and Bud wasn't quite sure why. 'I've become a bit of a health nut, you want to know the truth,' he said. He patted his stomach. Better to draw attention to it himself. 'I've been letting myself slip the past year or so. Our current mayor is a bit of a nincompoop and sometimes it's like I'm running the city myself. It's so much damn work that I haven't taken time for Bud. But I'm changing all that. You know, watching the fats and the starches, that sort of thing. Green tea instead of coffee.'

'I reckon I'll have to go that way myself down the line,' Gina said. Way sounded like why. 'But I like my partying too much for now. Low key, y'know. A little alcohol, a puff here and there. All things in moderation, right?'

'What kind of puff?'

'You know. A bit of the weed.'

Bud smiled at her. She had to be getting tipsy, with the beer she'd put away, and now the Glenfiddich. 'You know,' he said carefully, 'I'm not adverse to a little recreational use myself from time to time. You know, to help you relax. Especially in a private situation.'

She smiled her beautiful smile. 'Right, man. A little pot or whatever.'

'I like to smoke,' Bud said. 'But I'm not into pot so much.'

'What're you into?'

'I like cocaine, once in a blue moon. I like rocks.'

'Crikey. You wouldn't have some, would you?'

Bud got to his feet. 'I just might, you know. I think I might have some in the bedroom. Want to come see?'

'Yeah.'

Yeah sounded like yeah.

FIFTEEN

She was meeting Peter Dunmore at a coffee shop a block away from the courthouse downtown. He was there when she walked in, looking a little uncomfortable in a sports jacket and tie over a white dress shirt. She wondered if he'd dressed up for her. She was aware that he had a crush on her and she was feeling slightly guilty about it. Actually she was feeling guilty that she was not exactly discouraging him. She had arranged to meet today, calling him at the paper the day before.

Seeing him in the jacket and tie made her feel under-dressed, in her jeans and baseball jacket. She was using just one crutch now and as she moved across the floor he stood, as if to help her into her chair, but she sat quickly, sliding the crutch under the table.

'Look at you,' she said.

'I'm covering court,' he explained. 'Figured I'd put on a tie for a change. The boss likes it. Old school, you know.'

'You look nice.'

'So do you.'

She was sure that wasn't so. Maybe to him it was, though. She ordered coffee and he asked for a refill. She watched his hands as he drank. His nails were down to the quick and he wore a signet ring of some description on his right hand. She wondered about the significance of the emblem but decided not to ask.

'Why were you in court?'

'Covering an impaired case,' he said. 'This guy, some contractor, is trying to say his dentist gave him a shot of something, caused him to rear-end a school bus. Meanwhile his blood alcohol was twice the limit.'

'Gee, my dentist doesn't even have an open bar.'

He smiled and took a drink of coffee. 'People will try anything. If they spent as much effort obeying the law as they did trying to beat it, they'd be better off.'

'It's the little boy caught stealing cookies,' Kate said. 'He's not sorry he stole, he's just sorry he got caught.' She tried the coffee but it was too hot to drink.

'I'll have to remember that one,' he said.

She could see that he didn't know what to say, that he was not good at small talk. She suspected he lacked confidence in general and maybe he'd become a journalist because of it. If he couldn't tell his story, he'd tell the stories of others.

'How's your knee?' he asked.

'It's OK. Taking longer to rehab than they thought.' She gave the coffee another try. 'The physiotherapy was aggravating the soft tissue, or something like that, so I had to stop for the time being.'

'That has to be disappointing,' he said. 'And you're an athlete too. Must be frustrating not to be able to do the things you like to do.'

'I'm not sure I'm an athlete.'

'You play baseball.'

'Well, slow pitch.' She paused. She couldn't recall telling him how she'd injured her knee. 'How did you know I played?'

'Oh, I saw you once,' he said offhandedly. 'Over at Lions Park. I was on my bike and just happened to notice you. You were playing third base.' He suddenly began to apologize, for no reason. 'I should join a team. I need to get in shape. Spend all my time at a damn desk, staring at a computer screen. I'm going to start working out, though.'

His earnestness bordered on desperation, like a man determined to fit in, who stood out because of it.

'Well, no workouts for me,' Kate said. She thought it odd that he'd been watching her play baseball, but she let it go. That wasn't why she was here. 'I have to find other pursuits to keep me occupied.'

He smiled uncomfortably, knowing where she was going.

'Were you able to find out anything?'

'Not really,' he said reluctantly. 'I only had the one source on the department and he's clammed up.'

'Why has he clammed up?'

'He says he can't reveal any details that might be part of an investigation.'

'So the police are still investigating The Mayor?'

'Well, he didn't exactly say that.'

'According to Grant, they're not.'

Dunmore hesitated. 'Then it's a dead file. Right or wrong, the man was acquitted. It wouldn't be fair to—'

'Please don't tell me what is or isn't fair.'

He fell silent, lifting his cup to his lips but not drinking. He put the cup down and looked at her forlornly, wanting desperately to please her but having no notion how.

'Just tell me what the guy said,' Kate demanded. 'He didn't tell you they're still investigating him because they're *not*.'

He put the cup down. 'He said . . . he says that there could be accusations out there that just aren't true. And it wouldn't be right to release that kind of information to the public. Not after the man's been cleared in a court of law.'

'So that's what I am – the public?' Kate asked. She hated herself for resorting to the tactic. But she did it anyway.

'Well, no.'

'Besides, I'm not asking for information. I just want the names.'

'To do what with them?'

Kate considered the question. The truth was that she really had no idea just what she would do with the names. She sipped the coffee.

'To do what?' he asked again.

'I'll let you know when I know,' she said at last.

'It doesn't matter anyway,' he said. 'I have no access to them.'

'So much for your source.'

'Hey, I tried.'

Kate could see that he despaired at the very notion of disappointing her. 'I know you did,' she told him. 'I appreciate it.'

He drank off his coffee and looked up at the menu board. 'I'm hungry. Would you like some lunch? I'm buying.'

She reached for her crutch. 'No thanks.'

'You sure? We could go somewhere else.'

'I'll take a rain check.' Kate got to her feet.

'Wait a minute,' he said then, clearly not wanting her to leave. 'I did hear a story. Not from the cops but from somebody at the paper. I have to say, it's pretty far-fetched.'

Kate sat again. 'What is it?'

'Apparently the cops busted a woman last spring who later claimed her son was The Mayor's kid. Said he raped her up at the lake a few years ago. But it was obvious she'd been reading the papers and made up a story to match. Maybe thinking she could leverage it, hoping they wouldn't charge her, I don't know.'

'What did they bust her for?'

He rolled his eyes. 'She had a grow-op in a tent in her back yard. Big circus tent she found somewhere. She sewed plastic panels in the roof for sunlight. One day a huge wind storm came along and the tent blew over. And there's all the plants. What they call plain sight. One of the neighbors made a phone call and the cops showed up.'

'When was this again?'

'This past spring. She hasn't gone to court yet. I don't see her going to jail though, not for a half-assed operation like that. Plus she's got the kid, he's eight or nine, no father around. They won't lock her up.'

'You have her name?' Kate asked.

He hesitated. 'Yeah, I found it. The paper buried the story, not sure why.'

'To protect the fucking Mayor?' Kate suggested. 'That cross your mind?'

'Maybe,' Dunmore admitted. 'Not to protect him necessarily. But this was just before the trial. The paper's always mindful about running things that might slant public opinion. Let's face it – it's a pretty wild accusation.'

'Right,' Kate said. 'So who is the woman?'

'Elaine Horvath. Lives on Cleary Avenue.'

'Thanks.' Kate picked up her crutch again and got it underneath her.

He stood, in his clumsy manner both helpless and hopeless. 'Hey, I wish I could do more. I really am on your side, Kate.'

'Don't worry about it. You have your job to think about.'

'I have you to think about too. I can do both.'

Shit, she thought. 'I'd focus on the job if I were you. I might be a bit of a lost cause. I'll see you, Peter.'

'What are you going to do?'

'I don't know.'

'You're not going to talk to her?'

'I just might.'

'You realize it's just a story, don't you? Like the guy and his dentist. People will say anything.'

'I know,' Kate said. 'Sometimes they even tell the truth.'

She left him standing there, in his jacket and tie and too polite ways, his puppy dog eyes on her and his heart on his sleeve.

She drove home and went into the kitchen to make a cup of tea. Her knee was a dull throb. Taking a Demerol, she changed her mind about the tea and unplugged the kettle and mixed a Bloody Mary instead. She was sitting at the kitchen table when David came in.

'Hey,' she said. 'What're you doing home?'

He held up his right hand. There was gauze taped expertly around the gap between his thumb and forefinger. 'Cut myself on some scrap steel. I had to go to emergency for a couple of stitches so the foreman told me to take the rest of the day off.'

'Are you OK?'

'Just four stitches.' He gestured at her glass. 'Lunch?'

'Getting my vitamin C.'

He went to the fridge and took out a bottle of water. 'So what did you do today?'

'Nothing. I enjoyed it so much yesterday I thought I'd do it again.'

'How you feeling?'

She gave him a look. 'So-so.'

David sat down across from her. 'Maybe it's not just the knee. Maybe you should go in for a check-up.'

'I don't need a check-up.'

He tried to make a joke. 'Get it in writing. Get a doctor to say you don't need a check-up, and I'll quit bothering you about it.'

'Or you could just quit bothering me about it.'

'Am I not supposed to care about you? I know you're not sleeping, Kate. You were watching TV at four o'clock this morning.'

'Like I'm gonna miss a *Friends* marathon.' She sighed when he didn't smile. She wasn't in the mood for this particular conversation. 'I'm all right. Just . . . you know, feeling sorry for myself.'

'You're allowed to feel sorry for yourself.'

'So tell me – just how long am I allowed to feel sorry for myself? Can you give me a ballpark on that?'

'Maybe the longer you do it, the harder it is to stop. At some point you have to let it go. You did everything you could.'

'I'm not so sure about that,' she said.

'What's that mean?'

She shook her head. 'I'm not trying to be cryptic. It means I'm not so sure about that.' She stared into the glass for a moment, then suddenly looked up. 'Let's go someplace.'

'Where?'

She thought about it. 'Florida,' she said. 'We planned to go this winter anyway. Let's go now.'

He indicated her cast. 'With that?'

'Sure,' she said. 'You can play golf and I'll ride around in the cart with you. I'll be your beer caddie. We can lie in the sun. We can have drunken sex on the beach at night. Come on, David. Let's do it.'

'You mean right now?' he asked.

'Yeah. Let's get out of here.'

'I can't,' he said, after considering it. 'I'm training this new guy at work and there's no way I can get away. They'd freak if I even asked.'

'Shit.'

'I like the drunken sex part.' He smiled. 'We could do that here, you know.'

She sighed and drank from her glass before setting it aside. 'I need to get away, though. I really need to get the hell out of here.'

'We'll go this winter,' he promised. 'Your leg will be better then. OK?' He watched, waiting for a response. 'OK?' he repeated.

She nodded unhappily. 'OK.'

SIXTEEN

She pulled into the mall parking lot and drove along the row of stores until she spotted the Lincoln Town Car, parked across from the pharmacy. She turned and drove to the back of the lot, where she parked. She reached into the back seat for a ball cap, tucked her hair up underneath, then pulled it low over her eyes and waited.

She took the coffee from the holder on the dash and had a drink. She hadn't been sleeping well and she was a little wired from too much caffeine and too little food. Her knee ached, especially at night, even though the surgeon kept telling her she should be pain free by now. Him saying it didn't make it so. She'd smoked a dozen or so cigarettes in the past couple of days. The pack was in the glove box right now, and she told herself she would throw it out when she got home. She'd quit smoking when she was twenty-five but for some reason a few days ago had decided she needed one. The first cigarette had taken her unawares, catching her breath and ballooning her lungs. She had stubbed it out after a few drags. But the next day she'd had another and that time it had been smoother. Trickster.

She was lighting a cigarette when The Mayor came out of the store. He was wearing a golf cap with a Callaway logo, and pale blue pants and a yellow knit shirt. He carried a small bag with the drugstore's brand on it and wore his standard benign smile. A couple approached him to say hello. They were his age or maybe a few years older, retirees out shopping, Kate guessed. She saw him nodding his head and speaking and then the couple laughing at whatever he'd said. They chatted for some time. Kate smoked the cigarette and lit another before The Mayor looked at his watch and moved off toward the Lincoln, waving to the couple as he did.

Kate knew he'd be heading to the golf course next. He played at Grand River National, Mondays and Wednesdays and Fridays. There was a nine-hole seniors' league that teed it up at one in the afternoon those days, and he rarely missed. Kate waited until the Lincoln was out of the lot and moving toward the parkway before following. She hung back in the light traffic, and when he accelerated through a yellow light she lost him for a time. It really didn't matter – she knew where he was going; but still, for a brief moment, she allowed panic to set in. One day he might break from his routine.

When she drove past the golf course a few minutes later, the Lincoln was parked by the clubhouse and he was lifting his clubs from his trunk. She slowed down, then on an impulse pulled into the lot, idled past him, almost wishing he would look her way. He didn't, and she continued on, out to the highway. She headed for the medical center.

Her appointment was for half past one but she didn't get in to see Dr Song until after two. He had just come from surgery at the hospital across the street and appeared hurried and harried both. At his instruction, Kate removed her pants and sat on the examining table. He looked at the incision before working her knee a couple times, and feeling the tissue behind the leg.

'No swelling,' he said. 'Can you describe what you're feeling?'

'Like there's something in there that shouldn't be there,' she told him. 'Maybe it's scar tissue.'

He shook his head, dismissing the suggestion, and felt the leg again. 'And you have discomfort?'

'It's really not much better than right after the surgery,' Kate said. 'There's no chance something could have been left in there? You know, during the operation.'

'If it had been, you'd have an infection by now,' Dr Song said. He gave her a look. 'And I don't leave things in there during surgery.'

He stood up and indicated that she could put her pants on. He crossed to his desk and looked at her file there. 'You're still taking the painkillers?'

'Yeah, and I'm just about out.'

He looked again at the file. 'You shouldn't be.'

As she hesitated, his cell phone rang. He reached for it. 'My purse was stolen out of my car at the mall,' she said quickly. 'I lost my last script.'

He nodded and turned away as he answered the phone. He

told someone he was on his way and ended the call. He looked at her.

'We'll give it another week and then try the physiotherapy again,' he said. He wrote a new prescription. 'I think you have some inflammation that's limiting the flexibility of the joint.'

Kate stood up and took the slip of paper from him, wondering if he was telling her what he might tell her if he didn't know what was wrong with her knee.

'I have to go,' he said. And he left before she could say anything more.

She found Elaine Horvath's street address in the phone book. The neighborhood was part of an older subdivision in the east end, a cluster of attached semis and wartime houses that the years had not been kind to. The streets ran every which way into dead ends and cul-de-sacs and it took Kate a while to find Cleary Avenue.

It was Friday afternoon and Elaine Horvath was sitting on the front porch when Kate pulled up in her car. The house was a single story bungalow with dented aluminum siding. The roof had a sag in it and the screens in the windows were either ripped or missing altogether. The lot was narrow, with no more than ten feet separating the houses on either side. Behind the house, though, Kate could see that the yard stretched out toward a garbage-strewn industrial lot beyond. Presumably that was where the circus tent had been poorly pitched.

The woman on the porch was roughly Kate's age, she guessed, although she could have passed for older, with yellow blond hair showing black at the roots and a couple of inches of stomach hanging over her belt. She wore jeans and a t-shirt with a NASCAR logo, and she was reading a paperback while drinking coffee from a take-out cup. Her skin was terrible, her cheeks splotchy and red.

When Kate got out of the car the woman looked up from the novel, her mouth turning slightly as if encountering a bad taste.

'Well, aren't I the popular one?' she said.

'I beg your pardon?' Kate said.

'You people from family services. You got nobody else to bother?'

Kate approached the porch and stopped by the bottom step. 'I'm not from family services. Are you Elaine?'

The woman looked past Kate to her car, trying to figure out who she was, as if the vehicle might tell her. 'Who are you?'

'My name is Kate Burns.'

'What do you want?'

Kate had decided on the drive there that she would get right to the matter at hand. 'I want to talk about Joseph Sanderson.'

'Then you're a cop? It's about fucking time.'

'I'm not a cop. Joseph Sanderson raped me, seventeen years ago.'

Elaine Horvath smiled then. She didn't have a lot of teeth and those that were there weren't impressive. 'You shitting me? Why would you come here? You wanna start a club?'

Kate stepped up on to the porch and moved to sit on a wooden chair. 'I'd like to hear your story.'

'And what's that gonna get us?' Elaine asked. She took a closer look at Kate. 'Wait a minute. You're one of 'em that took him to court.'

'Yeah.'

Elaine drew the cigarette down to the filter and dropped it into the coffee cup, where it sizzled briefly before going out. 'What the fuck you doing coming here?'

'Did he rape you?'

'You got a smoke?'

'Yeah, I do. In my car.'

Kate was aware of the woman watching her as she went for the cigarettes. It seemed that a decision was being made in the time it took her to walk to the curb and back. They both lit up and then Elaine settled back in her chair, looking over at Kate with the same amused expression, as if she knew something that Kate did not. Maybe Peter Dunmore had been right. It had been a tall tale all along.

'Well?' Kate asked.

'Well what? Did he rape me?' Elaine pulled on the cigarette and exhaled. 'Make you a deal – I'll tell you my story and then you decide.'

'OK.'

'Me and my girlfriend Jill went camping up on Lake Sontag.

Nine years ago this summer. Bunch of us used to camp on the government land there. You weren't supposed to but nobody ever bothered us. We had a little tent, couple bottles of wine, some joints. Maybe mushrooms that time, I can't remember. My friend dropped us off, there was a couple guys supposed to meet us there but in the end they never showed. So we got no car, right? Anyway we set up camp, built a fire, got high. Ended up crashing, I don't know, late. Next thing you know there's this wicked fucking thunderstorm happening. Tore the tent pegs out of the ground, tipped the thing over. We came crawling out and then the wind blew the fucking tent right across the lake. Thing was bouncing like a ball across the water.'

'You don't have a lot of luck with tents,' Kate said.

'Aren't you fucking amusing? You want to hear the story or not?'

'I do.'

'So it's pouring rain. I mean you can't hardly see the lake it's raining so hard. And it's cold too. Me and Jill start walking and we end up at this guy's cottage. Well, guess who?'

'Yeah.'

'He's there by himself. And he invites us in, it's gotta be three in the morning at this point, and he gives us dry clothes, and he pours us drinks even. Then he gives us both a bedroom. We said we'd share but he's like, no, you each get a room. And we go to sleep. We're both baffed, right?'

She took another long drag on the cigarette and looked at Kate, as if to see if she was still listening.

'Next thing I know, I wake up. And he's in the bed with me. All he's wearing is a t-shirt. And he's got a hard-on and he's trying to push it into me. Got my panties off to one side and he's on top of me. Fucking freaky. So I try to push him off, and I'm like – I'm like I don't even know what's happening. I'm half asleep, half stoned. I tell him to quit, and he doesn't say a word, he just keeps pushing. And after a while, I don't know – I'm just so fucked up, after a while I quit fighting him. And he came in like two minutes and he got off me and walked out.'

Kate was staring straight ahead, trying to focus on the woman's story but instead seeing herself, seventeen years earlier, in nearly the identical situation, possibly even in the same bedroom. The old man pushing her down. The noises emanating from him, grunting like the pig that he was. The attitude afterward, the dismissal, as if the encounter meant nothing more to him than a handshake.

Now Elaine Horvath leaned forward and glared at Kate, as if challenging her. 'So you tell me. Did he rape me?'

With an effort, Kate brought herself back to the present. 'Did you want to have sex with him?' she asked.

'No fucking way.'

'Then he raped you,' Kate said, knowing it was the truth, knowing all along it was the truth.

'Thanks for telling me what I already knew.'

'What happened in the morning?'

'What do you mean?'

'Did he say anything about it?'

'Not a fucking word. The storm was over and he basically kicked us out. Said he had to get back to the city. But we saw his car there later, so I know he was lying.'

'You never told anybody at the time?' Kate, knowing the answer, wondered why all the stories were alike.

'I never even told Jill. It was just so fucking weird, like maybe I had imagined it or something. Didn't seem real. It just . . .'

Kate saw her eyes look up the street then and she turned to see a boy of eight or nine approaching on a bicycle. The boy's hair was shorn and he was riding the bike carelessly, weaving back and forth across the sidewalk. A woman out walking had just passed the house, and she had to step off the concrete to let the boy pass. He rode on to the narrow yard of the house and flopped the bike down while it was still moving. He noticed Kate and glared up at her. He had scars on his head and a fresh cut on his lip, or maybe a cold sore. His eyes were gray, familiar-looking.

'Hi honey,' Elaine said to the boy. 'How was school?'

'Sucks.'

Inside the house a phone began to ring. Elaine stood and went inside to answer it, flicking her cigarette butt over the railing. When Kate turned back to the boy, he was staring openly at her.

'Who are you?' he demanded.

'I'm Kate. What's your name?'

'Gimme some money.'

'What?'

'Gimme some money. I want to go to the store.'

'I'm not giving you any money.'

The boy scowled. 'You're ugly,' he said.

'Nice,' she said. 'That ought to get you lots of cash.'

'You're ugly,' he said again and went into the house.

When Elaine came out she didn't sit down but walked to the top of the steps to lean against the newel post there. 'So there you go. And I don't need to hear your story, if you don't mind. I read the papers when the trial was on. I knew he'd win. I coulda told you that all along.'

'What's your son's name?'

'Bobby.' She offered her challenging stare again. 'You wanna ask, go ahead and ask.'

'OK. Who's his father?'

'You know the answer to that. Or you wouldn't be here.'

The phone rang again and Kate could hear the boy answer inside. He said something and then walked out on to the porch. 'It's Aunt Rene.'

Elaine nodded slightly, but kept looking at Kate. 'So why you here? The cops told me to go screw myself. So where you going with this?'

'I don't know.'

'You ain't going nowhere. Nobody like you ever beat anybody like him. Don't you know that?' She went inside to the phone.

Kate got up and walked down the steps to the sidewalk. She sensed the boy following her.

When she got into her car, she picked up her cell phone and rolled down the window and took his picture, him standing there on the dying lawn, his hateful eyes on her.

'Now you gimme some money,' he said.

'Sorry,' she said, and she drove away.

Prosecutor Grant held the phone with the photo in his hand a moment before passing it back to her. He got up and walked around his desk to close the door behind where she sat. It was Monday morning and they were in his office at the courthouse. He was about to try a city man for second-degree murder. The accused was one Dwayne 'Big Dog' Reese, a street punk and convicted drug dealer who had gotten into a fight outside a tavern and, pulling a handgun, fired several shots at his antagonist. One of the shots had killed a woman just leaving the bar.

'I'm about to present a second degree murder case that is ironclad,' Grant had been saying a few minutes earlier. 'I've got eyewitnesses, I've got forensic evidence, I've got ballistics. Not only that, but I have a perp with a record as long as the Mississippi River. This is as pure a slam dunk as I've ever seen. But I'm not going to get a conviction for second degree. In the end this guy will go down on manslaughter, because he wasn't actually trying to kill the woman in question. He was trying to kill somebody else, but that's not why he's in court. He'll get double time for the eighteen months he's been in custody, and be out on the street in a couple years. There's your justice.' He sighed. 'My mother wanted me to be a pharmacist.'

All this information had come tumbling out of the prosecutor when Kate first arrived. She'd been hoping to find him in a more optimistic frame of mind.

'Yes, I know who Elaine Horvath is,' he said now.

'And you know her story,' Kate said.

'Oh, yeah.'

Kate waited for more but it didn't come. 'It isn't something you wanted to pursue?'

'No,' Grant said. 'When we first heard about her last spring we'd already built the case against The Mayor using you and the other three women. We were just a couple months from going to trial. Then the narc squad tells me that they've busted this grow-op over in the east end, and the grower has stories about The Mayor. Did I want to talk to her? Well, I had to talk to her. Did I want her within a mile of the courthouse? I most certainly did not.'

'Why not?'

'You've met the woman,' Grant said. 'Would she have a chance against Miles Browning?'

'Not on her own,' Kate agreed. She showed him the picture again. 'But this changes everything. Doesn't it?'

'You're operating on the assumption that he really is The Mayor's progeny.'

'I'm operating on that assumption.'

'OK, let's get hypothetical. Let's say I presented this in court and demanded a DNA sample. If the blood work showed that The Mayor was *not* the father, then suddenly the rest of my case is every bit as suspect as that. I wasn't about to risk everything on a story by a woman looking to make a deal on a drug bust. You can understand that, Kate.'

'But what about now?'

'Now?'

'You've got nothing to lose,' Kate told him. 'Go after the DNA test now.'

'Unfortunately, that's not even an option,' Grant said. 'Browning and The Mayor and his cronies have managed to sell this whole thing as a witch hunt. The buzz is that he'll run for mayor again next fall and I have no doubt it's true. To present this now would suggest that somebody is trying to hurt him politically and probably open us to a lawsuit.'

'Not if he turns out to be the father.'

'First of all, he would never willingly submit a sample. We would have to pursue him, get a ruling, put the woman in the spotlight, which we've already agreed is not a good idea. It's very unlikely. The people who run this department would never allow it.'

Kate glanced at the hateful face in the photograph. 'And it doesn't matter if this little shit is The Mayor's son?'

'No,' Grant said unhappily. 'At this point it doesn't matter if that little shit is The Mayor's son.'

SEVENTEEN

F all was the busiest time at the farmers' market in Rose City. And October was River Valley Farm's most lucrative month of the year. Like December for most retail concerns, October could make or break a produce farmer.

The second week into the month Frances and Perry loaded the root vegetables on to the truck Friday night and then the tomatoes and peppers and corn at four the next morning. Last to go on the truck was a skid with six dozen gallons of fresh cider. Frances had bought a new apple press that year and she no longer used metabisulphite in the juice. The result was a cider which, although one hundred per cent pure, would start to ferment if not kept refrigerated. So it was last to be taken from the coolers and loaded. Frances attached stickers with a picture of an inebriated Barney Fife to the jugs advising consumers either to drink the cider within a few days or to risk the consequences.

She and Perry were on the road before the sun showed above the treetops across the river. Frances had pricing placards to make up on the way so she had Perry drive. The truck balked and sputtered as they left the farm but it had settled down by the time they reached the highway.

'Motor's just cold,' Perry said.

Frances had little faith in Perry's understanding of things mechanical but in truth it was a cold morning. She'd kept a watch on the thermometer, going to bed and getting up. There had been no frost but it had been close, the warming effect from the river probably keeping the temperature above the line. As they drove toward the city, and away from the water, Frances saw frost in abundance on rooftops and parked vehicles. She decided to hire some pickers to harvest the remainder of the tomato crop before it was lost. She had sixty to seventy hampers of Romas yet to pick. What she didn't sell at market she would use to make River Valley Farm Organic Salsa.

It was just daylight when they reached the city. Perry took the access on to Brunswick Avenue and when he stopped at the first set of lights the truck engine began to cough again, then to rattle and vibrate. The light turned green and they started forward, lurching along. Perry kept pumping the gas pedal but it wasn't helping.

'Shit,' Frances said. They were a half dozen blocks from the market. 'Keep it going if you can.'

'The motor's just cold,' Perry said.

'The motor's not cold,' she told him. 'We've been driving for half an hour.'

They continued to lurch along, the engine occasionally roaring to life and then faltering again. Twice it stalled completely and each time Perry, pumping the gas pedal furiously, got it running again. They were lucky to hit three green lights in a row. Frances dug her cell phone out of her purse.

'If we can make it to the ramp, we can coast down to the market,' she said.

'Who you calling?' Perry asked.

'Carl. We might be able to roll down the ramp but we sure as hell aren't gonna roll back up.'

'We don't need Carl. I can fix it.'

'You're a good man with a hoe, Perry, but you couldn't fix a sandwich.' She punched the number in and Carl answered on the first ring. 'Shit,' she said, 'I just realized it's seven in the morning.'

'I'm up,' Carl said.

'What are you doing?'

'Counting flowers on the wall.'

Frances explained her predicament and he said he'd drive in and take a look. As she shut the phone off, the truck finally quit for good. Perry put it in neutral and they coasted to the ramp and managed to roll down the incline to the market. At the bottom the ramp curved to the right and Perry struggled with the steering, which was no longer powered. They made the turn, though, and entered the market area. Perry abruptly hit the brakes.

There were two Parnelli Farms trucks there. One of them was parked in the space reserved for River Valley Farm.

'What the hell is this?' Frances said as she climbed down from the truck.

The man Arnie was already set up in his regular spot. Two

other men – a different pair than before – were in the process of setting up in the second stall. Frances's stall. One was a big man, six foot four or so and heavy, with thick arms and the huge sloping shoulders of a gorilla. He had the numeral 13 tattooed on to the side of his shaved skull. The other was young, maybe early twenties – skinny, with a pockmarked face, wearing baggy-assed jeans and a sleeveless t-shirt and a dirty ball cap. They were hauling vegetables in hampers out of the big stake truck parked in behind.

Frances moved past them and headed for Arnie. Her blood was up and she told herself to keep calm. As she walked past, the big man smirked at her before glancing at his skinny partner. Apparently they were in on the joke.

'All right,' Frances said. 'What's going on?'

'It's market day,' Arnie said. 'What do you need, lady?'

'I need you to get the hell out of my stall,' Frances said.

'These are my stalls. I paid for them. Check with the office.'

'You're full of shit. This has been my spot for four years.'

'Don't tell me I'm full of shit, lady. These are my stalls. I booked them and I'm using them. Check with the office.'

'This is bullshit.'

'I'll be outa here early afternoon, you wanna wait,' Arnie said.

'You'll be out of here a lot quicker than that,' Frances told him.

The office door was locked. She waited twenty minutes until a young woman Frances had never seen before arrived and opened up. She introduced herself as Debbie and, after checking a ledger, she told Frances that Parnelli Farms had indeed booked her spot.

'I have the stall for the season,' Frances said. 'How can they book it?'

'I don't know. It says here they did.' The woman named Debbie offered over the ledger for Frances to see.

Frances didn't look at the book. 'Where's Gwen?'

'Home. She's probably sleeping.'

'I bet she wakes up when she hears her phone ringing.'

It took Debbie a moment to realize that she would be the one causing Gwen's phone to ring. While she dialed the number Frances turned and looked out the plate-glass window at the market. A few customers were already there, scouting the stalls.

The early birds tended to look the same. Young married couples, the men in Gap khakis and sweaters, the women in long wool skirts and jackets in deference to the cool of the morning. Sometimes they brought their dogs, Airedales and Bouviers and American Standard Poodles. They wandered about with serious looks on their faces, examining pears and zucchinis like diamond merchants appraising stones. They were the ideal demographic for River Valley Farm. They liked local produce, chemical free, whether it was organic or not. This particular couple would not be buying from Frances today, though. Not with her product still on the truck.

At the end of the lot, Parnelli Farms continued to do business. The gorilla had disappeared; Arnie and the kid were working the tables. Perry had the hood of the stalled truck open now and he was standing there, looking at the engine. He might as well have been looking at the plans for the space shuttle.

When Frances turned Debbie was talking on the phone, while making a point of not looking at Frances. 'All right,' she said into the receiver. 'No, I can find it.'

She hung up and went into a drawer and found another notebook. 'Someone called yesterday and cancelled your stall. Um . . . it wasn't you?'

'It wasn't me. I didn't call yesterday and cancel my spot and then show up this morning with two tons of produce on my truck. I didn't do that.'

'You don't have to be sarcastic.'

'I feel like I have to be something,' Frances said.

Debbie found the page in the book. This time Frances stepped forward to have a look. In a margin was scrawled in freehand: River Valley cancel Saturday 10th.

'Somebody cancelled it,' Debbie said.

'Gee, I wonder who,' Frances said. 'All right . . . I'm going to deal with this later. Right now I need a stall.'

Debbie grimaced like she had a pain somewhere. 'We don't have anything. I mean, everything is booked. This is harvest season.'

'I'm aware of that,' Frances said.

By the time she walked back across the market, Arnie was in the process of selling a quart basket of sweet red peppers to a couple wearing matching cable knit sweaters. Frances waited until the transaction was done, reasoning that couples who wore matching sweaters deserved to be fooled into thinking that imported California peppers were grown locally. Arnie took their money and went back to arranging tomatoes in baskets, ignoring Frances.

'I don't know who you're working for and for the time being I don't care,' she said to Arnie. She indicated the skinny kid. 'But you need to tell Leroy there to move that truck and then you need to get that produce out of my stall. Now.'

'We booked these stalls,' Arnie said. 'Maybe you shoulda booked one yourself. You know, before you hauled your stuff down here.'

'I'm not going to play this game where you pretend you don't know what's going on here,' Frances said. 'I *will* report this shit to the market board later . . . but right now I need to set up. So move the fucking truck.'

'Go sell your shit on the street,' the man said, and he turned away.

Frances looked at his broad back for a moment, her pulse pounding. Before she allowed herself to do anything foolish she walked over to the GMC, where Perry was still behind the wheel, watching the proceedings with an indignant look on his face. Frances stood by the running board a moment as Parnelli Farms went about their business. *Her* business.

Across the walkway from the market stalls was a triangular corner that was off limits to the vendors. Marked by yellow diagonal lines, it was reserved for emergency vehicles or the maintenance staff. Where it widened into the pedestrian lane there appeared to be just enough room for a couple of tables. Frances turned to Perry.

'We're going to set up there,' she said, indicating the area.

'You're not allowed to,' he told her.

'Let me worry about that.'

By the time they had the tables up and half their produce on display Debbie from the office was hurrying toward them across the market square.

'Um,' she began, 'you know you can't sell from there.'

Frances indicated the spot occupied by Parnelli Farms. 'I intended to sell from there.'

'I'm sorry about that,' Debbie said. 'But this area is for emergencies.'

'As far as I'm concerned, this qualifies.'

Debbie stayed for a bit, shifting her weight from one foot to another, and then went back to the office, presumably to wake Gwen up again. Frances and Perry finished with the displays and began to sell. The spot, however, was just isolated enough from the rest of the market that business was not great. The place had a flow; people moved down one side and up the other, and most didn't bother to wander over to the corner where Frances was. The Parnelli Farms stalls, in the market proper, were doing much better. It seemed to Frances that every time she looked over there Arnie was selling something, while taking time to smirk in her direction. The smirking bothered her more than the selling. She tried to put it out of her mind. It was one day and one day only.

Soon a few of her regulars stopped by and most of them commented on her new location.

'I've always been an outsider,' Frances took to telling them.

It was the best she could come up with. She didn't feel up to explaining the situation to her customers. Neither could she explain to herself why, when the dilemma with the Parnelli bunch arose, she hadn't called Martin. It would have seemed the natural thing to do, and she'd even thought of it while walking to the office. But she didn't call Martin – partly because she knew Carl was on his way. Six months ago, she would have called Martin anyway. But today she hadn't. They'd spoken a couple times since having dinner at the farm a week ago. He'd asked her to a play that evening, in fact, but she'd begged off, saying she had no idea what time she'd be back from market. In the past she would have brought clothes and stayed in the city, letting Perry drive the truck home. But not this time.

Carl arrived and parked beside the GMC. He was lifting his tool box from the back of his pickup as Frances walked over to tell him what had happened. When she was finished talking, Carl was staring over at Arnie and the skinny kid, at work on their sales.

'Why don't I ask them to move?'

'Tarzan, no,' Frances told him. 'It's not a big deal. Pisses me off though that they're selling more than me. Most of it is shipped in from the south.'

She went back to her makeshift stall and Carl carried his tools to the GMC. After starting the engine and having it stall a couple of times he opened the hood, and came out from under it a few minutes later with a cracked fuel filter. He walked back to his own truck but before he got in he stood there for a moment, looking from the Parnelli Farms stalls to where Frances was set up. He got into his truck and drove off.

He was gone for the better part of an hour. When he returned he installed a new filter in the GMC and started the engine, revving it up before allowing it to idle for a few minutes, smooth as silk. Closing the hood, he walked over to his pickup and dropped the tailgate. In the back were two white placards, four feet square, and a package of stencils, along with a spray bomb of black paint. He went to work making up two signs, a little crude in design but serviceable. Then he parked his truck squarely in the expanse between Frances's temporary stall, tucked away in the corner, and those of Parnelli Farms. He propped the signs up on his tailgate, side by side. One had an arrow pointing toward Frances:

GROWN LOCALLY

The other pointed toward Parnelli Farms:

IMPORTED

Even Frances was surprised at how quickly things changed. Within fifteen minutes she was selling as much as Parnelli Farms and in half an hour she was moving twice as much produce.

'The power of the pen,' she admitted to Carl.

'Spray bomb,' he told her.

At first Arnie laughed when he saw what Carl was doing. As he began to lose customers, his mood changed. Finally Frances saw him walk around his truck to open the passenger door. The gorilla with the tattooed head was sleeping there, sprawled across the seat. Frances had wondered where he had gone.

The man sat upright, rubbing his eyes, like a toddler. It seemed to take him a few moments to comprehend what Arnie was telling him but finally he looked over to take in the scene on the market floor. He was scowling as he climbed down from the van and started over. Arnie hung well back, watching.

Carl was by over by the GMC stake truck, putting his tools away. The gorilla walked past him without a glance and headed straight for Frances. Perry, standing behind the other display table, made a timid attempt to run interference. The big man straight-armed him in the chest, knocking him backwards several feet.

'Get lost, scarecrow,' he said before turning to Frances. 'All right, lady. Move the pickup truck *and* the signs.'

Frances smiled. 'Somebody woke up grumpy.'

The man's eyes widened, as if he wasn't sure what she'd said. 'You hear me, bitch? Move the fucking truck.'

'It's my truck,' Carl said. He wandered over, hands in his pockets.

The big man turned on him. 'Then you move it, asshole.'

Reaching the table, Carl casually picked up a butternut squash and examined it, like a customer might do. 'I don't think I will,' he said. 'Now you run along. And do some work on your people skills, will you?'

The gorilla was clearly aggravated at being awakened from his nap and maybe that was what caused him to overreact. Or maybe it was just his nature. He swung at Carl with a roundhouse right. Carl easily slipped the punch and with the butternut squash hit the big man flush in the face with such force that the squash exploded in his hand. The big man took two staggering steps backwards before crashing on to the adjacent display table, snapping the wooden legs like twigs. Falling to the pavement among the ruins of pumpkins and peppers and tomatoes, he groaned slightly and lay still.

Arnie, in full and sudden retreat into his own stall, was dialing somebody on his cell phone. Frances stepped around the fallen gorilla and headed toward him. 'Calling the cops, Arnie? Good idea. I'd like a word with them myself.'

Arnie turned away from her and listened to the phone ring before shutting it down and tossing it on the table. No answer, so he hadn't been calling the cops, Frances thought. He pushed by her and went over to where the big man lay on the pavement. The skinny kid was already there; he'd decided that splashing water in the man's face might bring him around, and it did seem to be working. The man's legs were moving as if he was trying to walk, even though he was still flat on his back.

Keeping watch on them, Frances picked up Arnie's phone from the table and pressed re-dial. She noted the number before putting the phone back. Walking over to her own display, she wrote the number down on a paper bag and slipped it into her pocket.

After the gorilla made his way unsteadily back to the stake truck, the crew from Parnelli Farms vacated not just Frances's stall but their own as well. Apparently they'd had enough of market life for the day. When they were gone, Frances moved into her usual spot. She had a pretty good Saturday in the end. It was a glorious fall day, with temperatures above normal, weather that attracted market shoppers. She sold all seventy-two gallons of the cider, and could have sold half that amount again. Gwen showed up at ten o'clock and apologized for the cancellation. She didn't mention Frances setting up in the restricted zone, although she surely would have heard about it from Debbie. She had no idea who phoned in to cancel Frances's booking, although she did recall that it was a man's voice.

'It's a mystery,' she said.

'Some things are more mysterious than others,' Frances told her.

Carl hung around for the day, finding other things to do. He bought two-by-fours at a lumber yard and repaired the table the fat man had crushed. He decided that the windshield wipers on his truck needed replacing. After lunch he took a grease gun from his tool box and crawled under the River Valley truck to lube the front suspension. He accomplished all this under Perry's sour surveillance and he was still there when they packed up for the day.

'You're about as subtle as a billboard,' Frances told him. 'Stop by the house on your way home. I'll buy you guys a beer.'

She was including Perry in the invitation, but he pretended not to hear. He'd grown increasingly unhappy, having Carl around for the day. Market day was the one time when he had her, in a manner of speaking, to himself. Carl coming to the rescue was not sitting well.

'That was a matter for the police, not for Carl,' he told Frances as they drove out of the city. 'That man was a thug.'

'The police weren't there,' she told him. 'Carl was.'

'Carl's a thug too.'

Frances smiled. 'Ah, but he's our thug.'

'This isn't funny, Frances.'

It was after five when they got back to the farm. Perry backed the truck up to the warehouse dock and they unloaded the empty hampers and baskets and the few items that hadn't sold. Frances was suddenly tired, but in a purely physical way. A good tired.

'Come up for a beer,' she said to Perry.

It seemed he was thinking about it but just then they heard a vehicle approaching, and Carl pulled up to the farmhouse.

'No thanks,' Perry said.

'Come on, for Chrissakes. It's been a long day.'

'No.' He turned on his heel and walked away into the failing light. She watched him go, his shoulders squared, chin thrust out defiantly, like a man who was taking the high road.

Inside the house, Frances and Carl sat at the granite counter that separated the kitchen from the dining area and drank Moosehead lager. Frances saw that the knuckles on Carl's right hand were raw from the punch he'd landed on the gorilla. Apparently the squash hadn't provided much padding. Frances had never seen anyone knocked unconscious with a butternut squash before. She doubted anyone had.

'Rufus was right,' Carl said.

'About what?'

'He said Hofferman would get somebody to do his bidding.'

She gave him a long look. 'So you and Rufus Canfield have been discussing my well-being down at Archer's?'

'What makes you think it was at Archer's?'

'The fact that I'm not an idiot?'

'Well, he was right.'

'That reminds me,' Frances said, and she walked over to her jacket by the door. 'I want to know who our boy Arnie was calling. I got the number from his phone.'

'You're a pretty devious woman,' Carl said.

'Fire with fire.' Frances got the number and brought it along with her laptop to the counter. She went online.

'All right,' she said as she began to type. 'Reverse telephone directory. So you're betting he was trying to call Hank Hofferman?'

'I didn't know we were wagering,' Carl said. 'He could have been calling his mother.'

Frances looked at the screen. 'You're right. He could have been calling his mother.' She closed the laptop. 'If his mother's name was Bud Stephens.'

EIGHTEEN

The Mayor crosshatched some kindling in the clay fire pit and lit the paper underneath. There was a bottle of forty-year-old Dalmore on the patio table off to the side, along with a couple of cut crystal glasses.

'Go ahead and pour,' The Mayor said as he watched the kindling ignite.

Bud got up from his chair and walked over to the whisky. 'Well, well. Where did you get this?'

The Mayor shrugged. 'Somebody gave me a case of it.' He fanned the flames. 'I couldn't tell you who.'

Bud poured a couple of ounces in each of the glasses and pulled a chair close to the fire pit. It had been a fine fall day, sunny and clear, but now the temperature was dropping. The Mayor added a birch log to his fire, then picked up the Scotch and sat down. Bud breathed out into the night air to show his breath.

'Look at that,' he said. 'Louise got her tomatoes covered?'

'I don't know,' The Mayor said irritably. 'I have no idea what she covers or doesn't.' He stared at the fire while he took a drink.

Bud glanced toward the house; through the windows he could see Louise and Deanna in the living room, where Deanna was displaying her photos from Portugal. When Deanna had pulled the tablet with the pictures from her purse, The Mayor had immediately suggested that he and Bud have a drink out on the patio. Louise had given him a look, but remained silent, as usual.

'So what happened down there today?' he asked.

'Same old song,' Bud said. 'Half the day was spent on the landfill issue. You know our current mayor – he wouldn't step into a wading pool without hiring five engineers to tell him how deep it was first.'

The Mayor rubbed the rim of his glass across his chin. 'And how will it go?'

'Cost-wise, Talbotville is the right choice. It's only thirty miles away. But there are environmental concerns. And you know how that plays these days. Sudbury's a better spot in that respect. It's all rock up there.'

'You going to sit there and drink my Scotch and tell me what I already know over and over?'

Bud was stung. He looked at the fire and had a drink. Swallowing, he spoke very slowly, and he didn't look at The Mayor until he finished. 'Hofferman has got money, and he has the land. And he's connected. All the pork he produces goes to Beaver Lodge Farms, the Montpelier family. They've helped him circumnavigate environmental issues in the past. If they don't get bogged down by that grassroots bunch out in Talbotville, it's a go. That's what I think, Joe.'

'OK,' The Mayor said. 'We have a year until the election. If Hofferman can pull this together, then we can make it a tax issue. Send the trash north and everybody in the city is going to see a tax increase. Send it to Talbotville and it's the status quo.'

'So all you need to do is back Hofferman,' Bud said.

'I have no intention of backing that shit-kicker until I know he can make this happen. Do you hear me, Bud?'

'Yes.'

The Mayor got up and added a couple more sticks of birch to the fire before walking to the table to pour more Scotch for himself. He didn't offer the bottle to Bud. As he drank he moved to the fence at the rear of the property and looked off into the night.

Bud watched the older man's back a moment and then thought, fuck it. If he was going to be abused, he might as well drink the good liquor while it was available. He stood and went for the bottle. After pouring he glanced over to where The Mayor was still standing by the fence, a quizzical look on his face. After a moment, he turned toward Bud.

'Do you smell cigarette smoke?' he asked.

Bud indicated the clay pit. 'You've got a fire going, Joe.'

'I said cigarette smoke.' The Mayor turned toward the fence again. 'Don't you know the difference?'

Kate stubbed the cigarette out in the dirt beneath where she sat and then hobbled away from the fence where The Mayor was standing, scant yards away. There was a ravine behind the house and she scrambled down its length, using her crutch as a pivot. A hundred yards along she tripped over a root and tumbled head first to the ground, her arms flung forward to protect herself. She skidded across the grass and bent her wrist back as she stopped. Jumping up, she ducked behind a cluster of scrub pine trees. She looked back. A yard light had been turned on and she saw The Mayor and the man named Bud standing outside the fence now. The sound of them talking carried clearly down the ravine.

'You're imagining things,' the man said.

'No,' The Mayor said flatly. 'Somebody was here.'

Kate's car was parked on the shoulder of McClung Road, a quarter mile away. She limped to it, got in and drove off. She took her cigarettes from her pocket and lit one and as she did she remembered that she'd left a butt in the dirt outside the fence. Actually, she'd left a half dozen butts there. He'd find them, if not tonight, then in the morning. Kate wondered if fingerprints could be lifted from a cigarette butt.

David was waiting for her in the living room. It was his hockey night and she'd been thinking he wouldn't be there. She went into the kitchen to pour herself a drink and he followed. She offered the vodka bottle toward him and he shook his head.

'Look at you,' he said.

She glanced down at her dirty jeans, the grass stains on her hoodie. Her wrist hurt where she had jammed it into the ground. She went into the fridge for orange juice.

'I don't know what's going on with you,' he said.

After pouring the juice she took her cigarettes from her shirt and lit one, blowing smoke into the air above her head as she looked at him.

'And smoking again,' he said.

She took another drag.

'I'm afraid to ask what you've been doing,' he said.

'Then don't.'

'Is that how you want to play it?' he asked.

'I'm not playing anything, David.' She looked away from him as she took a drink.

'OK,' he said in resignation. He turned and walked out of the room. Seconds later, he was back. 'Fuck it,' he said. 'I have to say it. I know you're seeing somebody else.'

'What?'

'Please don't lie to me, Kate,' he said. 'Don't make it worse. I know you've been seeing that fucking guy from the *Times*. Dunmore.'

'Jesus,' she said. 'I haven't been seeing him.'

'Don't lie,' David said. 'I saw you with him the other day.'

'What are you talking about?'

'The day I cut my hand. I was at the medical center downtown. I saw you with him in a coffee shop on Main Street. I knew he was calling here but you always said he was doing a story. Well, the story never ran and I finally figured things out. You're never home, Kate. And tonight, shit, I don't want to know what went on tonight. You're a goddamn mess.'

'I'm not seeing Peter Dunmore,' she said. 'Not like that anyway.'

'Not like what? You're either seeing him or you're not.'

Kate took a drink, her eyes down. 'I'm not proud of it but I've been using him,' she said. 'He's been giving me information on The Mayor.'

'I'm going to believe that?'

'Whether or not you believe it doesn't matter,' she told him. 'It's the truth. So you might as well know the rest. I've been following him.'

'Who?'

'Who do you think?'

It took him a moment. 'Sanderson?' He stared at her. 'No.'

'Yeah.'

David sat down. He put his hands flat on the table and stared at them as if they might tell him something. He looked up. 'Are you out of your fucking mind?'

'Possible.'

He indicated her clothes. 'Where were you tonight?'

'I was outside his house and I almost got caught.'

'Jesus Christ,' he said. He looked at Kate as if he didn't know who she was. 'Do you have any idea what you're doing? This is stalking. You're going to get yourself arrested.'

'I know,' she said. She took a drink. 'I need to be more careful.'

'You need to be more careful?' he repeated. 'That's your reaction?'

'Yeah. Because I need to be more careful.' She tried to smile at him. 'The good news is – I'm not screwing around on you.'

'The bad news is – you've lost your fucking marbles,' he said. 'You need to stop this.'

Kate shook her head. 'I don't think so. Not right now.'

'Why not?'

'Because,' she said, taking another drink, 'somebody has to keep an eye on him.'

'And why is that?'

'You know why.'

'I do?'

'You're the one who told me,' Kate said. 'Once a cat-killer, always a cat-killer.'

Bud Stephens had a precinct office on Balmoral Street, a five-minute walk from his condo. Council didn't sit Monday mornings so Bud was in the office from ten o'clock on. Miriam was taking calls. When he arrived Bud read some e-mails and listened to a couple dozen phone messages before sitting back with the morning paper. Monday was a slow news day, from a local standpoint at least, and since Bud was little interested in anything other than his own bailiwick, he skimmed through the paper quickly. Tossing it aside, he felt a presence and looked up to see a stranger standing in the doorway. Miriam was behind the man, her eyebrows raised to say that it wasn't her fault, he'd barged past her.

'This gentleman wants to see you,' she said.

The guy was a roughneck, tall and lean, maybe fifty or so, wearing jeans and a navy t-shirt. Scuffed work boots and three days' growth, his whiskers going gray, his face tanned like he'd been working outside. He could have been one of the guys who unloaded cargo on the docks, back when there was still cargo to unload. He was looking for either a job or a handout. Bud had already decided he wouldn't get either, not here. He got to his feet. 'Does the gentleman have a name?'

'Carl Burns,' the man said.

The name struck a chord with Bud but he couldn't say why. He met a lot of people during the course of a day. He would have offered his hand but he sensed that it wouldn't be welcome. He asked the man to sit down. Miriam went back out to her desk where she opened her laptop and began to type.

'What can I do for you?' Bud asked. 'I assume you're a constituent?'

Carl Burns took the chair across the desk from Bud. 'No,' he said.

'You're not a constituent?'

'I'm a friend of Frances Rourke.'

'Frances Rourke,' Bud repeated. 'Why do I know that name?'

'She has a farm outside of Talbotville,' Carl said. 'She's fighting the landfill that you and Hank Hofferman are pushing. On Saturday you had some jokers from Toronto try to run her out of the farmers' market here in the city.'

And just like that Bud knew who Carl Burns was. He'd heard all about the dust-up at the market, but until this minute no one had been able to identify the man who had done most of the dusting. Bud got up and walked to the bar fridge in the corner to retrieve a root beer. Carl watched him quietly, waiting.

Bud popped the tab on the can and came back to sit down again. 'That's quite a story,' he said. 'And those are some pretty serious charges. Let's be clear on this – you're suggesting I had something to do with it?'

'I know you were behind it. One of the jokers called your number in the middle of it.'

Bud hesitated before taking a drink of the soda. His cell phone had been off at the time. After all, it had been early morning. There'd been no message though, and Arnie hadn't mentioned it when he'd called later that day to fill Bud in. Of course, there'd been no reason to mention a missed phone call.

'You're mistaken about that,' Bud said.

'He called your number.'

'Put it this way, I didn't receive any call,' Bud said. 'I'm a city councilor, Mr Burns. I suppose if there's a problem at the farmers' market, then someone might start calling city councilors. Are you in town today to visit all of them?'

'Just you,' Carl said.

'Just me,' Bud said. He set the soda can aside and laced his fingers together across his chest. 'Now why I would be involved in a disturbance at the farmers' market? It's not even in my ward. You care to explain that to me?'

'You want me to explain something you already know?' Carl asked.

'If you don't mind.'

Carl shrugged. 'Hofferman threatened Frances, and she told him to pound salt. You and Hofferman are Frick and Frack on the landfill so Hofferman went whining to you and you set up the deal with the jokers from Parnelli Farms to try to intimidate Frances. I don't know what you paid the jokers, but if I were you, I'd be asking for a refund.'

'You have a wild imagination, my friend,' Bud said. 'My only interest in the landfill is that this city finds a suitable place for its trash. I couldn't care less about Hank Hofferman, or Frances Rourke either, for that matter. I'm an elected official of this city. I don't threaten people, and I don't arrange to have people threatened. Understand?'

'I understand that you're a liar,' Carl said. 'I expected that you would be and I don't care that you are. As long as you understand that you're not going to bother Frances Rourke again.' He stood up and leaned over the desk. 'You do understand?'

'Oh my,' Bud said. 'Are you a tough guy?'

'No,' Carl told him. 'But I doubt I'd have to be.'

And he left.

As soon as he was gone Miriam was standing in the doorway. 'You know who that was, don't you?' she asked.

'Should I?' Bud asked.

'I did a search. He's the guy who burned down that pig barn out in Talbotville. The firefighter was killed. Twelve years ago.'

'Shit, the arsonist named Burns. I knew it rang a bell. Didn't he go to jail?'

'For two years,' Miriam said.

'Looks to me like he's a slow learner,' Bud said. He sat thinking a moment. 'But the fact is he killed that fireman. He can't be real popular around Talbotville even now.'

'Probably not,' Miriam said. 'Why?'

Bud shrugged. 'Just something to keep in mind. You know, if he's determined to make a pest of himself.'

*   *   *

It was raining when Carl left the city and traffic was slow. By the time he got back to Talbotville it was noon. He grabbed a sandwich at the sub shop and ate it in the pickup as he drove out to River Valley Farm. He had finished the exterior of the warehouse addition and moved inside now, where the weather wouldn't bother him.

He parked in the warehouse lot and walked in the drizzling rain to the addition. The farm was a muddy mess, water running in rivulets through the muck toward the ditch to the river. Most of the fields were bare now, although some squash and cabbages remained. Frances had mentioned that she wanted everything picked by week's end. The rain had put a stop to any harvesting today and there was nobody in sight.

Inside, he began to run wire for the overhead florescent lights, working off a twelve-foot stepladder. He could hear activity in the front part of the warehouse, where the online orders were being processed. Telephones ringing and printers operating. Lost in the work, he didn't hear Frances enter.

'Little late this morning,' she said.

'It's afternoon,' he told her.

'Even later then.'

She was standing at the foot of the ladder, wearing jeans and a sweater with a vest over-top. Her hair was tied back and she had a slightly pissed-off look about her. And the comment itself was out of the blue. Carl worked his own hours and she had never questioned him on it.

'Mondays,' he said. 'Moving kind of slow.'

Frances made a point of looking at her watch. 'I was thinking you were moving pretty fast. You've been to the city already, had a little talk with Bud Stephens, drove back here and now you're stringing wire and acting dumb.'

Carl stripped the ends of the cable. 'Can't anybody keep a secret anymore?'

'Apparently not,' Frances said. 'He called me two minutes after you left. You want to tell me about it?'

'Didn't he?'

'I'd like to hear your version, Galahad.'

'I told him I knew it was him behind that shit at the market.'

'Thought you were going to keep out of it.'

'I said I would stay out of the landfill situation. I didn't say I was going to let Bud Stephens push you around.'

'Bud Stephens is not going to push me around,' Frances said. 'You do realize that this whole notion of you protecting me is rather sexist, don't you? I hired you to build this addition. That's it.'

Carl connected the wires before turning to look at her. 'OK, how about this? If these guys try to run you out of the market it could affect your business, and if your business suffers, I could be out of a job. So really, I did it for selfish reasons.'

'That the best you got?'

'I thought it was pretty clever,' Carl said. 'You know, for spur of the moment.'

'I'll let you know when you're being clever,' she told him. 'And this morning didn't qualify. I'm not the schoolmarm and you're not John Wayne.'

'I don't want to be John Wayne. Can't do the walk.'

She wasn't smiling.

'All right,' Carl said. 'So what did Bud say?'

'Same thing he said to you, I'm guessing. He lied about the whole thing, said he had nothing to do with it. Said it's not his style. Why do guys like that always think they have style?'

'That was it?' Carl asked.

She shrugged. 'Pretty much.'

He caught her hesitation. 'What else?'

She took a moment. 'Nothing you want to hear.'

'Let me decide.'

She sighed. 'He brought up Red Walton and then he suggested that you were a disreputable character. Told me I shouldn't be associating with you.'

'He's probably right.'

'Oh, he probably is,' Frances said. 'But I'll be goddamned if I'll let Bud Stephens make that call. I'll let you get back to work, Carl.'

'Yes, ma'am.'

'And don't ever call me ma'am again,' she said, and left.

NINETEEN

The seniors' golf league finished in early October and The Mayor's schedule changed accordingly. His new routine included euchre twice a week at the Masonic Lodge and a walk in Fisher Park most afternoons. Fisher Park was across the ravine from The Mayor's house. It bordered a blue-collar neighborhood, loosely referred to as 'the west end', that stretched all the way to the lake. The ravine was a buffer zone that separated the older estate homes on the ridge from the graffiti-marked walk-ups and clapboard bungalows below. The park had a checkered past, a home to drug dealers and keg parties and gang fights. That element had largely moved on but some of the older residents still referred to the park as 'the combat zone'.

As a crow would fly it was only a quarter mile from The Mayor's back yard to the center of the park, but that quarter mile was the ravine itself, consisting of brush and rock and scrub, as well as the meandering, shallow stream that was Fisher Creek. The Mayor took the long way around, driving to the park every day in the Lincoln Town Car, usually arriving around two o'clock.

Kate knew this because most days she was at Fisher Park, waiting for him. She'd discovered a spot near the old stone pavilion where she could sit with her coffee and her newspaper and watch the two parking lots below, one on Millburn Street, the other off Nash Road. The pavilion was on a rise behind some dying white pines, and she could be relatively inconspicuous there.

Once she determined his schedule – and he was if nothing else a creature of habit – she made certain to arrive in advance. With her knee still on the mend, it took a while to climb the hill to the pavilion. She would sit on one of the picnic tables scattered on a gravel patio along the south wall of the building and elevate her leg while she waited for him.

She had been taking Percocet now as well as the prescription painkillers and it felt good to sit in the sun. She'd scored the Percs from a woman with pink hair who played slow pitch in the same league as Kate, after the woman had told her about her own problems post knee surgery. Kate suspected the woman was strictly dealing and the knee story was a cover but that was OK with her. She needed the extra meds.

Some days The Mayor wouldn't show and she would pass the afternoon there anyway, watching the goings-on of the park. The drugs took the edge off her anxiety and convinced her that there was purpose in her actions. Everyone required a sense of purpose.

The park had seen better days. The concrete of the basketball courts was cracked and potholed and the ball diamonds were weed-infested, the screens rusting. There were still pickup games in progress some days but in general the place was a hangout for kids smoking pot or playing music while they danced or rode their skateboards on the courts. Seniors from the area walked their dogs on the grass, and once in a while an optimistic angler would make his way down into the ravine, pole in hand, heading for Fisher Creek.

She had been puzzled when The Mayor had first begun his visits there. There was a much nicer park within walking distance of his house, a well-kept expanse of red oaks and hard maples and stone fountains, along with a band shell where a jazz quartet played on Friday evenings in the summer. Decades earlier the property was bequeathed to the city by a woman on the condition that the park be named after her late son, a bankrupt lawyer as well as a drunkard and a wife-beater, character traits that were not mentioned on the plaque bearing his name.

It didn't take long for Kate to realize the attraction of Fisher Park for The Mayor. Most days there was a handful of teenage girls who after school played pickup basketball on the court near the wading pool. They were girls from the neighborhood, wearing sweats or jeans or cargos, bandanas and ball caps turned backwards, tough chicks but probably not nearly as tough as their poses. They trash-talked and strutted on the court, multi-pierced and tattooed and profane.

It was obvious that The Mayor's routine put him at that particular court at a specific time. He parked in the small gravel lot off Millburn Street at shortly after two, got out and retrieved a tartan carry bag from his trunk. He would stroll the full length

of the park, stopping often to chat with someone or to sit on a
bench in the sun. The tartan bag contained, among other items,
breadcrumbs and peanuts which he would sometimes feed to the
birds and the squirrels.

He rarely climbed the steep hill to the pavilion where Kate
sat and watched from the pines, her face hidden by a hoodie or
baseball cap and shades. When he did, she would see him well
in advance and move away, down the other side of the slope and
into the ravine.

His meander up and down the park would usually take the
better part of an hour but he would always arrive at the benches
by the basketball court by three o'clock. There he would sit and
take a thermos from the bag and pour himself a cup of something.
Coffee or tea, Kate guessed, but she couldn't be sure. It could've
been Scotch or gin.

He would take a book or magazine from the bag and sit there
reading while he sipped from the cup. By arriving no later than
three he was always there when the girls showed a half hour or
so later. So he was not an old man showing up to ogle young
girls. He was there first.

It hadn't been long before he'd started up conversations with
a few of them. Kate had no idea what the subject matter might
be. But soon he was laughing with them, and offering snacks
and power bars from the bag. There was one girl in particular
whom he talked to more than the others, primarily because she
was a lousy player and preferred to sit out. It seemed she was
there as part of the group of friends. She was tall and slim, with
straight blond hair that reached halfway down her back. She was
reticent in her body language; there was a shyness about her that
resonated even from a hundred yards away. From time to time
she would sit beside The Mayor on the bench, and once he
showed her something in the book he was reading.

One day The Mayor arrived carrying a large shopping bag
and when the girls gathered for their game, he presented them
with a new ball. The girls made a huge fuss over him, hugging
him and urging him on to the court to shoot a few baskets. He
laughed and waved them away.

He left early that day, having made his impression, Kate
thought. Her car was parked on Nash Road, on the far side of

the park. When she saw that he was leaving, she made her way quickly to it and followed him as he pulled out of the lot on Millburn Street. He did not head home, though, but turned right and drove toward the lake. She kept him in sight until he reached Lakeshore Drive and turned off on a side street. She stopped by the entrance to the street and watched as he parked and got out and went into a building. She drove down the street. The building had a sign out front and she stopped to read it.

When she got home, David was standing in front of the garage, fixing a broken handle on a rake. There were leaves piled here and there in the yard. Kate parked and started for the house.

'Hey,' he said.

'Hi.'

She sensed that he wanted to talk but she went inside. She expected him to follow but he didn't. She drank a vodka and tonic and smoked a cigarette, limping on one crutch from the kitchen to the living room. He was still in the yard, bagging leaves and placing the bags by the curb for pickup. She got her notebook from her room and wrote down the day's events.

When he finally came in, Kate was on her second vodka. Writing about her day calmed her, gave her a sense of accomplishment, even though in her heart she knew that the notion was false. Still, there had been a new development today and she wanted to get it on paper, even though she couldn't decide its significance. She was finally beginning to feel tired. She wasn't sleeping very much at night, although the painkillers helped. Her eyes were closing when she heard the door and she looked up to see him standing there.

'Are you OK?' he asked.

'Sure.'

'You don't look OK.'

'Gee, thanks.'

'Where you been?'

Kate took a drink. 'Fisher Park. That's where I've been.'

'What did you accomplish at Fisher Park?'

'Nothing.'

'Maybe there's nothing to accomplish there,' he said.

She rubbed her eyes with her fingertips. 'He bought a puppy today.'

'What?'

Kate reached for the drink. 'When he left the park, he drove over to a kennel by the lake and bought a puppy. A Golden Retriever.' She glanced up. 'Why would he buy a puppy?'

'Who the fuck cares?'

'I have a theory on why he bought a puppy,' she said.

David put his hands in the air, like a man being held at gunpoint. 'I don't want to hear it.'

'That's OK. You don't need to.'

'I don't know what's going to happen to you,' he told her.

'It already happened,' she said.

The blond girl's name was Lindsay. A few days after picking the pup up at the kennel, The Mayor began to take the dog to Fisher Park with him. The tartan bag now contained, among the usual items, dog biscuits and bottled water as well as a miniature drinking bowl. The Mayor's routine remained the same. But now, when he arrived at the basketball court, he was no longer by himself.

Teenage girls love puppies and the tough chicks from the west end, with their tats and their nose rings and their trash talk, were no exception to that truth. From the first day The Mayor had shown up with the dog, the animal had been greeted with squeals of delight and smothered with affection. Soon the girls were bringing presents – dog treats, rawhide bones, slices of cheese. One removed her own bandana and put it around the puppy's neck.

The Mayor couldn't have integrated the group any better if he had passed out hundred dollar bills. Later that same week Kate saw him give the blond girl a book from the carry bag. Kate had come closer that day, limping cautiously along the ravine's edge, wearing shades and a toque. She was near enough to see the look on the blond girl's face when The Mayor gave her the hardcover. After a moment The Mayor took the book from her and found a particular passage to show her. The blond girl read it with the little puppy sitting on her lap. Kate dropped down into the ravine and leaned her head against the mossy bark of a maple tree. She felt as if she was going to throw up. The blond girl was Kate, seventeen years earlier. Kate was out of earshot but it didn't matter. She could hear the old man's line of bullshit, the flattering remarks, the grandfatherly advice. And the blond girl soaking it in, as Kate had, unknowing, naive. Like Kate, looking for approval. Liking the attention. It was human nature for a kid that age, especially a kid who had grown up with large emotional gaps in her life. And the old man knew it. He more than knew it: he had made it his life's work.

Later that day she learned the girl's name. When The Mayor clipped the leash on the pup and left, Kate didn't follow. She moved to the rise and watched the Lincoln pull out of the parking lot and head for the concrete bridge that spanned the ravine. He was going home.

The basketball game was still in progress. Kate got her crutches beneath her and moved toward the court.

The book was *To Kill a Mockingbird*. The blond girl was reading the first chapter when Kate hobbled over to plop down on a bench a few feet away. She felt her knee, as if evaluating something there, before glancing over.

'Hey,' she said.

'Hi,' the blond girl replied.

The girls on the court were watching Kate as they played. 'Great book,' she said.

'I'm just starting it,' the girl said.

'It was a movie too, you know.'

'Yeah.'

'So what's your name?'

The blond girl looked at Kate a second time before replying. 'Lindsay.'

Kate rubbed her knee again. 'Oh man, it's been tough rehabbing this thing.' She indicated the players. 'Blew it out playing this dumb game. You play?'

'Nah, I'm kind of a spaz.'

'You live around here?' Kate asked.

'Over on Ross.'

'With your folks?'

'Just my mom.'

Good Christ, Kate thought. It never changes. It was like watching the same movie over and over again. But why would it change? What had ever occurred that would require him to alter his methods? Or better yet – to cease and desist?

'That guy that was here – he give you the book?'

Lindsay put the book down in her lap. 'Yeah.'

She was looking at Kate closely now. Kate was suddenly aware of her clothes, her dirty jeans and hoodie.

'So what's his name?'

'We just call him Uncle Joe.'

Uncle fucking Joe, Kate thought. She glanced at the girls running up and down the cracked concrete. They were the tough ones, at least in this little circle. He hadn't chosen one of them. He'd picked this girl. She was the one Uncle Joe had decided was worthy of special treatment.

'You know what the book's about?' Kate asked. 'It's about an ignorant white asshole who assaults his own daughter.'

Lindsay wouldn't look at her now.

'What do you know about Uncle Joe?' Kate asked.

Glancing over at the other girls, Lindsay asked loudly, 'Who are you anyway?'

'I know about Uncle Joe,' Kate said. 'He's not safe to be around.'

'Yo, Lindsay!' one of the girls shouted. 'What's going on?'

'Who are you?' Lindsay almost shouted it this time.

A couple of the girls came off the court. Kate got to her feet, picking up her crutches. She was suddenly pissed off, angry that they would suspect *her* of something.

'Uncle Joe isn't what you think,' she told them. 'He isn't your uncle. He isn't your fucking grandfather. Wake up.'

'What she on about, Lins?'

'I don't know,' Lindsay said. 'I think she's high.'

'Get the fuck outa here.' The girls were laughing now. 'Get your Tiny Tim ass out of here with them crutches.'

Kate had no choice but to back off. She looked one last time at Lindsay before she moved away. As she made her way to the parking lot she could hear the girls, still mocking. When she got to her car, she turned back toward the court. The game was on again. Lindsay was on the bench, reading her new book.

When Carl pulled up to the warehouse with the plywood in his truck, he saw the dark blue Land Rover parked on the slope leading to the farmhouse. It was late afternoon, the day cooling off quickly as the sun descended behind the spindly pines at the rear of the barn. Getting out, he noticed Frances over by the chicken house. She was wearing red coveralls and black rubber boots and she was talking to the guy with the beard, the guy who drove the Land Rover. She gave Carl a little wave and as he nodded in her direction the guy with the beard raised a camera and took her picture. It seemed that Frances glanced sheepishly toward Carl, as if she was self-conscious about the whole thing.

Carl unloaded the plywood and stacked it along the wall. He put on his tool belt and walked over to the warehouse to get his saw and square. The building was locked. The office staff had gone home for the day, apparently forgetting that Carl was still working in the back. Frances would have keys. Carl really didn't want to go over and interrupt whatever was going on, but he had no choice.

The bearded man was still taking pictures as Carl approached. There was a portable propane burner near the door of the chicken house, with a large stainless-steel container of water resting over the flame, steam rising from within. As Carl neared, Frances put her hand up in front of her face.

'Enough,' she told the bearded man. She turned. 'Hi, Carl.'

Carl nodded and jerked his thumb over his shoulder. 'I'm locked out.'

'Right,' she realized. 'Carl, this is Martin Benoit. Carl Burns.'

Carl made to extend his hand but the man was fiddling with something on his camera and didn't so much as look his way. 'Good to know you, Carl,' he said offhandedly.

Carl said hello and turned to Frances again. She seemed even more embarrassed. 'The keys,' she said. She reached into her pocket, then apparently remembered she was wearing the coveralls. 'I'll have to go to the house.'

Martin looked at her. 'Get the man his keys, change your clothes and come with me. Forget about bloody work for once in your life, Frances. It's going to be a fantastic show.'

'I told you, I promised Henry he'd have the chickens for tonight's menu,' Frances said. 'He's a good customer.'

'Where's Perry? Can't he kill a chicken?'

'Perry went home sick,' Frances said. 'He does that a lot when we harvest the birds. He doesn't like the blood.'

Carl was growing both uncomfortable and impatient, waiting for the keys.

'Tell you what, Martin,' Frances suggested. '*You* help me with the birds and then we'll go to the theater.'

Martin looked down at his crisp cotton pants, his pale blue shirt. 'Not a chance. Besides, I don't kill things.'

'You've become a vegetarian?' Frances asked.

'I have not,' he said defensively.

'You'll eat animals so long as someone else is doing the killing?'

'This is going to turn into *that* conversation?' Martin asked.

Carl had heard enough. 'I'll be at the warehouse, Frances,' he said.

'See there,' Martin said, smiling. 'Now you've upset the carpenter.' He had yet to look at Carl.

'His name is Carl,' Frances said sharply. 'Go to your revue, Martin. I have work to do.'

Martin raised the camera. 'I love your color when you get angry. Hold that, will you?'

'Enough with the fucking pictures,' she snapped.

He took the shot anyway, still grinning inanely, and then backed away. 'I'll let you get to your important work.' he said. 'You're making a huge mistake, missing this show. You can catch up later, though. Call me on my cell.'

He turned and headed for the Land Rover, looking at the tiny screen on the camera as he walked. Carl watched him. He seemed like a ridiculous man. He turned to Frances.

'Yeah, yeah, the keys,' she said.

Carl smiled. 'Don't jump down my throat,' he said. 'I didn't take your picture.'

She hesitated before releasing an exasperated laugh. 'Sorry about that. Henry Bolton from Le Bistro called an hour ago and asked if he could get a dozen chickens for tonight's menu. Some last minute thing, he needs them by seven o'clock. Perry took a hike and then Martin showed up.' She paused to look at Carl a moment. 'Martin, the guy you've been wondering about.'

'Not really,' Carl said. 'I had a nice time talking to him, though.'

She smiled. 'I'll get the keys. I don't know why you don't have a set anyway.'

She walked up to the house and retrieved the key ring from where it hung inside the kitchen door. When she got back, Carl was walking toward the chicken house from the direction of his truck. He had removed his tool belt and pulled on a pair of overalls. It took her a moment to understand.

'You're not going to run home at the first sight of blood, like Perry?'

'I don't believe so,' he said.

'You ever kill chickens?'

'Ducks and geese,' he replied. 'I used to hunt a bit with my old man.'

Frances shrugged. 'Close enough.'

She did the killing and Carl dunked the birds in the hot water and plucked the feathers. They both gutted. They were finished in less than two hours. Frances brought a tote half filled with ice down from the house and they piled the carcasses inside, with Carl doing a count.

'Baker's dozen,' he said when he was done.

Frances nodded.

'Didn't you say twelve?' he reminded her.

'The extra one is dinner for the workers,' she said.

'The workers at the restaurant?'

'The workers right here,' she said.

TWENTY

I t had been Miriam's idea to arrange a field trip to the proposed site for the landfill, but Bud took credit when the plan was well-received. Miriam sent the invitations out and arranged the transportation. At eleven o'clock Friday morning a Greyhound bus left the city hall parking lot, headed for Talbotville and the rolling farmland beyond. On board were all of the city's councilors, planners from different departments, a couple of waste disposal engineers and a sizable contingent of media. Of those asked along on the trip, Mayor McBride was the only name of consequence who'd turned down the invitation. The mayor insisted he was fighting a flu bug and did not want to expose the others to the virus.

'He's got a bug all right,' Bud told Miriam that morning. 'It's up his ass.'

Miriam didn't make the trip as she had the office to run. But she had provided all on board with a box lunch from Merkel's Deli, along with coffee and soft drinks. Upon entering the bus everyone was given a binder titled The Talbotville Landfill Continuum, part technical primer on the landfill and part public relations flyer on the project. The cover of the binder featured a TLC logo in bold font splashed against a background of pastoral countryside.

There was something about a bus ride that brought out the adolescent in people, and this excursion was no exception. The councilors, a staid bunch at city hall, were loose and talkative with the media types, who were typically excited about the free food and drinks.

Bud hadn't anticipated the jocular mood but he hoped it would extend to the project itself. There were eleven other councilors on board. If Bud could bring a quorum on side today, it would be time for The Mayor to announce his support of the proposal. And Mayor McBride could take his opposition and put it in his soon-to-be-required résumé.

The air of camaraderie on the bus was unexpected. Bud had never felt accepted by his peers on council, or by anybody at city hall for that matter. He had always suspected that the general consensus out there was that he'd gotten elected six years earlier because The Mayor was his uncle and had campaigned for him. In truth, The Mayor was his uncle by marriage only; Bud's mother had been Louise Sanderson's older sister. And if Bud thought that his colleagues in council had their doubts about him, he was quite certain that The Mayor did as well, a fact that the old man did little to conceal after Bud was elected. Once, after being taken down verbally yet again by The Mayor, Bud had confronted him, asking why the old man had backed him for office in the first place if he was of the opinion that Bud was such a light-weight. The old man had replied by saying that he did it just to shut his wife up.

Before running for public office Bud had been, in quick succession, a university drop-out, half-assed developer, unsuccessful car salesman and consultant. The consultant title was basically nothing more than a decoy. When he ran for council he needed to tell the voters that he was currently *something*, and the term sounded genuine while remaining vague enough to pass muster, so long as that muster wasn't too closely examined. During the campaign his opponent, a retired shop teacher, never once thought to ask Bud just exactly what it was that he consulted upon.

With The Mayor on the sidelines, at least until the next election, Bud had been considering of late that the landfill just might be the issue which would finally give him some credibility at city hall. As for the old man, Bud really didn't care in the end if the old fucker liked him or not. But maybe, just maybe, he would have no choice but to grant Bud a little respect.

Hank Hofferman was waiting when the bus pulled up at the site, standing alongside the head of the engineering firm that had designed the footprint for the landfill. Both wore hard hats – for aesthetic reasons apparently, as there was nothing overhead but blue sky. A billboard version of the TLC logo had been erected on the property.

Although the day had arrived under full sun, it had rained for most of the week. The fields designated for the landfill had been tilled after the recent harvest and the area was now a quagmire.

Hofferman had that morning acquired fifty bales of wheat straw
from a local farmer which he and the engineer had spread over
an area large enough for the contingent from the bus to gather
and wander on.

Aside from the muck, the rain was actually a blessing in
disguise. Hofferman, seizing the opportunity, had a backhoe on
the site on Wednesday, digging a small lagoon within fifty feet
of the creek that ran through the property. The clay lagoon had
filled with rain water and was now holding that water. After the
introductions, the engineer led the group along a straw-strewn
path to the lagoon, where he proceeded to scoop a plastic pail
full to the brim from the pond. He placed the pail on the ground
in front of him.

'The clay is impervious,' he said. 'This test lagoon demon-
strates that. It's not going to leak, any more than this bucket is
going to leak. Any notions of problems with containment are
groundless, and are put forth by people who are ignorant of the
properties of the soil.'

As fate would have it, some of those ignorant people began
to show up. Tipped off by the farmer who had sold the straw to
Hofferman for three times the market price, several members of
HALT arrived, parking their vehicles along the road behind the
Greyhound. Frances came with Rufus Canfield, who had driven
out to River Valley Farm with the news, finding Frances slogging
through the mud behind the barn, loading cabbages on to a wagon.

'So Bud and Hank have taken it on the road,' Frances said as
they walked toward the demonstration. 'Not exactly Bob and
Bing.'

Hofferman was explaining how the landfill would be divided
into quadrants, with each section responsible for different types
of waste. Some of the councilors took notes while the TV crews
shot footage of the property, panning their Betacams over the
barren acreage and back again.

'That'll make for some exciting television,' Rufus said. He
was taking notes as well.

Some of the reporters noticed the newcomers and began to
wander their way. Frances wore a HALT button on her jacket.
She was approached by a young woman from the *Rose City
Gazette*.

'What's HALT?' the woman asked.

'Halt All Landfills in Talbotville,' Frances told her. A few feet away, Bud Stephens was watching. He was standing beside Hank Hofferman, nodding his head in compliance with whatever Hofferman was saying. But he was watching Frances.

'So you're against this project?' the reporter asked.

'I'm wearing a button that says Halt All Landfills in Talbotville and you're asking me if I'm against this project?'

'OK,' the woman said, obviously miffed. 'Why are you against it?'

Frances gestured. 'This is good farmland, and it's less than three miles from the river. That creek runs into the river. You know what goes into a landfill?'

'Um . . . what?' the reporter asked.

'Everything,' Frances told her. 'They can bag and bury whatever they want here. Toxic materials, paints, lead. You could tear the asbestos siding off your house and put it in a bag and it would end up here. Who would know?'

'The on-site engineer says the clay will contain everything,' the woman said.

'The on-site engineer hired by Hank Hofferman?' Frances asked. 'Did Hank's mom give it a thumbs-up too?'

She saw Bud approaching on a bee line, ignoring the straw path. His black jeans were muddy to the knees.

'Hello, Frances,' he said, smiling.

'Doing bus tours now, Bud?' she asked.

'This woman was saying she doesn't have faith in the containment assurances,' the reporter said to Bud. She turned to Frances. 'Um, what was your name?'

'Frances Rourke. You're new at this, aren't you?'

Bud gestured to the test lagoon. 'The proof is in the pudding.'

'That's pudding?' Rufus asked, looking up from his notes.

Bud kept smiling. 'Come have a look.'

When he and the reporter started toward the lagoon, Frances and Rufus followed. They stood by the little pond, looking at the murky water inside.

'This lagoon is just a few feet from the creek and it's totally contained,' Bud said. 'For the landfill itself, there will be setbacks of three hundred yards from any waterway. If this trial lagoon is safe at a few feet, then imagine what a three hundred yard buffer would give you.'

'What's with the bucket?' Rufus asked. The plastic pail, filled with water, sat where the engineer had left it.

'They were using it as an example,' the reporter said. 'Of how the lagoon held the water.'

'So the lagoon won't leak, just like that bucket won't leak?' Rufus asked.

'That's right,' Bud told him.

Rufus looked around and spotted an empty water bottle in the straw, presumably tossed there by someone off the bus. 'It could rain for forty days and forty nights and that lagoon would never leak?' he asked, picking up the bottle.

'You got it,' Bud said. 'And that's from the best topographical engineer in the country.'

Rufus knelt to fill the bottle from the lagoon. 'But what if it rained for forty days and forty nights – and the lagoon over-flowed?' He poured the water into the pail and the pail did indeed overflow, the water running in a tiny stream toward the creek. 'What then?'

The reporter watched the trickling water and began writing quickly in her notebook. 'I didn't get your name,' she said to Rufus.

Frances smiled. 'Did you bring along an overflow engineer, Bud?'

Bud turned to the reporter and then, realizing he had nothing to offer her, glanced toward the main gathering across the field. 'They need me over there. All the information is in the package you were given. Containment is a dead issue.' He pointed his chin toward Rufus and Frances. 'There will always be people who are against progress. They laughed at Thomas Edison.'

'They laughed at the Wright brothers,' Rufus corrected him. 'I believe they marveled at Thomas Edison.'

Bud gave him another look before starting back across the field, toward the imaginary summoning he had mentioned. Frances and Rufus mingled with the crowd for another half hour, talking to whatever reporters approached them. Many did not, perhaps remembering that it was Bud Stephens who had bought them lunch and taken them for a bus ride on a sunny fall day.

* * *

Rufus dropped Frances off at the farm before heading back to Talbotville to write about the field trip that he, a member of the local press, had not been invited to join.

Walking to the house, Frances noticed a red Camaro parked beside Carl's truck at the warehouse. The car was vaguely familiar but she couldn't say why. She went into the house and poured herself a glass of cider. Standing by the kitchen window that overlooked the farm, she thought about Bud Stephens, buying off councilors and media alike with a box lunch and cup of coffee. It had been a cheap day. As much as Frances had enjoyed Rufus embarrassing Bud, in the end she was left with little hope. There was real money behind it all, she knew, and that was why HALT would eventually fail. Frances had no intention of telling the members that. There was something to be said for tilting at windmills and the hope that springs eternal.

As she finished the cider, she suddenly realized whose Camaro was parked down the hill. She grabbed her jacket and started out the door.

In the warehouse, David was seated on a sawhorse and Carl was standing a few feet away, staring out the window at the muddy fields. Neither was saying anything, although the air was thick with what had already been said.

'Hey,' she said.

David nodded to her, but Carl never turned. Frances began to panic.

'What the hell is going on?' she demanded.

'Kate's been following The Mayor,' David said.

For a second Frances was actually relieved. She'd been afraid it was something worse. 'Why?' she asked.

David told her all that he knew, and he admitted that there was probably plenty that he didn't. Frances kept her eyes on Carl as she listened but he wouldn't engage her. He had taken a tape measure from his tool belt and he kept pulling the rule out and letting it snap back, over and over.

'She's got too much time on her hands,' David said. 'That's the problem.'

Frances turned to him. 'I think the problem's a little bigger than that.' She heard the tape snap back into the casing. 'Where does she follow him to?'

'He goes to Fisher Park every day,' David said. 'And she does too.'

'What's the attraction there?'

'I don't know,' David replied. 'Have you talked to her?'

'I talk to her maybe once a week,' Frances said. 'I don't get much out of her.'

'Join the club,' David said. 'She's still taking painkillers. I think she's been working her doctor for extra pills. Drinking too much. And she doesn't eat.'

'She home now?' Frances asked.

'I never know the answer to that,' David said. He looked at his watch. 'Listen, I'm on afternoons. I gotta go. I just thought you guys should know.' Here he hesitated. 'I was hoping you might talk to her, Frances,' he said. 'She thinks you walk on water.'

Frances walked with him to his car and thanked him for coming. When she came back inside Carl was insulating the rear wall of the addition, fitting the fiberglass batts between the studding.

'Have you talked to her?' Frances asked.

He kept working. 'She's never there, or doesn't answer. I leave messages but I never hear back.'

'I'm going to go see her.'

'That's good.'

'Do you want to come with me?'

He shook his head. 'She doesn't think that I walk on water.'

Frances nodded. 'What the hell do I say to her? Stop stalking The Mayor and have a nice day?'

'Be a good place to start.'

'Would it?'

'You could ask her why.'

'She might not know why,' Frances said. 'If she does, she might not want to tell me.'

'You can bet it's nothing good.'

'I would bet that.'

Carl looked at the wall he'd been insulating. 'Tell her I'd like to see her.' He turned to Frances. 'I guess it's too late to be her father, but I would like to see her.'

'Nobody said it was too late.'

'They didn't have to,' Carl said.

*   *   *

There was nobody at the house when Frances arrived so she waited in the car in the driveway, listening to the news on the radio. On the drive there she had rehearsed what she was going to say. None of it sounded all that convincing. She was still rehearsing when Kate pulled up.

For an instant it looked as if she might drive off again but she got out of the car and with a crutch beneath her arm hobbled over to where Frances was parked. She looked thin and her color was not good, her hair lank. She wore cargo pants and a wind jacket over a t-shirt. She pushed her sunglasses up into her hair. Frances got out of the car.

'Hey, honey.'

'What're you doing here?' Kate said. She smiled but her tone was flat.

Frances opened the rear door and retrieved an eleven-quart basket of apples and pears and plums. 'Brought you some fruit.'

'Great.'

'Oh, and I'm here to yell at you,' Frances said.

'I like the part about the fruit,' Kate said. 'Can I have a drink while you're yelling?'

She walked past Frances and went into the house. Frances hesitated before following. She found Kate in the kitchen, taking vodka from the freezer and orange juice from the fridge below. She didn't turn when she heard Frances come in.

'You want to have a drink with me, Frances?'

'Sure.'

The kitchen table was covered with mail unopened and newspapers unread. Frances put the basket on top of them and sat down. There were pizza boxes stacked in the corner by the fridge. Kate went into the freezer for ice cubes but the trays were all empty. She put the screwdriver down in front of Frances.

'No ice,' she said.

Frances took a drink while Kate retreated across the room. Using the crutch as a prop, she pushed herself up to sit on the counter. She lifted her glass toward Frances before she drank. Frances had a sip.

'You got a mirror in this house?' she asked.

'Why would you ask that?'

'Just wondering if you have any idea of how remarkably shitty you look.'

Kate smiled. 'You drive in just to tell me that?'

'Didn't know it until just now.'

'They say that beauty is in the eye of the beholder,' Kate said. 'I didn't know you were so shallow, Frances.'

'I'm not,' Frances told her. 'I was making small talk and now I'm going to quit. So David told me about you and The Mayor.'

'David has too much time on his hands.'

'He said that about you.'

'Yeah? What else did he say?'

'You haven't done anything stupid, have you?' Frances asked. 'You've just been following him, right?'

Kate went into her pocket for her cigarettes. She lit up and exhaled before looking over at Frances. 'Some people might say that just following him is pretty stupid.'

'They'd be right,' Frances said. 'But you haven't broken any laws. Not yet.'

'I don't think so.' Kate took a drink. 'Is breaking the law a bad thing? Seems like he gets away with it all he wants.'

'You're not him.'

'That's the nicest thing you've said to me in a long time.' She took a pull from the cigarette and exhaled before looking over at Frances. 'Did you know that there were actually thirty-six women who accused The Mayor of sexual assault?'

'I didn't know that,' Frances said slowly. She took a moment. 'Why didn't it come out in court?'

'Good question.'

'How do you know that's true?'

'It's true,' Kate said. 'Grant even admitted it to me. The *Times* knew it too, not that they ever printed it. Apparently he's been like this his whole life and getting away with it. Feeling women up in elevators. Grabbing waitresses by the ass and then apologizing, like it was all a little joke or something.' She took a drink. 'And everybody has always looked the other way. Even his wife.'

'I've wondered about her,' Frances said. 'She must have known.'

'She lied on the stand, Frances,' Kate said. 'When she said she never knew Maria's mother, she lied. I talked to Maria after-

ward. She didn't make that up. She didn't make any of it up.
Why would The Mayor's wife lie under oath?'

Frances thought about it. 'She's probably been living with it
for so long she thinks she's telling the truth. Denial is a powerful
thing.'

'And all along I was hoping that the truth was a powerful
thing,' Kate said. 'Do you know what he does every day now,
Frances?'

'No, I don't.'

'He hangs around a playground. How's that for a fucking
cliché? Right out of the pervert's handbook. He hangs around a
playground, talking to a bunch of young girls.'

Frances sighed. 'Well, shit.'

'Yeah.'

'All right,' Frances said. 'I can see what you mean. We need
to report this.'

'Report what, and to who?' Kate demanded. 'They've been
turning a blind eye to him forever. You think it's going to change
because he's walking his dog in the park? That's another thing.
He bought a puppy. You want to get close to some teenaged girls,
show up with a puppy. These chicks are as hard as nails and
they're falling all over the thing.'

'I'll go to the police with you, Kate.'

'I've talked to the cops, and I've talked to the prosecutor. I
even showed them a picture of a vile eight-year-old who is The
Mayor's son, a little memento of yet another *incident*. And all I
hear is that they had one shot at him and they missed. End of
story.' She pulled on the cigarette, squinting through the smoke.

'Why won't the *Times* run what they have?'

'They're all afraid of him, Frances. Newspapers are afraid of
lawsuits. According to Peter Dunmore anyway.'

Frances sipped at the drink. With no ice, it was growing warm.
'Then what can you hope to accomplish?'

'Well . . . I'm a little confused about that,' Kate admitted. 'I
guess I'm just keeping an eye on him.'

'Why don't you come out to the farm for a week?' Frances
said. 'We can talk about it. Maybe make a plan. I'll put you to
work in the warehouse, and I'll feed you some real food.'

'What if I can find something on him?' Kate asked. 'What if

I can stop him from doing it again? Is that not something worth doing?'

'It's worth doing,' Frances said. 'But I'm not sure it's up to you.'

'Who's it up to, Frances? Tell me and I'll go talk to them.'

'I wish I knew.' Frances had another drink. 'What if we warned the girls at the park?'

Kate laughed. 'I tried. They mocked me, Frances. Can you believe that? I'm trying to tell them what a fucking monster this guy is and they make fun of me and treat him like he's Santa Claus.'

'You did try, though. What else can you do?'

'That's the question I keep asking myself.'

'You said those girls are as hard as nails,' Frances reminded her. 'They won't fall for his act.'

'Be nice to think that.'

Frances studied her for a moment. 'Maybe you should talk to somebody else. Have you considered that?'

'Well, I'm talking to you. How's it going so far, Frances?'

'I didn't mean me.'

'You meant a shrink,' Kate said. 'I talked to a shrink. She told me to get on with my life.'

'Maybe she was right. Let somebody else worry about him. Come out to the farm.'

Kate flicked her ash into an empty soda can. 'OK, I'll let somebody else worry about him. But I don't need to come to the farm. I'm OK.'

'Gee, that was easy,' Frances said.

Kate smiled. 'You don't believe me?'

'No.'

Kate shrugged.

Frances took a sip, watching Kate over her glass. 'How much painkiller you taking?'

'Christ, David's got a big mouth,' Kate said. 'I'm taking what my doctor prescribes me to take. You want his phone number? You can ask him why my fucking knee isn't getting better.'

'Your knee is not the problem.'

'You're right,' Kate said. 'The judicial system is my problem. Maybe if it was a little more efficient, we wouldn't be having this conversation.'

Frances watched her in silence for a moment. 'You know your father is very worried about you.'

'No offense, but as a father he's about as capable as the judicial system.'

'You need to give him a chance,' Frances said. 'He's not who I thought he was. He actually came to my rescue the other day.'

'Was he riding a white horse?' Kate asked.

'Pickup truck.'

Kate smiled. Frances finished her drink and stood up. She knew better than to push too hard. 'I'm going to head back. I want you to think about this, Kate. Maybe you're not breaking the law but you need to think about where it's going.'

'I will, Frances. I will.'

'Will you come out to the farm and visit?' Frances asked.

'Yes.'

'I'm going to hold you to that,' Frances said.

TWENTY-ONE

The council session ran straight through until late afternoon. There were new problems with the chronically delayed Duck Creek Expressway, due to begin construction finally in the spring, and the matter took up the entire sitting. An obscure Indian tribe Bud had never heard of had suddenly decided that the expressway would be running through an ancient burial ground. A dozen members of the tribe had shown up at city hall that morning to announce their intentions to occupy the site until their concerns were met. The bunch must have been thrown together on short notice, as they were a little conflicted on what they wanted. Several were demanding a re-routing of the road, while others were looking for a cash settlement. Apparently the ancient burial grounds were sacred, but not so sacred that they couldn't be purchased.

The expressway was in the east end of the city, out of Bud's ward, and he had no interest in the matter. In principle Bud was not in favor of paying the Indians money to make them go away, but he had no intention of saying as much in open council either. Why piss them off for no good reason? Next thing he knew they'd be protesting outside his office, with their buckskins and feathers and Nike runners.

He normally would've headed home after council, to kick back for a couple hours and do a pipe or two if Deanna wasn't back from shopping yet. But he decided to stop at his office first to ask Miriam if the Indian tribe even existed.

Hank Hofferman was there when he arrived, sitting in the outer office, his cowboy hat on his knee. He looked like an extra in a Western movie. Miriam was across from him, at her desk, typing away on her keyboard. Hank's blond hair was molded to his head from wearing the hat and he was smiling like a poker player who had just bluffed his way to a large pot.

'Hello, councilor,' he said.

'Mr Hofferman,' Bud said. 'I wasn't expecting you.' It was

the first time Hofferman had been to the office and for Miriam's benefit Bud wanted to maintain a pretense of unfamiliarity with the man. Miriam knew most of what went on with Bud's political dealings but she didn't know everything and there was no reason that she should. Bud didn't trust anybody to that extent. He led Hofferman into his office and closed the door. He sat behind his desk and indicated the chair opposite.

'I think I make that little girl nervous, Bud,' Hofferman said, lowering his bulk into the chair. 'I couldn't hardly get two words outa her.'

'She grew up over a bakery on James Street,' Bud said. 'She doesn't know any guys like you.'

'Maybe I should take her for a ride in the old Hummer. I like a plump girl from time to time.'

'You're feeling pretty good about something, Hank.'

'Matter of fact, I am feeling good.' Hank took his hat in both hands and pinched the crease in the crown, then plopped it on his head and pushed back the brim with his thumb, a cocky cowboy move. 'I don't think we need worry about an environmental assessment after all.'

Bud was looking through a bunch of messages on his desk. He stopped. 'And why's that?'

'We're just finishing the paperwork on the last farm I bought. That piece in the southeast corner? Well, my lawyer was doing the title search and you will never guess what he stumbled on. You want to try and guess, councilor?'

'No. I don't want to try and guess.'

'There was once a county dump on that property. Opened in the nineteen fifties and operated for thirty years.' Hofferman paused. 'Get this – the zoning is still on the books. We're about to get grandfathered in, Bud. I talked to Big Ed Montpelier at Beaver Lodge and he talked to his contacts in the department. He figures they'll rubber stamp it.'

Bud smiled. 'And you never knew about this old dump when you starting buying property there?'

'No idea,' Hofferman said. He laughed loudly. 'Some days you eat the bar, and some days the bar eats you.'

'Right,' Bud said. He'd never gone in much for rural colloquialisms. Most he didn't understand. What the fuck was a bar?

'So what you're saying is that HALT can't appeal a re-zoning application because there won't be a re-zoning application. And they can't ask for an environmental assessment on something that already exists.'

'What I'm saying is that they can go fuck themselves.'

Bud got up and walked to the fridge for a root beer. Holding the door open, he looked at Hofferman. 'Hires?'

'You got anything stronger in there?'

'Nope,' Bud said, and he closed the door. 'This is the office of a dedicated civil servant, Hank. No alcohol on the premises.' He popped the top of the can and sat down. 'I think we need to make this public as quick as it's official. For a couple of reasons. One, it's going to ease the lingering concerns of my fellow councilors. Some of them are stewing about an assessment, saying it could take a couple of years. And two – it will knock that Talbotville bunch on their asses. Frances Rourke and that dickhead lawyer Canfield. Carl Burns too, for that matter.'

'Carl Burns?' Hofferman said. 'What's he got to do with it?'

'Carl Burns is the guy who kicked the shit out of that moron at the farmers' market. Yeah, the same Carl Burns who burned down your barn and killed the firefighter back in the day. You didn't know he was in the area?'

'I knew. He was at the farm the day I paid Frances Rourke a visit. So he wants a piece of this? I guess a couple years in jail don't have much effect on some people.' Hank fell silent for a moment, pulling at his nose with his thumb and forefinger. 'I don't like him hanging around. He don't know anything about rules.'

Bud laughed. 'Like we do?'

'I'm just saying. I might have to talk to that boy.'

'Maybe you should at that. First, you need to get your friends in high places to make the announcement about the zoning. That'll take care of HALT.'

Hofferman got to his feet, pulling his hat forward and down, like he was locking it in place. 'Don't worry about my guys. You handle things at city hall and we'll be up and running in eighteen months. Gonna be a nice thing for you, Bud. Best retirement savings plan you could ever hope for.'

'It's going to be a nice thing for you too, Hank. I'm nobody's charity.' Bud glanced toward the outer office, where Miriam sat.

'As far as my financial involvement goes, that's something we don't need to talk about. You do know the value of discretion, Hank?'

'Yup.'

'That's good,' Bud said.

He waited until Hofferman was gone and then he called The Mayor at home and told him the news.

'This should clear the deck,' he said when he finished.

'It should,' The Mayor said. 'If the information is solid.'

'It is,' Bud said. 'Hank Hofferman is a bit of a dufus but he knows his business.'

'Well then,' The Mayor said. 'It happens that I'm speaking at this dinner tonight. Rose City Arts something or other. There will be media there. It might be a good time for me to mention my concerns about our city's trash.'

'Let me guess,' Bud said. 'The current mayor wouldn't be attending this shindig, would he?'

'Wouldn't surprise me.'

'You think he'll get the message?'

'I don't care. Everybody else will.'

Rufus Canfield was acting as legal counsel for HALT, and it was he who filed the applications on the group's behalf for an environmental assessment on the landfill proposal. So it was he who was notified that the assessment request was suddenly a moot point, as the zoning had already been granted. A HALT meeting was called for that evening, at the River Valley Farm.

Rufus arrived early for the meeting and when he drove his old Volkswagen into the drive he saw Carl's truck by the warehouse. He walked down the hill and told Carl the news.

'So where do you go next?' Carl asked.

'Home, I fear,' Rufus said. 'We're finished.'

The executive consisted of Rufus and Frances and a half dozen others. Perry always attended the meetings too, probably because Carl did not, grabbing any opportunity to spend time with Frances when Carl wasn't around. But he rarely said anything. None of the group said much, in fact, after Rufus delivered the news. They sat around the big oak dining room table, drinking coffee and staring in resignation at the table top.

'Hofferman had to know this all along,' Jack Phillips said. 'Sonofabitch. That's why he picked that concession.'

Frances looked over at Jack, saw his red face growing redder. He was a beefy man who owned a two-hundred acre apple orchard across the river. He was confrontational by nature and not entirely rational, also by nature. As a teenager she had seen him punch a stubborn Belgian mare in the forehead. The mare hadn't blinked and Jack went to the hospital with a broken hand.

'Allegedly not,' Rufus said. 'I talked to the surveyors myself. They said it came up during the title search.'

'Doesn't matter one way or the other,' Frances said. 'Not now. It is what it is.'

'What the hell is the ministry saying?' Jack asked. 'That a little town dump from fifty years ago is the same thing as a landfill that's going to take all of Rose City's garbage? Is that what those idiots are saying?'

'They're pulling a Pontius Pilate,' Rufus said. 'They had a problem they didn't want to deal with. Hofferman's got pork belly friends with influence. The ministry sees an out here and they're taking it.'

'Write that up, Rufus,' Jack said. 'Tell everybody exactly how it happened, just the way you said it. We can embarrass the assholes.'

'But we can't prove it,' Rufus said. 'And these guys don't embarrass easily. They'll laugh at us. People from Rose City are already laughing at us. Granola, they call us. Flakes and nuts. They couldn't care less what we think.'

Frances went into the kitchen to make a fresh pot of coffee. While she was spooning the grounds into the pot, Carl knocked and walked in. He was still wearing his work clothes and carrying what appeared to be a roll of blueprints.

'Hey,' she said.

'Am I welcome at your meeting?'

'At this point it's not really going to matter.'

'Kind of a defeatist attitude, isn't it?' he asked.

'That's what happens when you get defeated.'

When Frances returned to the dining room with Carl she saw Perry stiffen and then glare across the table as Carl pulled up a chair and sat. Frances introduced him to the group.

'No offense, Carl,' Jack said pointedly, 'but with your history I don't know if it's a good idea for you to be here.'

'Now Jack, are you worried we might get on Hofferman's bad side?' Rufus asked. 'What do you have there, Carl – a copy of the Magna Carta?'

'Gas wells,' Carl said, and he opened the yellowed roll to reveal a map of the concession where the landfill would go. 'I ran into an old-timer named Lee Cumberland a while back, drilled gas wells in this area for fifty years. This is his map. There are twenty-six gas wells on that concession.'

Everyone except Perry leaned forward to have a look. The wells were marked with small circles with double lines through them.

'There are gas wells everywhere in the county,' Jack said. 'I've got two on my farm.'

'What's this about?' Rufus asked.

'I've been doing a little research on this,' Carl said. 'A gas well is basically a hole in the ground. There's a steel casing that goes down eight or nine hundred feet through rock, and it runs through the aquifers that feed the drilled wells around here. Every farmer's got a drilled well, some two or three. If the steel pipe for the gas gets old and rusted, anything that goes in that hole could contaminate the groundwater. And these aquifers are basically underground streams. One bad casing here could pollute a drilled well fifty miles away. A hundred miles away.'

'OK,' Rufus said. 'So what can we do with this?'

Carl indicated the map. 'If you wanted to put a landfill on that property, first thing you'd have to do is make sure all the old wells were properly plugged.'

'What's it cost to plug a well?'

'Ten or twelve grand.'

Jack scoffed. 'So it costs them two or three hundred thousand to plug some gas wells. We're talking about a landfill that's gonna make Hofferman tens of millions of dollars over the next twenty years. A couple hundred grand is nothing. I don't think you understand the situation here, Carl.'

'Boy,' Perry said, shaking his head.

Carl cocked his head toward Perry before turning to Jack. 'So Hofferman would just pay to cap all the wells on this map?'

'It's chump change,' Jack replied.

'What about the wells that aren't on the map?' Carl asked. 'The ministry records only go back to the thirties. But they started drilling gas wells around here in the eighteen eighties. Lee Cumberland tells me that for every well they know of, there's probably five or more they don't know about. That means there're over a hundred unknown gas wells on that property. If they were ever plugged they weren't properly plugged, because there were no regulations back then. Sometimes they'd throw a fence post down a well and that would be it.'

'Over a hundred wells,' Rufus said. 'And he can't plug them because he has no idea where they are?'

'That's right,' Carl said.

Frances looked at Perry, who had reverted to his scowl.

'So what do we do with this?' Rufus asked.

Carl shrugged. 'Make it a groundwater issue. Trash disposal's a pretty hot topic these days. But clean water is bigger.'

'Will the old guy help us out?' Frances asked. 'Cumberland, is it?'

'I don't know about that,' Carl said. 'He'd rather not have his name involved. I had to pry this map out of his hands. And it's due back tomorrow. He's nervous around this, but I think he's on your side. And there's something else – he showed me some archives from the early nineteen hundreds. Gas well records that are vague, which is exactly what you want.'

'Why is vague good?' Frances asked.

'One entry read "Gas well drilled front field Hoover farm August 1908",' Carl said. 'That's the entire record of that well. Makes a good argument that nobody knows where they are or how many.'

'Where's this guy live?'

'Right in Talbotville,' Carl said. 'He's got logs, maps, contracts. All originals. Somebody's got to convince him to hand them over.'

'I'll go see him,' Rufus said.

Frances tapped her forefinger on the map. 'OK, if we can suggest that the groundwater is at risk, we can get the health department involved. We convince *them* to ask for an environmental assessment. All we need to do is delay this thing for a couple of years. They'll have to go elsewhere.'

Perry got noisily to his feet, chair legs screeching across the hardwood floor. 'I think it's stupid. Nobody cares about old gas wells. Nobody's gonna listen to any of this. It's stupid.' He walked out.

'Who shit in his cornflakes?' Jack asked when he was gone.

'It's nothing,' Frances said. 'He gets a little resentful over things.'

'Over gas wells?'

Frances shrugged. 'I don't think it was the gas wells.'

'Is he with us or not?' Jack asked.

'Who knows?' Frances replied. 'Doesn't matter, one way or the other.'

The weather was getting colder. Kate thought constantly now of what would happen when the pickup basketball games stopped. There had been the occasional rainy day when the girls hadn't shown and on those days, if The Mayor showed at all, he would shorten his walk around the park before heading home. In her more optimistic moments she imagined that eventually he would just quit coming, and that the dread Kate felt regarding him and the blond girl Lindsay would disappear. But those moments were fleeting. Her gut told her otherwise.

In the meantime, The Mayor had continued his grandfatherly posturing, offering Lindsay little gifts and what Kate took to be earnest conversation. The gifts were books mostly, although one day he arrived with fudge for the whole group, and another time – on a particularly chilly day – he'd shown up with a large thermos of what appeared to be hot chocolate.

Kate had kept her distance since her encounter with the girls. If any of them had mentioned her to The Mayor she doubted he would have grounds to suspect her in particular. Presumably, the list of women who might hold a grudge against him would be long. Even so, she was now forced to keep out of sight of the basketball players, as well as The Mayor. One of them might decide to point her out.

This day Lindsay had taken the puppy for a walk along the edge of the ravine while The Mayor sat and watched the pickup game. With the changing weather the players were wearing more clothes. Sweats and hoodies, ball caps and toques, fingerless gloves. The Mayor wore a yellow windbreaker but was bare-headed. When the blond girl brought the pup back to him he spoke to her, thanking her maybe, and when he did he reached out and brushed some wind-blown strands of hair away from her face. Kate, hunkered down by the wall of the pavilion, watched the scene, the rage rising in her like a drug.

He left shortly after that. She watched as the Lincoln turned out of the parking lot, heading for the bridge, and home. Keeping out of sight of the players, she made her way down the slope to the lower parking lot, and did the same.

TWENTY-TWO

Bud walked out of the coffee shop and into the biting wind off the lake. Pulling his lapels close to his neck, he walked quickly toward his office. His cell phone began to ring and by the time he removed his glove and fished it from his pocket, it stopped. The display said Hank Hofferman. Bud called him back.

'I just left you a message,' Hank said.

'Yeah?'

'Where you been?'

None of your fucking business, Bud thought. 'What's up?'

'I gotta talk to you,' Hofferman said.

'You are talking to me.'

'I gotta see you. There's somebody you need to meet.'

Bud had been looking forward to getting home, kicking back; maybe order in tonight. Deanna was in New York City with her girlfriends, spending money. 'Come to Spinnakers,' he told Hofferman.

'This guy won't come into the city. Meet me at Brannigan's.'

'You sound like you're about to pop a fucking vein, Hank,' Bud said. He stepped into a doorway, out of the wind.

'You need to come to Brannigan's.'

Bud sighed. 'OK, half an hour,' he said.

He couldn't have picked a worse time to drive out of the city. All the ramps to the thruway heading south were jammed, and the side roads were even more congested. Bud's nature was such that he couldn't handle a simple thing like waiting in line at the bank. Sitting in traffic was a nightmare for him. It elevated his heart rate, made him antsy. He sat leaning forward over the wheel, as if his posture would speed up the pace, his fingertips drumming on the steering wheel.

'This had better be good,' he said out loud as he sat idling halfway up the John Street ramp.

It took an hour to get to the truck stop. Hofferman's Humvee was parked in the lot, dwarfed amongst the eighteen-wheelers. The man himself was at a booth inside, and with him was a tall skinny guy in jeans and a worn plaid work shirt and a dirty cloth cap.

Sliding into the booth, Bud gave the skinny guy the once over and the man looked away, made eye contact with Hofferman and looked away again. Finally his gaze settled on the waitress who stood behind the counter, pouring coffee for the truckers sitting there.

'My next project's going to be a new highway out of the fucking city,' Bud said to Hofferman. 'OK – what's got you all excited?'

'We've got a problem with HALT,' Hofferman said.

'You said the zoning was a slam dunk,' Bud reminded him.

'It should have been,' Hofferman said. 'But now they're claiming there's unknown gas wells on the site. They're saying there's a threat to the groundwater.'

'What's gas got to do with water?' Bud asked.

'The piping goes through the aquifers that feed the drilled wells,' Hofferman said. 'If they make drinking water an issue, we've got problems. A review could take years.'

'We don't have years,' Bud said. 'The city won't wait.'

'Think I don't know that?'

'Shit,' Bud said. 'So get your buddies at the capitol to take care of it.'

'I tried,' Hofferman said. 'They say this is a different animal. You start threatening people's drinking water and everybody runs for cover. Nobody wants to be the guy to OK things, in case it goes sideways down the road.'

Bud sighed and rubbed his eyelids with his fingertips. He had been really looking forward to going home and getting high. When he opened his eyes he was looking directly at the skinny guy in the work shirt.

'I assume you've got something to do with this.'

'He brought it to me,' Hofferman said.

'Well, let's hear it,' Bud said to the man. 'You got a name, pal?'

'Course I got a name,' the skinny guy said. 'It's Perry.'

*   *   *

Thinking about it afterwards, Carl knew that he should have seen it coming. He worked late at the farm Friday and when he got back to his room at the hotel he showered and changed his clothes and drove across town to Archer's for something to eat. He decided on the special, shepherd's pie. He sat at a table in the corner and drank draft ale while he waited for his food. He noticed Harold Sikes at the bar when he walked in, which was why he sat across the room. From what Perry had told Frances it was evident that Sikes had an over-active imagination. Carl had no intention of feeding it. Still, Sikes kept throwing looks Carl's way, which was typical, and when he wasn't doing that he was talking on his cell phone. Carl continued to ignore him.

The shepherd's pie might have been very good a few hours earlier but by the time it arrived in front of Carl it was overcooked and dry, probably from sitting under a warmer. He ate it anyway and drank another draft. By the time he got up to leave, Harold Sikes was making a concentrated effort *not* to look in his direction. It was another red flag and if Carl hadn't been tired he might have picked up on it.

They were waiting for him in the parking lot behind the bar, Hofferman and a guy Carl had never seen before, a short squat guy who looked like a gym rat. Carl slowed when he saw them and immediately heard shuffling footsteps behind him. He turned to see Sikes lumbering toward him, his arms swinging, chest puffed out, his face beet red.

'Payback is a bitch, asshole,' he said.

Carl hit him in the forehead with a hard right hand and then he hit him again, this time on the cheekbone as Sikes was going down. Carl turned at once, knowing full well that the other two would be coming on, but still he was too late. The gym rat clubbed him behind his right ear with a fist the size of a ham, and then he grabbed Carl around the throat with both hands and actually lifted him off the ground before slamming him on to the hood of a car. Carl kneed the rat in the groin but it seemed to have no effect. He tried to throw punches around the massive arms that held him down but they deflected off the man's shoulders. Then he felt other fists hitting him and he went down. The boots came next, as he knew they would. There were a lot of them, meaning that Hofferman, and probably Sikes, were joining in the fun.

The last thing he heard was Hofferman advising him to mind his own business.

When he woke up he was in the alley behind the bar, although it would take him a while to come to that conclusion. He came to with his face against the steel base of a dumpster, the acrid, rotting smell of the garbage inside the container strong in his nostrils. He got to his knees and remained there for a moment, his head swimming. The entire left side of his rib cage was racked in pain and it grew worse each time he attempted to inhale. It occurred to him that the pain was what brought him around. His nose felt as if a huge weight was pressing against it and there was dried blood in both nostrils and on his lips. He was suddenly nauseous and vomited on to the pavement before he could get to his feet.

He found he could barely walk because of the pain in his ribs, which he knew were broken. He could feel them grinding together as he made his way slowly to his pickup. Crossing under a streetlight, his left elbow and forearm pressed tightly against his rib cage, he looked at his watch and saw that it was quarter past three. He managed to get behind the wheel of his truck and drove back to the Queens.

In his hotel room's bathroom he took his shirt off and looked at his side. The flesh over the rib cage was already beginning to discolor, yellow and red. He knew there was nothing to do with cracked ribs other than live with them until they healed. He had a piss and was relieved to see no blood in the bowl. The entire side of his body was a mess but he would live. He suspected that the kicking must have continued after he'd lost conscious-ness. His jaw was swollen too but didn't appear to be broken. He had a cut, clotted over, beneath his left eye.

He stood in front of the bathroom mirror and reset his broken nose. It was a painful process and there was considerable blood. After a while, he decided that he would settle for a rough semblance of his old nose. He cleaned the blood from his nostrils and mouth and then he brushed his teeth. He had a long and painful shower and took a handful of aspirins and went to bed. He slept all day Saturday.

*   *   *

Lee Cumberland lived in a neat bungalow on Fairview Avenue in Talbotville. The house was part of a subdivision built thirty-five years earlier. Red maples and white pines and Colorado spruce, planted back then, were now twenty-five feet high. The houses in the neighborhood were for the most part immaculately kept, the lawns trimmed, and in the summer expansive flower beds of brilliant blooms were in evidence everywhere. The flowers were mostly dying now, but here and there a flash of color could still be seen, the plants persevering against the coming season.

Rufus spent the better part of an hour with Lee Cumberland and his wife, Shirley. They gave him coffee and banana nut muffins and information. More information than he had counted on.

Afterwards he decided to drive out to River Valley Farm to report to Frances directly. He thought that Carl might be there too, even though it was Saturday. Rufus wasn't sure if River Valley Farm had adopted Carl or if Carl had adopted River Valley Farm, but it was apparent that some connection of the sort had been made. Working for Frances made it possible for Carl to stick around. Rufus had no idea what would happen when the work came to an end.

It was growing dark when he got there. He found Frances in the front section of the warehouse, in a large area that served as a communal office, seated at a desk with her feet up, a computer keyboard on her lap. She wore jeans and a maroon sweater. She was looking through rimless glasses at a computer screen on the desk.

'Hello, Rufus,' she said when he walked in, her eyes still on the screen.

'Ms Rourke.'

'Just a sec,' she said. 'I'm e-mailing the government money. Unless you advise me that I'm really not required to.'

'Death and taxes,' he told her.

'You're a lot of help.'

Rufus heard a noise and he turned and looked through the open doorway to the main warehouse. Perry was pushing a skid of boxes across the floor toward a shelving unit against the far wall. He was focused on his task and if he'd seen Rufus arrive, he didn't let on.

'Done,' Frances said. She stretched and yawned. 'What do you know, Rufus?'

'I've just come from Lee Cumberland's house. Is Carl around?'

'I haven't seen him today. About time he took a day off. He's not exactly charging me the going rate anyway.'

'And why is that, Frances?'

'Nice try,' she said. 'Back to Cumberland.'

Before Rufus could reply, Perry appeared in the doorway.

'I guess I'll be going then,' he said to Frances.

'OK, Perry. See you Monday.'

Perry gave Rufus a look before going out the side door. Rufus could see him through the front windows, walking quickly toward the road.

'First time I ever saw that man in a hurry,' Rufus said. 'He's an odd one, isn't he?'

'I've quit studying the oddity of men,' Frances said. 'What about Cumberland?'

Rufus flopped down in the chair opposite her. 'The man has a mother lode of gas well information. And he's willing to help. We need to photocopy what he has, put it in a package and get it in the hands of the right people.'

'OK. When does that happen?'

'He's going to gather everything together and bring it to my office tomorrow for photocopying,' Rufus said. He paused. 'And there's something else.'

'What's that?'

'Hank Hofferman paid Cumberland a visit.'

'What?'

'My reaction precisely,' Rufus said.

'What the hell did he want?'

'He offered Cumberland a consulting job on the landfill.'

'I'll just bet he did.'

'So he knows that Cumberland has the goods. How he knows is another question. But he was there to pay the man off.'

'What did Cumberland say?' Frances asked.

'He showed Hofferman the door.'

'Good for him,' Frances said. She sat quietly, thinking for a time. Something wasn't right. 'So who tipped Hofferman off?'

'I don't know,' Rufus replied. 'Does it matter – if Cumberland turned him down?'

'Probably not,' Frances admitted. 'But it would be nice to know, either way.'

Carl was still in bed Monday afternoon when Frances showed up, although he'd been up earlier and gone downstairs for breakfast. His ribs were worse, if anything, and the skin over them was now several interesting shades of purple. When Frances knocked he pulled a sheet over himself, flipped the TV on and told her to come in.

'Jesus,' she said when she saw his face.

'What are you doing here?'

'You don't answer your phone,' she said.

'I've been under the weather. What's up?'

She took a long look at him. 'I had a discouraging meeting with Rufus Canfield and I thought you should know about it. You going to tell me what happened to you?'

Carl gave her a mild version of the incident in the alley, suggesting that the entire fight had consisted of a couple of wild punches being thrown. There was a chair by the bureau and Frances moved to sit in it while she listened.

'We're going to the police,' she said when he finished.

'No,' Carl told her.

'Why the hell not?'

'Because we're not.'

She stood up and walked across the room to the window overlooking Main Street. She looked down on the street for a moment, then glanced toward him. He turned slightly to follow her movement and when he did, he grimaced. He saw her eyes fall on the sheet covering his torso.

'What's this about Rufus?' he asked.

'Rufus took the Cumberland data to Natural Resources this morning. They got back to him in a couple hours, which was surprising. The bad news is that they say it's an environmental issue. But the Ministry of the Environment has already signed off on it. And they'd rather not take another ministry to task. Guess they don't step out on one another, these ministries.'

'Even if it means doing their job.'

'Even if it means that.'

'Well, shit,' Carl said.

'So the message Hofferman sent you behind Archer's was for nothing. It's a non-issue.'

Carl shifted in the bed. 'What makes you think that had anything to do with Cumberland?'

'Hofferman found out about the maps and the rest of it. He tried to buy Cumberland off.'

Carl thought about that. 'How would he know about it?'

'That's a very good question. I have a theory on that.' Frances took two quick steps and grabbed the sheet covering Carl and pulled it back. 'Jesus Christ! Look at you. OK, I'm taking you to the hospital.'

'I'm all right, Frances,' he told her. 'I've had broken ribs before. They'll heal.'

'Why do you have to be so tough?'

'If I was tough then Hofferman would be the one on his back.'

'You need a doctor, Carl. Will you listen to me?'

'A doctor's gonna tell me I've got broken ribs and I should stay in bed. I'm already doing that.' He smiled.

'Don't you smile at me,' she snapped. 'You're a frustrating man.'

He shrugged. 'Have you heard from Kate?'

'I guess we're done talking about you seeking medical help,' Frances said.

'I was hoping.'

She shook her head at his obstinacy. 'I haven't heard anything. I left her a couple messages but nothing.' She paused. 'She said she'd come out to the farm. I keep hoping she will.'

Carl nodded. 'So what about the landfill? What's next?'

'Nothing's next,' Frances replied. 'Who were we trying to kid anyway? You can't beat these guys, Carl. It's money and it's politics. They won't stop.'

Carl lay back on the pillow and looked at the ceiling. He'd spent most of the past three days in bed and yet he was tired. His sleep had been ragged. Every time he moved, the pain in his ribs woke him up.

He opened his eyes. 'Got to be a way.'

'Last time you got thinking that way, you went to jail,' she

reminded him. 'You get some rest. I still think you should go to
the hospital but I'm not going to fight you over it. You could use
a shave, you know.'

Carl's hand went to his chin. He hadn't shaved since his run-in
with the gang behind Archer's. There were too many sore spots
on his face. He watched Frances as she walked to the door. She
was wearing a skirt and a sweater under a leather jacket, and her
hair was hanging loose to her shoulders. Usually she had it tied
back when working at the farm. It was the first time Carl had
seen her in a skirt since he'd returned to town. She had nice legs.

'I ever tell you that you're a good-looking woman?'

She turned. 'I wondered when you'd get around to it. Did it
take a blow to the head?'

'Well, I was married to your sister,' he said. 'And then there
was some guy in a Land Rover. Taking your picture every ten
seconds.'

'The guy in the Land Rover drove off into the sunset. He took
his camera with him.'

'Well,' he said.

She kept watching him until he looked away. She shook her
head.

'Slow but sure,' she said, and she left.

He smiled as he lay back and closed his eyes. He thought
about her legs for a while. Then he thought about Kate and what
she was doing. He wished he could talk to her. But everybody
else had, and he didn't know what good it had done. Maybe she
would come to the farm, as Frances said. That would be something, at least.

Thinking about Frances made him think about what she had
said about the landfill.

She was right about one thing. It always came down to money
and the money always won. Carl's mother had died broken at
the side of the highway, her life leaking out on to the gravel
there in the dusk, while the money that caused it had motored
on unchecked toward the city. The same money had sucked the
marrow out of Carl's father, sitting on that back porch, drinking
case after case of Old Stock Ale, unable to talk about what
happened to his wife, or what didn't happen to the man who had
run her down.

It was money that had lured Carl to that half-constructed pig barn that night. Of course, it was money. He realized he hadn't thought about it in years. It was supposed to be a simple thing. A midnight fire, a victimless crime – unless anyone considered Hank Hofferman a victim, and Carl didn't. All it took was a gallon of gas and a single wooden match. Douse the studding and the truss system and strike the match. The building was fully engulfed by the time he walked through the bush lot to his truck, parked on the side road a half mile away. He met the fire trucks as he drove back into town.

The next morning he learned that Red Walton had died at the scene. Carl hung around the house for most of the day and at five that afternoon he turned himself in to the police. He could have lived with the arson but not the dead firefighter. Hofferman had dozers on the site the next day and a week later the barn was being rebuilt. And Carl was in jail, waiting for trial.

The money won again.

She sat huddled in the wool coat, a cigarette cupped in her hands as she tried to light it in the wind. She was against the pavilion wall, on the lee side, but still the breeze whipped around her. It had snowed earlier, before the wind had risen, large wet flakes which had floated through the air like indolent falling leaves before melting immediately upon hitting the ground. Kate pulled on the cigarette and took a drink from the take-out coffee at her feet.

The wind abated and rose again, strong enough to whip the wet leaves from the ground. She was content with the cold. It meant the end of pickup basketball for the year. She was counting on that meaning the end of The Mayor's visits to the park, the end of his gift giving and his benevolence, to the basketball players in general but most specifically to the blond girl Lindsay.

Still, she couldn't resist coming today. She needed to know firsthand that the weather had ended his Fisher Park schemes, that the girl was safe. The Mayor could walk his dog in the ice and snow if he wanted. But there would be no girls for him to charm, no more lambs stumbling blindly into the path of the lion.

Butting the cigarette beneath her shoe, she got up and walked around to have a view of the basketball court and wading pool. The park was deserted. Leaning against the wall, she fished in her jeans pocket and brought out the container of Percocet and opened it. She took two and washed them down with the tepid coffee.

It was time to stop this, she knew. Maybe she needed the onset of winter to show her that.

It seemed that everyone else was of that opinion. David, Frances. Even Sasha had called from Shoeless Joe's, asking how she was doing. She could tell by what she said, and what she didn't say, that she'd been talking to David. And David had been staying at his brother's the past week or so. He said he couldn't watch her anymore. Wouldn't watch her anymore.

So she would quit. When winter set in, The Mayor would lose contact with the girls at the park, and that would be that. He was getting old. Maybe it was finally time for him to quit too. But how could she know that? Maybe he hung out at hockey arenas or schools during the winter, inventing some excuse to be there, to insinuate himself. How could she know?

She couldn't, but maybe that was a good thing. She needed to get on with things. First and foremost, she had to make things up with David; she knew it had been a terrible time for him. He'd stood beside her for as long as he could. In the end it was almost as if she'd deliberately driven him away because she couldn't stand to see him watching her. The way she was.

As she was considering the matter of the rest of her life she heard a car and turned to see the Lincoln as it pulled into the Millburn Street parking lot. After a moment The Mayor got out, carrying the little pup. He bent over to clip a leash on to the dog's collar and then he straightened and started into the park. He was wearing a fedora with little ear flaps, and a tan trench coat.

Kate moved back behind the corner of the pavilion wall to watch him. He looked forlorn and even older than his years as he trudged along the gravel pathway, the energetic pup straining the leash. Maybe he was harmless at long last. Maybe that was all she would ever have. Knowing that he was finished. A lion with no teeth wasn't much of a lion at all. Time had done to the animal what his victims couldn't, and the law wouldn't.

Then she saw Lindsay, walking across the grass from the direction of the housing development, wearing jeans and a nylon coat and a ball cap. She was smiling as she approached The Mayor. Kate watched in horrid fascination. It was no chance meeting. When the two met on the pathway, The Mayor reached into his coat and pulled out a book. Another fucking book. He presented it to the blond girl and then he embraced her, briefly and chastely. Kate couldn't watch and she went around the corner of the building, out of sight. She sank down, kneeling there, for a few moments, her breath coming in spurts. When she looked past the corner again, the two of them were on a park bench, side by side, talking. The pup was off its leash and was running zigzag courses across the dying grass of the park.

And so that was it, Kate thought. She was willing to stop but he wasn't. He would never stop, not on his own.

Somebody would have to help him along.

Carl met with Rufus at his office and laid out what he had in mind. He'd been expecting an argument but Rufus, to Carl's surprise, had warmed at once to the plan. Carl called River Valley Farm and left a message for Frances with Grace, who worked in the shipping office of the warehouse. Ten minutes later, Frances called back.

'You said they'd use their money to win,' he said.

'I guess I did,' she said. 'Why?'

'Then let's make them use a little.'

'What does that mean?'

'I need to talk to you,' he said. 'I'm going to drive out there today and tell you a story.'

'Can't you tell me over the phone?'

'I have to tell you in person. And Perry has to be there.'

'Perry has to be here,' Frances repeated slowly. She considered this. 'All right. Should I set out some cheese?'

'What do you mean?'

'For your trap.'

'You're a smart woman, Frances.'

'You're just full of compliments lately,' she said.

'You know me. Slow but sure.'

She was laughing as he hung up the phone.

*   *   *

When Carl arrived at the warehouse a half hour later, Frances and Perry were disassembling a steel shelving unit and moving it from one side of the room to the other, an obvious make-work project. Frances looked suitably surprised when Carl walked in.

'There you are,' she said. 'We were wondering where you've been. We were just talking about it. Weren't we, Perry?'

'Yeah, we was real worried about you,' Perry said. 'What happened to your nose?'

'I slept funny,' Carl told him.

Perry smiled and moved away to lift an end frame on to the tow motor. Carl turned to Frances.

'I just had a visit from Lee Cumberland,' he said.

'Oh,' Frances said. She hesitated, waiting.

'He's getting cute,' Carl said.

'Cute in what way?'

'Well, he's suddenly decided the gas well info is a valuable commodity. He wants money for it now.'

'Shit,' Frances said. She frowned at Carl, looking for a lead.

'The stuff is for sale,' Carl said. 'The good news is he's giving you first refusal on it.'

Frances caught on now. 'Does Hofferman know it's for sale?'

'Not yet.' Carl shrugged. 'I'm just a messenger, Frances. It's up to HALT to decide what they want to do.'

Perry was keeping himself busy while the conversation went on. When his back was turned Carl gestured to Frances, rubbing his two fingers against his thumb.

'What's his asking price?' she asked.

'He says he wants five thousand dollars,' Carl said. 'Can HALT swing that?'

'That's a good question,' Frances said. 'I doubt it. Not on short notice. If we had some time . . .'

'You have time. I just don't know how much.'

'We can call a meeting tonight. Is the stuff worth it?'

'I say yes,' Carl said.

Frances regarded Carl for a moment, then turned to Perry. 'What do you think, Perry?'

Perry had a socket wrench in his hand, loosening bolts from the frames. He looked at Frances. 'I don't know nothing about this stuff.' He pointed the ratchet at Carl. 'Ask him. He's the one supposed to be so smart. Maybe he ain't so smart after all, by the looks of that nose.'

Perry returned to his work. Carl looked at his back for a moment. 'Well, if I stick around here, I'm just gonna get my feelings hurt,' he said. 'I delivered my message.'

Frances followed him outside to his pickup.

'I got a question,' she said. 'What if Hofferman knows that we got nowhere with Cumberland's information?'

'Either way, he doesn't want this in the news,' Carl said. 'It's about drinking water. As long as that threat is out there, he's going to want the evidence off the market.'

'That's pretty optimistic.'

'It's my nature.'

'The hell it is,' she said. 'Where you going now?'

'I have to check back with Rufus. I might have a security system to install.'

'You going to tell me where this is going?'

'Eventually.'

'How about right now?'

He smiled. 'You don't need to know everything right now. Some of what I'm doing is not exactly ethical.'

'That makes me feel a lot better.'

He leaned in suddenly and kissed her softly on the mouth, then turned and got into the truck. The window was down.

'I've been thinking about that for a while now,' he said, and drove away.

TWENTY-THREE

Bud wheeled the Escalade in and out of the crawling traffic on the thruway as best as he could. It was raining hard and the road was full of dawdlers. One minute Bud was doing eighty-five miles an hour and the next he was down to thirty. As he drove, he muttered constantly to himself. Two drops of rain and people start driving like they're in a mine field. Hit the gas or stay the fuck at home.

Hofferman was sitting in his Hummer in the rear corner of the parking lot at Brannigan's. The lot was flooded from the downpour, the potholes overflowing. When Bud pulled up, Hofferman got out and climbed in the Cadillac's passenger side.

'I was beginning to think you weren't coming.'

'Fucking traffic,' Bud said. 'I swear, people drive like that just to piss me off. OK, what are we going to do with this dickhead?'

'We're going to enter into a business transaction with him,' Hofferman said.

'What the fuck does that mean?'

'All on the up and up,' Hofferman said. 'That's the way to play it. He has some documents that are pertinent to the landfill proposal. Information that we need to ensure that things are done safely and in the best interests of the public.'

'In other words, we're going to buy him off.' Bud was intrigued that Hofferman had suddenly dropped his shit-kicker persona and was now talking like a Philadelphia lawyer.

'You can phrase it any way you want.' Hofferman pulled a thick envelope from his pocket and offered it over. 'But I think you should tell him that it's all for the public good. Make the old guy feel like he's contributing to something important.'

Bud pushed the envelope away. 'What do you mean – I should tell him?' he asked. 'I'm not going anywhere near the guy.'

'Yes, you are,' Hofferman said. 'I met with him last week and it didn't go well. He's been led to believe that I'm some sort of greedy opportunist. The guy doesn't like me, Bud. But you can present yourself as a civil servant. With the interests of the people at heart.'

Bud was clearly not happy with the development. 'Why do we even need this shit?'

'Maybe we don't.' Hofferman shrugged. 'But we know that the other side is willing to pay for it. What's that tell you?'

'That they're stupid?'

'I don't think we can assume that,' Hofferman said. 'This is what you call containment.'

'Christ,' Bud said. 'I don't want to fucking do this. Don't you have somebody you can send?'

'Gotta be you, Bud.'

'Shit.'

'You'll be in and out in five minutes.'

Bud stared out the windshield. The rain had picked up now, along with the wind. The tattered banners outside the restaurant were whipping crazily in the storm. 'What do I say to this guy?' Bud asked. 'What's his name again?'

'Cumberland. Tell him you want everything he's got. Make sure he understands that. Everything.'

Bud finally took the envelope from Hofferman. He stared at it in his hands for a moment, as if it might tell him something. 'Jesus Christ. I don't even know what we're buying here. How am I going to know if he's being straight with me?'

'This old geezer's too nervous to try anything,' Hofferman said. 'You telling me you can't handle this, Bud?'

Bud sighed. 'I can handle it. If he wants to deal, that is.'

'He wants to deal.'

'But does he want to deal with us?'

'Look, he's about to get five grand for a bunch of stuff that a week ago wasn't worth five cents. Why would he give a shit where the money comes from?'

'I guess we'll find out,' Bud said. Looking around, he sighed. 'These fucking people. I'm getting sick of them all. And I'm getting sick of coming out here too. I don't even like leaving the city, you want to know the truth.'

'Thought you went to Portugal,' Hofferman said. 'That's way out of the city. How was it anyway?'

'A fucking nightmare,' Bud said. 'The only one there who spoke English was my fucking wife. If I wanted to talk to my wife, I'd have stayed home.'

'You need to learn to relax, Bud.'

'So I keep hearing. You know what bothers me even more?' Bud asked. 'Hearing that Carl Burns is still mucking around in this. I've seen slow learners before but this guy takes the cake.'

'I might have to hurt the man.'

'I was under the impression you did hurt him,' Bud said.

'Thought I did too,' Hank said. He laughed. 'I must be getting old, Bud. We beat that guy like a rented mule and three days later he's got his nose in where it doesn't belong. Again.'

Bud shook his head. 'Back in ancient times the Romans, or somebody, would cut a man's nose off for sticking it where he shouldn't.'

'The Romans did that?'

'Somebody like that,' Bud said. 'Might have been the Vikings.'

Lee Cumberland was alone in the little bungalow when Bud arrived. The old man seemed surprised that he was there, but after Bud introduced himself and dropped Hofferman's name, he invited him in. He said that his wife was out getting groceries. He was quite insistent that they sit at his kitchen table. He was acting on the nervous side but then Bud had never met the guy before. Maybe that was the way he was.

'What's this about?' Cumberland asked when they were seated.

'I think you know what it's about,' Bud told him.

'I can't say that I do.'

Bud leaned forward over the table. 'Listen, Methuselah, I don't have time to play ring around the rosie with you. You might be a little slow on the uptake but this transaction couldn't be simpler. I'm going to give you five thousand dollars in cash and you're going to give me those logs and maps and whatever else you got pertaining to that landfill site. Surely you can grasp that.'

Cumberland fell silent for a moment, chewing his bottom lip. 'What do you want with it anyway?'

'What do I want with it?' Bud repeated, leaning back in his chair. 'Do I really have to spell it out? I want it so other people can't use it to oppose the landfill. You realize that the landfill is a good thing, right?'

'I've heard both sides of that argument.'

'Well, you best listen to my side. Because I'll give you the straight dope. The landfill represents progress. What would you do with tons of trash – throw it out in the street? Those fuckwads who are against it don't know what they're talking about.'

'I won't have that language in my house.'

'Sorry,' Bud said. Even he realized how insincere he sounded so he showed him his palms and apologized for the apology. 'I really am sorry.'

'And you claim to be a city councilor. With a mouth like that.'

'Well, I'm not here as a city councilor,' Bud told him. 'This matter is between you and me. Now, are we going to do business or not?'

Cumberland paused again. He seemed genuinely conflicted. 'I suppose,' he said.

'You suppose?'

'Fact is, I could use the money. Did you bring a check?'

'Cash,' Bud said. 'We deal in cash. And another thing, you don't ever mention this to anybody. I was never here, you never met me. You got that?'

'I guess so.'

'You'd better do more than guess so.'

Cumberland nodded. 'OK.'

'You never met me.'

'I never met you.'

'Now where is this stuff?'

While Cumberland went into another room, Bud took the money from his coat pocket and counted it out on the table. It was in hundreds and he made five piles of ten each, stacking them neatly. Cumberland returned with a thick manila envelope. Bud opened it and had a quick look inside; he wasn't going to go through it all because he wouldn't know what he was looking at anyway. He got up to leave.

'Now listen, old-timer,' he said, standing in the doorway. 'Come next week, you're not going to suddenly remember some other shit you got stashed away and come looking for more money? Because that's not the way this works.'

'You have no worry there,' Cumberland said. He had followed Bud to the door. 'Far as I'm concerned, we have a gentleman's agreement.'

'Well, that's good,' Bud said.

'Even if we might be one gentleman short,' Cumberland said.

Bud stopped and glanced back at the old man for a moment. Cumberland was no longer looking at him. Bud let the comment pass and left.

Frances and Rufus waited until Bud Stephens drove off before coming out from Lee Cumberland's spare bedroom. Cumberland was in the kitchen, spooning coffee into an old-style percolator. He smiled at them, looking like a mischievous boy when he did.

Rufus retrieved the camera from inside the cupboard where Carl had concealed it and connected it to his laptop and the three of them watched the video replay. The tape looked good. The sound was excellent. Modern technology at work.

'A hand nicely played, Mr Cumberland,' Rufus told him.

'I never done nothing like that before,' Cumberland said. 'I was shaking the whole time.'

Frances put her hand on his shoulder. 'Nice parting shot, by the way.'

'So now you write this up in the newspaper?' Cumberland asked.

'But not just my little weekly,' Rufus said. 'I'll have copies of this tape all across Rose City by the end of the day. Bud Stephens has always loved media attention. He's about to get his wish.'

'Will it stop the landfill, though?' Cumberland asked.

'It should stop Bud Stephens, and the landfill is his baby,' Rufus said. 'This thing gets rank enough and everybody's going to want to get away from the smell.'

Carl was connecting the electrical panel in the warehouse and waiting to hear from Frances. She'd been adamant about him staying away from Cumberland's place and he knew that she had been right. After the incident behind Archer's he didn't need to be near Hofferman right now. He could barely bend over to tie his work boots.

Late morning he went into the front warehouse for coffee but the urn there was empty. He walked up to the house. It was a warm day for the month, and the sky was clearing after the rain earlier. The maple trees in the yard had been the last to lose their leaves, and they were thick on the grass underfoot as he walked. He crossed the patio and went into the kitchen and made a pot of coffee. After pouring himself a cup, he went back outside.

And came face to face with Kate.

'Hey,' he said.

'Hi, Carl.' She hesitated, glancing past him toward the house. 'Frances not around?'

'She's in town. Be back soon. I hope.'

'You hope?'

'She'll be back soon,' Carl said. 'You want some coffee? I just made some.'

'Um . . . yeah.'

'You want to come in?'

'Let's sit out here,' she said. 'It's nice.'

He went inside. Seeing her had thrown him for a loop. She didn't look particularly good. She seemed worn down, weary in a way that had little to do with being tired. Carl knew the feeling.

But she was there.

Not knowing how she took her coffee, he carried the cup, sugar bowl and cream outside and put everything on the wooden table. She splashed a little cream in the cup and they both sat down.

'It's good to see you,' Carl said.

'You too, Carl.' Saying it, though, she wasn't looking at him, her eyes darting restlessly, over the farm, down to the river. Finally she turned to him. 'Did you ever think you'd end up working for Frances?'

'That's one thing I didn't see coming.'

'Do you usually see things coming?'

'You got me there,' he said. 'I guess I've never really seen anything coming. Take today, for instance.'

Kate smiled at that as she sipped at the coffee. 'Well, I promised Frances I would come by.'

'How's the knee?'

'Coming along. I'm using a cane now. I left it in the car.'

'You're not back to work yet?'

'No.' She put the cup down, and this time she really did look at him. 'Do you remember taking me fishing? Off the pier?'

'Yes.'

'We caught all those fish and we went back to your place. You lived in that little yellow house by the textile mill. It smelled funny there.'

'It did?'

'Not the house, the air. Maybe the smell was from the mill,' she said. 'You cleaned the fish and I watched. I didn't want to touch the guts and stuff. Then we cooked them outside, with fried potatoes.'

'We went downtown for ice cream afterwards.'

She smiled brightly and Carl's heart nearly broke in half. 'Yes. I forgot about the ice cream.'

'How old were you?'

'I was thinking about that,' she said. 'Maybe eight or nine? That was a fun day.'

'Yeah.'

She went into her pockets then, searching for something. 'Do you still smoke?' she asked.

'No.'

She gave up and had another drink of coffee. 'Maybe we would all be better off if there was no such thing as memory.'

'Some memories are good.'

'Some of them are.'

Carl watched her but she wouldn't return his look. 'I should've listened to you that day,' he said. 'I should've . . . made you tell me what you were trying to tell me. It was my fault you didn't.'

'No,' she said. 'It wouldn't have changed anything. What would you have done?'

'Probably something stupid.'

She laughed. 'In that case, I wish I had told you.'

He was glad that she could laugh. There was something off about her though, something wired and jumpy, as if she was thinking of a thousand things at once. Behind her, he could see a large cloud approaching from the southwest. They were about to lose the sun.

'But I don't want him dead, not really. I just wish he'd never lived. That doesn't make any sense, does it?'

'It makes perfect sense.'

'It doesn't matter,' she said. 'Hey, maybe someday they'll figure a way to program your memory, like a computer. You can just delete the stuff you don't want. Wouldn't that be nice? You could keep on file the fishing trips and the walks for ice cream.' She paused. 'And delete all the rest.'

'I'd sign up for that.'

The cloud moved over them now and within seconds they were in shade. The air grew cooler immediately. There was loud clucking from the direction of the barn. The chickens were heading for the brood house on the run, the slight change in the weather setting off some alarm. Carl kept his eyes on Kate as she watched them.

'You want more coffee?'

She hesitated. 'No, I'm OK. I should get going.'

'Frances won't be long.'

'Oh, I can come back. I've got some stuff to do. I need to use the bathroom, though.'

Carl waited while she went into the house. She was limping and trying not to, it seemed. He was at once elated and anxious. Thrilled that she had shown up, fearful she wouldn't come back. But he felt as if something had broken today, and in a good way.

When she came out he walked with her to her car. He thought for a moment that she might hug him but she didn't.

Frances arrived less than five minutes after she left. Carl had washed the cups and spoons in the kitchen and was walking back down the hill. When he heard her pull in the driveway, he stopped and came back.

'How did it go?' he asked.

'Bloody perfect, as Rufus put it.'

'The tape looked OK?'

'It looked better than OK,' Frances said. 'Hofferman didn't show with the money.' She paused. 'Bud Stephens did.'

Carl smiled. 'You don't say.'

'I do say. We went fishing for a pig farmer and landed a big city councilor instead.'

'Could be an interesting couple days in Rose City.'

'Yes, sir.' Frances pointed her chin to the west. 'I could've sworn I met Kate on the road.'

'You did.'

'She was here?'

'Yeah. We had coffee together.'

'You had coffee together,' Frances said. She smiled. 'Is there any left?'

'Yeah.'

'Then come on and tell me about it.'

TWENTY-FOUR

When The Mayor came downstairs from his shower, Louise was at the kitchen table, the day's edition of the *Times* in front of her. As he walked toward the refrigerator, The Mayor could see the picture of Bud on the front page. He poured himself a glass of orange juice and stood looking out the window to his yard and the ravine beyond. There were rumors of coyotes in the area and he had awakened in the night, thinking he had heard yelping.

'This is a mess,' Louise said.

'What's a mess?' he asked without turning. He watched outside as the pup came trotting around the corner of the house, a tennis ball in its mouth. It was raining and the dog's feet were muddy from its travels. Louise could clean the animal up.

'This business with Bud.'

He turned. 'Isn't it?'

She pushed the paper away from her. 'This is so obviously a set-up. A hidden camera, for crying out loud. It makes no sense whatsoever to even suggest that he would bribe somebody. He's a city councilor, for God sakes.'

The Mayor drank the orange juice and put the empty glass in the sink. 'I'm going to take a drive up to the lake house. I want to be sure that the lines have been drained and that the place is secure. All the break-ins last year.'

'You're not going there today?'

'I am.'

Louise indicated the newspaper. 'How can you think of leaving the city in the middle of all this? Your name is connected to that landfill.'

'Not for long,' he told her. 'I'll make a statement in a day or two.'

'Well, you have to support him.'

'Bud? The hell I do. He's finished. He'll resign before the week is out. And that landfill project is toast. Environmental will have no choice now, with this all over the newspapers. They'll have to call for an assessment.'

'Bud is my sister's only son. And your friend.'

'Bud is an idiot who got caught on video tape. I'm supposed to feel sorry for him? I don't think so.'

He turned and walked out.

Bud Stephens, who as a point of pride never wore a hat, was wearing one today. It was a baseball cap his wife had picked up somewhere, pink with NYC across the front. Bud also wore sunglasses and a London Fog raincoat, the collar turned up. He left his building through the back entrance at seven thirty, daylight just showing, and was both grateful and yet somewhat surprised that there were no reporters around. They might have been in the lobby, though, or in front of the building. The phone had rung constantly the night before, until Bud finally unplugged it. Deanna saw the video of Bud and old man Cumberland on the six o'clock news and left shortly thereafter to stay with a friend. She didn't even say goodbye. She didn't say anything at all. Bud had sat up half the night drinking Scotch in the dark before finally falling asleep on the couch.

He made his way through the alley to the next block and then walked quickly to the park on the waterfront. With the sun just showing, there were joggers here and there but they were, typically, into their own thing and never gave Bud a glance. He walked over to the benches along the waterline and waited for Hofferman to show up.

It was less than twenty-four hours ago that Hofferman had called to tell Bud that he needed to meet him out in Talbotville to deal with what he had referred to as the 'Cumberland situation'. Bud had been tempted at the time to tell Hofferman to take care of the Cumberland situation himself, but he hadn't, primarily because Bud didn't trust anybody to attend to details.

How had that turned out?

He heard the Hummer's noisy approach and turned to see it pulling into the lot at the far end of the park. Hofferman sat there for several minutes and Bud realized that he, too, was wary of any media types that might be in the area. Finally he got out, his black cowboy hat on his head and a take-out coffee in his hand. When he was a few feet away, he smiled.

'Up with the chickens.'

'Yeah,' Bud said.

Hofferman walked to the railing above the beach, leaned back with his elbows on the top rail.

'This is a major cluster fuck,' Bud said.

'It's all of that.'

Hofferman took a sip of the coffee and looked into the park. There were more joggers out now, a few roller-bladers with dogs on leashes. Hofferman watched them for a moment. He was as calm as Bud was not.

'That fucking old man sat across from me at his kitchen table—' Bud began. He stalled there.

'And?'

'And?' Bud repeated. He took a moment. 'He sat across that kitchen table and proceeded to shove that landfill right up my ass. And I walked in of my own accord and let him do it. Stupid, stupid . . .'

'No point in me arguing with you on that.'

Bud turned an eye on Hofferman. 'Thanks a lot. The question is – what are we going to do about it?'

Hofferman walked over and leaned down to Bud's level. 'Who is this *we* you're talking about?' he asked. 'You got a mouse in your pocket?'

Bud hesitated and then got to his feet. 'What's that supposed to mean?'

'Hey, you got your pecker caught in a thresher,' Hofferman said. 'You're gonna have to get it uncaught by yourself. If you can.'

'You should be on that fucking tape with me and the old man,' Bud snapped. 'You would have been, if you hadn't rubbed him the wrong way—'

'Rubbed who the wrong way?'

'The old man.'

'Cumberland?' Hofferman asked. 'We got along just fine. Matter of fact, he personally asked me to deliver the money to him. I told him I was busy.'

Bud stared at him. 'You sonofabitch. You set me up.'

'Why would I do that?' Hofferman asked. 'But I had no intention of setting myself up. You always need a buffer, councilor.'

'You prick.'

'I'm only going to take so much of that name calling.'

Hofferman's tone backed Bud up a bit. 'OK. What about the landfill?' he asked.

'I suspect the landfill is a dead duck,' Hofferman said. 'And even if it's not, your involvement with it is. You realize I'm going to have to make a statement saying how shocked I am at your behavior.'

'Not so fast,' Bud said. 'You forgetting about the deposits you made to my account?'

'You won't find my fingerprints on a nickel of that money,' Hofferman said. 'Did you miss that part about the buffer? Now I have to get going. I have business to tend to.' He tipped his Stetson and started to walk away.

'You're going to be stuck with all that property!' Bud called after him.

Hofferman replied without stopping. 'Haven't you heard, Bud? You never lose money on land. They don't make it anymore.'

Carl's ribs weren't up to installing drywall yet so he took the next day off. He told Frances he would give them the rest of the week and the weekend to mend.

In the morning he went down for breakfast and then returned to his room, where he took more aspirin and lay down on the bed. Just the act of walking up and down the stairs of the hotel aggravated the pain in his side. He wished he could sleep for a couple of hours but he was not tired in the least. He replayed the conversation he'd had with Kate in his head, as he'd already done countless times since he'd seen her. From there his mind wandered to the thought of Frances's legs again, a thought that had been increasingly present in his consciousness of late.

Even though Carl had married Suzy, he had oddly enough never really developed anything resembling a friendship with her. She'd been great to party with, and to have sex with, and even interesting to fight with because of the sex that usually followed. But he'd never really shared anything else with her – which was why, of course, they had broken apart. Carl had been twenty and Suzy eighteen when they got married. There really should be a law against that kind of behavior.

But he had become friends with Frances these past few months and if that surprised Carl, he was pretty sure that it shocked the hell out of Frances. Carl had come looking for Kate and found Frances. He'd never considered the possibility that he and Frances would become friends and yet that was what they were, at least in his mind. And now he was thinking about having sex with Frances. He had no idea if she was thinking the same. But when he had kissed her, there had been no resistance. And maybe even a slight encouragement.

While he was thinking about kissing her the phone rang. It was Frances, and she was in a panic.

'Was Kate in the house yesterday?'

'In the house? Yeah.'

'My father's gun is gone,' Frances said, the words tumbling from her.

'Slow down. What gun?'

'He had an old police issue Smith and Wesson. It's always been locked in the desk drawer. I think Kate took it.'

'Why do you think that?'

'It's always been locked in my father's desk. It was there on the weekend and it's gone now. The key's above the book shelf. She knew that – she grew up here, Carl. That's why she came here yesterday.'

Carl was on his feet now, trying to think. 'What would she do with a gun?'

'Nothing good.'

'I'll head to the city,' Carl said. 'I can get there before you.'

'Where you going to go?'

Carl took a moment. 'David said she follows him to Fisher Park. I'll go there. You go to the house. Get moving.'

When she got to Fisher Park she parked in the Millburn Street lot and turned the ignition off. She sat there a moment, pressing the palm of her hand against her forehead with great force, as if the effort might clear her thoughts. Her head had been pounding since she woke up that morning, although she could hardly describe what she had been doing before that as sleeping. She had taken the last of the Percocet about an hour ago. She was going to have to find the pink-haired woman again.

Or quit, one or the other. It wasn't something she could think about right now.

She had no notion how it would end but she knew with certainty that it would. She couldn't continue like this. He hadn't shown at the park yesterday and neither had the girls, with the weather. But he was coming back, she knew. Maybe today or maybe a week from now. The thought of a week made her head hurt even more. She didn't know if she could last that long.

Kate knew nothing about the blond girl Lindsay. But she did know what it was like to live a life with the memory of The Mayor lurking. Still, Kate wouldn't say that what had happened to her defined her. She had always hoped that she was stronger than that. On the other hand, she had no way of knowing what her life would have been like without it. Certainly she wouldn't be here today, wired on painkillers and vodka, looking for a delete button that didn't exist. She couldn't deny what had happened and so she would have to live with it.

But she had decided that Lindsay wouldn't.

He left the puppy at home. He would tell the girl that the dog had taken sick, was throwing up, and couldn't ride in the car. He'd arranged to meet her, not in the Millburn Street lot where he usually parked, but in the lower lot off Nash Road, out of sight of the shabby townhouses across from the park.

The rain had stopped and the clouds to the west were breaking up. She was not yet there when he parked the Lincoln. He got out and walked over to the edge of the ravine, still thinking of the coyotes. He'd never seen a coyote, except in pictures or on film, and it surprised him that it was so. He had an old .30-30 Remington in the attic at home, his father's gun. Perhaps later that day he would take it down and clean it. Maybe he'd get a shot at one of the wild dogs before the city brought trappers in to take care of them. He imagined the *Times* carrying a picture of him and the dead animal. After all, they had run the picture of Bud that morning and he was as dead now as the coyote would be. He just didn't know it yet.

He walked a hundred yards or so, looking down into the overgrown gully, and when he turned he saw the girl coming over the crest of the hill. He started back toward the parking lot.

She was smiling, wearing a red toque and a quilted vest and track pants. She had a backpack hooked over one shoulder.

'Hey,' she said when she drew near.

'Hello there,' The Mayor said.

'I brought a pack to put the books in.'

'Good idea,' he said. They met by the front of the Lincoln. 'I think the rain has finished. Be a glorious day for a drive.'

'How far is it?'

'An hour and a half each way. You'll be home for supper.'

'Where's the puppy?'

The Mayor told her the story of the dog falling ill as he walked around and unlocked the passenger door and opened it. He watched as the girl unslung the pack from her shoulder and moved to put it inside. He reached out and touched her hair, felt it clean and soft in his fingers.

Kate hurried toward the parking lot from the slope above. She'd watched The Mayor arrive and waited in her car as he'd walked along the ravine, looking into the brush as if he was searching for something. When she realized that he didn't have the puppy with him, she knew something wasn't right, that this wasn't just another day in the park. A chill ran through her, a dark and frightening feeling of premonition.

As soon as she spotted Lindsay walking across the grass to meet him, she jumped out of her car and started for them. In her haste she left the cane behind and she limped badly, trying to run on her balky knee. Up ahead the two of them were by the Lincoln, talking. As The Mayor opened the passenger door, he reached out and caressed the girl's hair.

'Hey!' Kate called out.

The old man and the girl both turned. Kate came forward, her hands thrust in the pockets of her windbreaker and her cap pulled low. Stopping, she pointed her chin at the blond girl.

'Get the hell out of here.'

The girl looked at The Mayor, who held his hand out to reassure her. 'It's OK,' he said, his tone more curious than anything else.

'Get out of here,' Kate said again, her frustration rising. She waited a couple seconds more and then pulled the revolver from her pocket and pointed it at The Mayor. 'Run, you stupid girl,' she yelled. 'Run!'

The girl ran. Dragging her pack in one hand, she turned and sprinted up the hill. She did not look back, not even a glance. The Mayor watched as she disappeared over the rise before turning to Kate. She saw the recognition come to him.

'You,' he said.

'Yeah.'

'Well, I'll be damned.'

'I think you can count on that,' Kate said.

'You look like something the cat dragged in,' The Mayor said.

He was still amused, it seemed, not threatened in the least. Kate felt suddenly light-headed. She put the gun back in her pocket. 'Well, I've had a rough time of it,' she said.

'It's about to get rougher,' he said. 'You realize that I will have to press charges against you this time. This is more than just a case of false accusations.'

'There won't be any charges,' Kate told him. 'Go home, old man. You're finished.'

He grew irate. 'How dare you tell me what to do?'

'It's time somebody did,' Kate said. 'Where were you taking the girl?'

'I don't answer to you,' he said. 'But you're going to answer to the police. You can make up whatever story you want. Nobody believed you before and they won't believe you now. I'll be going now.'

He turned but she moved with him, cutting him off. She reached into her other pocket and brought out her cell phone. 'Hold on,' she said. 'I got something for you.'

She stepped closer and held out the phone. Showed him the picture of the eight-year-old boy from Cleary Avenue. 'Say hello to Bobby Horvath. You know his mother. You raped her nine years ago at your cottage. Remember – the girls who got caught in the storm? Or were there so many you can't recall them all?'

Almost against his will, The Mayor looked at the screen.

'Truth is, he's a nasty little prick, but what can you expect?' Kate asked. 'That's genetics for you.'

Who would have thought that after all the decades of deceit and unchecked brutality, the reckless assaults and the denial of the same, the sheer arrogance – who would have thought that a picture on a tiny screen would finally cause him to crumble? Not Kate, and presumably not anybody else. He was the epitome of self-control, in everything he did, and it seemed impossible that anything could change that. Maybe the effort of maintaining that self-control was what did it. Until this point his reprehensible history had existed only in the abstract. He had made false any allegations merely by declaring them so, by convincing himself, even. Maybe the strain of that finally caught up to him.

Or maybe it was something simpler than that. Maybe it was just that he was finally face to face with who he was.

He lunged forward, seizing the phone and tearing it from her hand before grabbing her by the neck and spinning her around, slamming her spine against the front fender of the car. Kate attempted to pry the fingers from her throat but he held on, squeezing. All along she'd been thinking he was an old man, spent, and now she was stunned by his strength. His full weight was on her and she could not push him off. He was grunting, animal-like noises from somewhere within.

Kate attempted to knee him with her good leg but the other leg would not support her. She tried to scream but couldn't make a sound, her throat constricted. She realized she was being stran-gled. Squirming beneath his weight she managed to turn sideways from him.

Her right arm came free.

Carl, on foot, crested the ridge that ran the length of Fisher Park. And stopped.

In the parking lot below was The Mayor, standing by a new Lincoln sedan. Kate was a few feet away, holding something out to him. It appeared to be a cell phone. Suddenly The Mayor leaped forward, grabbing Kate and slamming her viciously against the car.

Carl began to run.

With each step, the pain in his ribs cut into him like the blade of a sickle. But still he ran, as the scene below him unfolded. The Mayor pushed Kate backwards over the hood of the car and began to choke her. She was fighting him but he kept his weight on her, his hands on her neck. He must have weighed twice as much as her; she couldn't push him off. As Carl came off the slope to the gravel lot he saw her turn sideways beneath him. Her right arm came up.

The shot echoed along the ridge like a firecracker.

When Carl got there, The Mayor was seated on the ground by the open passenger door of the Lincoln, his back against the rocker panel. The underside of his chin, where the bullet had entered, was bleeding, and his silver hair was wet where the slug had made its exit. His eyes were wide open, as if his dying had surprised him. Kate was standing sideways to Carl, coughing and fighting for breath, the gun still in her hand. Her eyes were glazed and her mouth slack. She looked as if she had no notion of where she was. Of what had happened.

As she turned toward him, Carl hit her on the cheekbone with a short right hand, and then caught her before she could fall to the ground. She was out. He carried her to the grass alongside the parking lot and laid her there. He felt her pulse.

He picked up the gun from where she had dropped it, then stood up and looked around the park. There was nobody in sight. Pulling his shirttail out, he wiped the revolver clean of prints, keeping watch on the ridge as he worked.

When the gun was clean, he took it in his right hand and walked to The Mayor's body. He glanced around once more, then cocked the Smith & Wesson and fired a bullet into the old man's chest. He stuck the revolver in his belt.

He walked over and sat down on the grass. He gathered his daughter in his arms and held her there while he waited for the police to arrive.

TWENTY-FIVE

Prosecutor Thomas Grant had been away for most of the month, first attending his niece's wedding in Victoria and then taking a week's vacation in Mexico. He had been back in his office for just two days. He spent the morning alternately on the phone and the computer, attempting to arrange his caseload into something that resembled order. At quarter to twelve, his secretary came in and told him that Rufus Canfield was there for his appointment. Upon hearing the name, Grant drew a total blank.

'The lawyer from Talbotville,' his secretary said.

'Right.'

Rufus Canfield was unkempt, with a bushy mustache and a pronounced limp that required the aid of a cane. Grant had never heard of him until a couple of days earlier. The two men sat on leather chairs in the inner office.

'Carl Burns,' Grant said to begin. 'This is a sad case. You're his lead counsel?'

'His sole counsel,' Rufus said.

'Well, it's good that we can touch base early on like this,' Grant said. 'But unless he plans on entering a straight guilty plea, we aren't even looking at a preliminary until spring at the earliest.'

'The charge is first-degree murder. There will be no guilty plea.'

'There's not much wiggle room on this,' Grant said. 'A prominent citizen was murdered here.'

'I'm inclined to disagree on that,' Rufus said. 'You see, it is all about perception.' He made quotation marks in the air. 'Some might look at this as "pillar of the community gunned down". Others might see it as "serial rapist shot by victim's father".' Rufus smiled. 'Perception, Mr Grant.'

'I know all about Joseph Sanderson and his past,' Grant said. 'You should know I did my level best to convict the man, and I failed. But that's not going to mean a hell of a lot where this is concerned. Right now, we have an honored civil servant shot in cold blood in a city park. Most people believe that the man was innocent of those other charges.'

'But we know different, you and I,' Rufus said.

'What we know and what we can work with are two different things,' Grant said. He leaned back and clasped his hands behind his head. 'Nothing's going to happen for a few months. Let the dust settle and I'll see if we can quietly make a deal for second degree. I'll recommend parole after twelve years.'

'No chance,' Rufus said.

'No chance?' Grant repeated. 'I hope you're not going to tell me you're looking to plead him to manslaughter? I don't have to remind you that manslaughter is, by definition, killing without intent. The evidence says that your client fired one thirty-eight caliber slug into Joseph Sanderson's brain, and another into his heart. I have a distinct feeling that there was intent there. So you can forget about manslaughter, Mr Canfield.'

'I have no interest in a manslaughter plea,' Rufus said. 'Nor in first degree, nor second either. Any charge related to murder and I will plead my client not guilty. Pardon my insolence, but I'm now about to remind you of something that *you* know quite well. When you prosecuted Joseph Sanderson the third, you did so on the testimony of four victims. You and I know, however, that there were, in fact, thirty-six women who came forward with tales of sexual assault at his hands. Assaults that covered a period of nearly thirty years. Most of these women are still alive and I will call each and every one of them to the stand. Not only that, but I will add Elaine Horvath to the list. And I will make her little boy part of it as well, once a DNA test proves what I think it will. How do you think the Sanderson family will react to a bastard child tacked on to the great man's legacy?'

'Probably not well,' Grant admitted. He looked at Rufus for a moment. 'You're going to conduct a trial within a trial? You'll try to prosecute a dead man?'

'I'll do more than try, I'll bloody well do it. And this time he won't have Miles Browning to attack the credibility of these women. It will be up to you, Mr Grant, to take on that task. It will be your job to call these women whores and drug addicts and liars. Do you have the stomach for that? Will you be the man who defends Joseph Sanderson this time around?'

Grant exhaled heavily and pinched the bridge of his nose. 'Seven days ago I was lounging off the coast of Mexico, casting for tarpon and drinking cold *cerveza*. Seven days ago I had never heard your name. Do you really think that Carl Burns is going to walk on this murder charge?'

'I do,' Rufus said. 'I will do my level best to make certain that every member of the jury is the parent of a daughter. And then I'll show them a man who raped a multitude of daughters, and who was in the process of viciously attacking a former victim. Until the father of that girl put an end to it. Yes, I'll take my chances on that defense.'

Grant looked at the shelves across the room which held his law books, and then back to the rumpled lawyer from Talbotville.

'Do you have a daughter, Mr Grant?' the rumpled lawyer suddenly asked.

'As a matter of fact, I do have a daughter,' Grant said. He shook his head. 'What are you looking for?'

'Criminal negligence,' Rufus said. 'Throw in unlawful discharge of a firearm if you want to tack on an extra conviction. Six months less time served.'

'You're out of your mind,' Grant told him. He got to his feet and walked across the room to look out the window to the street below. It was a gray day, the sidewalks nearly empty. When he turned, his eyes went to a framed photo on a shelf that held various pictures, awards and other bric-a-brac. The photo was of himself and his family. His daughter Katherine.

He crossed the room to his desk. 'Criminal negligence causing death. Plus unlawful discharge. Two years for each, the sentences to run concurrently. He keeps his nose clean, he'll probably be out in a year.'

Rufus stood up. 'I can live with that. I think my client can live with it.'

'I have to sell it first,' Grant said. 'I'm going to take a lot of heat for this.'

'But you'll do it,' Rufus said. 'You'll do it because you know in your heart that it's right. The law can be an ass, Mr Grant, but sometimes the law can be a great leveler too.'

Grant walked Rufus to the door. 'You haven't seen the disclosure yet, I assume?'

'No,' Rufus said. 'I've been waiting for it.'

'There's something odd in there,' Grant said. 'A few hours after the shooting, Kate Burns tried to claim that she was the one who killed the old man.'

'Indeed?'

'Trying to protect her father, I guess. His were the only prints on the gun. She was pretty incoherent, according to the police report, but she also said that there was a young girl there that day. Nobody's ever come forward.' He paused. 'You know, I like Kate Burns. I hope she's going to be OK.'

'I think she has a chance,' Rufus said.

'We all have a chance, Mr Canfield.'

'Isn't it nice to think so?'

If the various media outlets across the country were salivating at the prospect of the trial of Carl Burns for murder, they were destined for disappointment. There was no trial. The plea bargain took place at ten o'clock on a Wednesday morning. Present, along with the judge and various courtroom personnel, were the defendant, the prosecutor Thomas Grant and the Talbotville lawyer Rufus Canfield. Frances was in the gallery, with Kate and David.

The whole procedure took less than ten minutes. The murder charge was dropped and Carl pled guilty to the lesser charges and was sentenced to two years. As he was led out of the court-room, he glanced over to the gallery. Kate met his eyes and held them until he was gone.

Frances came to see him the next day. They were holding him at the old Rose City jail while they decided where to send him to serve his sentence. The courtyard at the jail was accessible to inmates and visitors who wanted to smoke. Neither Carl nor Frances smoked but they sat out there anyway, on a bench by a stone wall. Above them, two guards behind a glass partition watched the yard.

'You were all over the news last night,' Frances said.

'So I hear.'

'And the *Rose City Times* this morning is outraged.'

'I'll bet.'

'Oh, they're probably just pissed that they got cheated out of covering the trial,' Frances said. 'You should know that a lot of the other coverage was on the sympathetic side. The *Gazette* even suggested that The Mayor had skated on the rape charges.

They didn't make you out a villain. Don't get me wrong, they stopped short of calling you a hero.'

'I would hope so.'

Frances paused before continuing. 'They got a quote from Sanderson's wife.'

Carl took a moment, not certain he wanted to hear it. 'Oh?'

'She said she was satisfied with the plea bargain.'

Carl was surprised. 'That seems strange.'

'Maybe not,' Frances said. 'Maybe she finally took the blinders off. If so, it was a long time coming.'

It was a frigid November day. There had been rain earlier in the week and the puddles of water that had accumulated in the courtyard were frozen over. It had snowed at River Valley Farm overnight and Frances had wakened to a light dusting over the fields behind the house. The sky had cleared and the sun was out now, the light glancing off the ice puddles in the yard.

'I talked to Rufus,' Frances said. 'He told me you'll probably be out by next fall.'

'He told me that too.'

'If you behave,' she said pointedly.

'There's always a catch.'

'Did you hear about Bud Stephens?' she asked.

'I heard he resigned.'

'He did. There's a council seat open in Rose City if you're interested when you get out.'

'I believe I'll pass.'

'Then what will you do?' she asked.

'Look for a job.'

'I had to fire my last hired hand for duplicitous behavior. So I happen to have a position open. If you're interested.'

Carl shrugged, looking at the guard behind the glass. The guard was looking back.

'I hope you don't think I'm going to beg you,' she said.

'I'm not so sure I want to be a hired hand. At my age.'

'There's room for advancement,' she said. She watched him a moment. 'For the right applicant.'

He smiled. 'Then I might be interested.'

'Let's not be hasty,' she said. 'What are your qualifications?'

'I can swing a hammer and I'm a fair-to-middling chicken plucker.'

Frances laughed. 'I'll keep your application on file.'

He turned to her now. 'How is she?'

'She's pretty damn good. Better than I imagined and better than she should be. She wanted to come here today but we decided she should stay away for the time being. There's media out front of this place right now, probably waiting for her to show.'

Carl nodded. He pulled his hands from his pockets and blew into them.

'She and David are talking,' Frances said. 'I don't know how that's going to go. But I think he's a good man.'

'I think so too.'

'And she's . . . different. This might seem wrong, but I think she started getting better the moment The Mayor drew his last breath.'

Carl considered this but said nothing.

Frances hesitated. 'There's something else. She's pretty foggy on exactly what happened that day, Carl.'

'That's probably a good thing.'

'She told me she thinks she shot him.'

'I shot him,' Carl said. He stood up and blew into his hands again. 'I shot him.'

After a while he walked her to the front entrance and they stood there, waiting for the guard to work the bolt to the door.

'How are the ribs?' she asked.

'Better and better.'

'You know, I had half a notion of crawling into your bed that day in your hotel room. When you were banged up and refusing to go to the hospital. You remember that day?'

'You were wearing a skirt.'

'You do remember. I was afraid your ribs wouldn't be up to it. If I had known you were going to get yourself locked up, I think I would've risked it.'

'You willing to wait?'

'Maybe.'

'You going to make me beg?' he asked.

She put her hand on the back of his neck and kissed him on the mouth for a long time. 'I'll wait.'

The bolt slid open and clanked into place. Carl watched as Frances walked down the corridor and through the doorway into the brilliant autumn sunshine outside.

ACKNOWLEDGEMENT

I owe a debt of gratitude to the Ontario Arts Council for their support of an early version of this novel.

Thanks to Helen Reeves, Lorraine Kelly and Alison Clarke for being in my corner.

Thank you Kate Lyall Grant and the team at Severn House.

And a very large *efharisto* to the lovely and tenacious Jen Barclay. You are my editor first, my agent second, and my friend always.